Remi DeWitt was born in Southampton in 1954. Adopted into an agriculture family, he left the farm to work in both the brewing industry and civil engineering, completing a degree in physics along the way. He has since returned to the countryside and now takes long walks in between writing.

SOMEWHAT LOST

"It Was One Bottle of Wine!"

REMI DEWITT

CHAPTER ONE

There's a very bright light, so bright I have to close my eyes again. This is weird. Even if the bedroom lights were left on when I went to bed, they've never been this bright.

Unless—no way! Did I die in my sleep? Is this one of those near-death experiences? Oh come on, that's not fair. Okay, that was an entire bottle of wine last night in front of a very weepy movie. Guilty as charged, but a mom's gotta do something when her other half takes the kids to visit his parents for the weekend. That's what me time is for. The small price of a hangover in the morning wouldn't have been at all surprising. But dying in my sleep? That's not fair at all.

As my eyes get used to it that light becomes round and high, in the apex of what appears to be a dome-shaped chamber. There are things hanging down around it, metallic tendrils, each one with some nasty-looking instrument at the end of it. Well, this isn't what heaven's supposed to look like. Where are all the angels? Where's the choir invisible? Where are all my dead relatives waiting to greet me? Where's God?

Or is this the other place? No one goes to the other place in a near-death experience. Correction: Almost no one goes to the other place in a near-death experience. Well, isn't this just peachy? My near-death experience is the other place: an eternal visit to the dentist, probably with no anesthetic. We left fairness behind a long time ago.

Time to wake up. My body is waiting for me in a nice, warm, cozy bed, which this surface I'm lying on most definitely isn't. It's cold and very hard. Moreover, only my eyes can move. I peer down over my cheeks to find four figures standing in a semicircle around my feet. They look like doctors, very short doctors but all of them wearing white scrubs. They should be wearing surgical masks and caps as well. Instead, this bunch seems to be wearing Halloween masks: green triangular things with a small mouth at the bottom, two big almond-shaped black eyes above, and nothing more than two nostrils in between.

There's a name for this, sleep paralysis, and it usually involves being abducted by aliens. Wait. You cannot be serious. Abducted by aliens! Things like that don't happen to me. I'm normal, ordinary. I live in a normal, ordinary house in a normal, ordinary neighborhood with my normal, ordinary family. The weirdest thing that's ever happened to me is finding my car keys aren't where I swear I left them.

This has to be a dream, a really unpleasant one that has me sweating between the sheets because my heart is racing and I really would like to wake up now. Come on! Wake up! Except now one of those creatures is stepping forward. Its three-fingered hand reaches for one of those instruments hanging down from the light. It wants me to have a look at it, the big grip with the thinner nozzle that's several inches in length. See? It's wonderful, perfectly crafted for its purpose.

And look. When this button is pressed, this thin sliver of a very long needle slips out the end of it.

No! No! Don't you come near me with that thing. Don't you dare come near me with that thing. My eye. You are not going to stick that thing in my eye. Don't you even think about sticking that thing in my—you goddamn son of a—

There's a sound, hissy like a snake with a stutter, and the probe alien's head explodes.

What the hell!

As what's left of it slowly collapses, a fountain of green gunk splatters everywhere, some of it onto me. The snake spits again and the other three lose their heads too, with a whole lot more green gunk splattering everywhere.

Oh my God! Oh my God!

In the deathly silence that follows, because it isn't even possible for me to scream, something moves into my field of vision. It's a woman. She's tall, with short, dark hair and a slim, athletic body. She's also holding a very big gun which she continues to point at the bodies on the floor. That's okay by me. My head's fine where it is, if it's all the same to you.

After a few moments, satisfied that all four of them are now very dead and no longer a threat, she looks down at me through deep dark brown eyes, coolly unconcerned with the slaughterhouse she's just made of this chamber.

"Are you harmed?"

No, not physically anyway, but getting the hell off this table would be nice. That comes out as a series of muffled squeaks. Somehow she understands and, reaching down and under the table, she does something. The invisible hand pinning me here disappears and I'm on my feet, backing away from her and almost slipping up on all that green gunk.

"What did you do? You killed all the alien guys. Where are

you from, Chicago? They were aliens, weren't they?"

"If by aliens you mean not of your kind, then yes. Would you prefer me not to have killed them?"

Standing in among them now, and looking back at all those tendrils ending in nasty instruments, the answer to that question is pretty damned obvious.

"No! Who are these guys anyway, and what were they going to do to me, apart from sticking that needle in my eye for who knows what reason because they're a bunch of sadists who get off on that kind of thing? For that matter, who are you?"

"I don't know. I can't remember. They tried to memory-block me. It's rather like having a corrupted data file inside your head. I can remember bits and pieces here and there but everything in between is gone. For instance, right now we're aboard their ship. There's a planet below us. It's blue but I don't know what planet it is. I don't know what part of the universe we're in either. Nor do I know why I'm on this ship."

"Wait. We're on a ship? You mean a spaceship?"

"Yes. Why? Where did you think you were?"

"I thought I was in bed dreaming, or at least I hoped I was. So I actually have been abducted by aliens and we're on a spaceship orbiting Earth. That's what we call that blue planet. It's my home, and I think I'd rather like to go back now."

"You can't."

"What? Why?"

"Because I think I killed them all, but there might be one or two left. If so they will have sent a distress call. When that call is received, others will come and they'll be looking for this ship. They'll be looking for us too. Before that happens we need to be a long way from here."

"A long way from here? Are you serious? I can't just leave.

I have a family. I have friends. I have a cat."

"You don't have a choice, unless you want to be here when they come looking. Your Earth, your family, and your cat are not a threat to them. They'll be perfectly safe. We aren't. We need to be a long way—"

"You can't be sure of that. You said your memory was blocked, like a corrupt data file."

"It is, and I'm not. Do you want to take the chance? Now get dressed. We've wasted enough time already."

Oh my God, she's right. Look at me standing here butt naked and covered in green gunk. It's sticky, it's yucky, and it has a very peculiar smell. "Ew. Do they have any showers on this ship?"

"I don't know. I haven't come across any, but don't worry, it's not corrosive. Here, use this." She tosses a shirt at me. It comes from among all the clothing piled against the curved wall like flotsam on a reef.

"My God, how many people have these aliens abducted, and what happened to them if their clothes were left— corrosive! What do you mean, corrosive? This stuff isn't going to eat through the hull, is it?"

"No. It hasn't eaten through you, has it? So why would you think it might eat through the hull?"

It was rather a silly thought, put like that, and this woman, whoever she is, clearly doesn't do silly. "No reason. It's just something I saw once. It doesn't matter."

The shirt does a moderately good job of wiping me clean, enough to live with anyway. After that my own clothes are easily found: a dark green t-shirt and tartan pajama bottoms because that's what they abducted me in. It's not exactly what anyone would call a fetching ensemble, but then who expects to be abducted by aliens in the middle of the night? Some dingy sneakers that almost fit finish it off. Whoever owned them when they were taken isn't exactly going to kick up a fuss about it.

"Okay. I'm good to go. What? You don't like it?"

She's dressed all in black: flat-heeled boots, skin-tight pants, and a jacket that might be leather, might be faux or might be something else entirely. Either way it's very functional, and yet at the same time quietly chic. She could walk a catwalk anytime she wanted to on Earth. She's even got that sense of hauteur they do it with, or it might simply be more of the total lack of emotional engagement she's shown so far. Then again, it could be fascination because it's not what I'm wearing she's looking at. It's my hair, shoulder-length and now swept back behind my ears.

"What color is that? I don't think I've ever seen hair that color before."

"I'm a redhead. Or a ginger if you want to be a dick about it."

"And does everyone on your planet have hair that color?"

"No. My ancestors came from a place where the sun only came out once a year and the rest of the time it rained. UV is not our friend."

She nods slowly, fascinated enough to briefly forget any sense of urgency. Then she snaps out of it, and without another word spoken, leads the way out of this chamber. I'm expected to simply follow on behind apparently. Not a very promising start to a relationship, but then the only other choice is to wait here for more of them to turn up. It'll be the strong, silent mass murderer for me then, and we'll get to work on her communication skills later.

The passageway beyond is dimly lit but just as littered. So are all the ones that follow and all the rooms leading off them. Housekeeping may be a chore, but really, if this were my spaceship I'd be ashamed to bring abductees aboard. But then it's not my spaceship. It's not theirs anymore either. It's my new best friend's. It's also a maze, one I'd be lost in instantly, and it's by no means certain she knows her way through it either. It's pretty obvious where she's come from though because of all the headless aliens she's left behind, which might be what she's following.

"My God, how many of these guys did you kill?"

"A lot but, like I said, there might be the odd one or two left so keep your voice down and your eyes open."

For a while we walk on in silence. It's horrible. This isn't a ship so much as a crypt filled with ghouls who might jump out at us at any moment, except these ghouls are green aliens. Not that it really matters. Ghouls or aliens: If they're out to get you, they're out to get you, and these guys, if there are any of them left, are definitely out to get us. The silence is becoming oppressive, morbid even, cloying and stifling like too much cheap perfume. Finally it just has to be filled.

"So what should I call you? Only I forgot to ask."

She gives a little shrug. "I don't know. I can't remember."

"Because they memory-blocked you. How does that work?"

"I don't know. I know they have that kind of tech because they used it on me. It's highly likely they were going to use it on you too. That way you wouldn't have been able to remember any of this once they'd finished with you."

"I don't know about that. There are an awful lot of people on Earth who do remember, or at least they think they do."

"Yes. Judging by all that clothing these aliens have been busy, which is interesting. And with that many people, it's hardly surprising if some of them were ineffectively blocked. As for me, I think they were going to block me entirely and then dump me on your planet with no way home, wherever home is, but it didn't go so well. I woke up and the training kicked in, or at least I'm assuming it's some kind of training. That's something else I can't remember."

"That's the second time you've called it my planet. Does that mean you're not from Earth? You certainly look human."

"Yes, I've been thinking about that too. Unfortunately I don't have an answer. I know I'm not from Earth because this isn't the only spaceship I can remember being on. I can remember other planets too, and the beings who live on them. One in particular feels like home. I remember a big city filled with tall buildings and bright lights. The streets are teeming but no one is in a hurry. Everyone is very polite. Everyone is quietly happy."

"Can't be New York then. They'll eat you alive as soon as look at you."

Still lost in memories, she doesn't hear me. "There's a building too, with lots of security. There are people in uniforms. I think I must be one of them but I can't remember who they are."

"Sounds like a police precinct or maybe even the Pentagon. Wait a minute—that works. You're some sort of agent. Yeah, someone sent you out here to get on board this ship and they memory-blocked you and now you can't remember why. That would also explain your training. You're some sort of super spy."

This time she does hear me, although it might have been better if she hadn't. There's a glance, mildly indulgent, as if I'm prattling on about Santa Claus or the tooth fairy.

"Do you always run off into flights of fantasy like that?"

"Pretty much. That's who I am, and by the way, my name is Debbie. Since you can't remember yours, I think I'll call you

Ellen because she was good at kicking alien ass too."

We turn into another passageway. This one ends in a blank wall with a strange bluish tinge to it, as if it is covered in a layer of cellophane. It's fascinating to look at, but a dead-end is a dead-end. There aren't even any headless aliens so it looks like the maze has finally defeated her.

"We're lost, aren't we? We could be wandering around this ship forever, slowly dying of thirst in orbit around a planet that's three-fifths water. That's if more of these aliens don't turn up first. Where are we supposed to be going anyway?"

"We're trying to get to the bridge. This—I know this. It's some sort of door. It could take us straight there if I could remember how it works." Reaching out a finger, she stabs at it, causing little ripples to spread out around her fingertip. Apart from that, nothing happens.

"Maybe you're supposed to tell it where you want to go, like it's voice-activated."

She thinks about it, shrugs, and stabs again. "Bridge."

Still nothing happens.

It must be some kind of AI, the kind that's so sophisticated it completely fails to understand anything said to it. *I'm sorry, could you repeat that?* And we're still gazing at a blue-tinged wall, a very uncooperative blue-tinged wall. Maybe this AI is waiting to hear the magic word because somebody decided even machines have feelings. *I'm sorry; your request cannot be processed at this time due to your lack of courtesy. Please try again later when you've learned some manners.*

Reaching past Ellen, I try a tap of my own. "Bridge, please."

An even more indulgent gaze is turned on me. "You actually thought that would work?"

"It might have."

"Well, it didn't, so it looks like we're walking. Come on."

She heads back the way we came, which strikes me as giving up way too easily. They might not call it the bridge. They might call it something else, like Helm or Command Center.

My first tap produces nothing and she's calling back to me, "Come on. We're walking."

My second tap causes the wall to shimmer. Now we're getting somewhere. "Ellen. Look, I've made it work."

Or not, because gazing back at me from the other side with its big black eyes is one of them. If its triangular face with that tiny mouth could wear something as recognizable as a smirk, it probably would be. Who knows, perhaps it is. It can gurgle though, which might be laughter. Well, the joke's on you pal. My friend has a really big gun and you don't. But then, I don't have one either.

"Ellen!"

There's no answer. It's just me and the gurgler, and the gurgler might as well be saying, "Run if you want but I'm still gonna getcha."

This is not good.

"Ellen!"

Feet slap the floor behind me. There's the end of the passageway. Which way did she go: left or right? I don't know. I wasn't paying attention. Maybe she's gone left. Maybe she's gone right. Those feet are closing on me. There's nothing to choose between the passageways. In both directions there's a growing gloom and the certainty that this passageway will run into a dead-end at some point.

"Ellen! Help! Now would be good."

I run to the left, with those feet slapping harder and closer. Please God, let there be something more than a dead-end ahead of me—and there is. It's an opening to my left that leads into a long chamber filled with benches. Clutter is everywhere. It looks like some kind of laboratory. There are all sorts of science stuff like glassware, more nasty-looking instruments and strange apparatus: small bench-top things and big, bulky stand-alone things with control panels filled with lights. My situation just got very much worse. Rats don't walk into laboratories, let alone run, especially when they're being chased by a mad scientist. The one chasing me is now very mad—gibbering mad, in fact. As it leaps up onto a bench and sees me scurrying along the floor, my pursuer picks up one of those bench-top things, a particularly big and heavy-looking one, and launches it across the chamber, only narrowly missing me.

The instrument bounces off the edge of a bench and clatters to the floor, which only serves to infuriate my pursuer further. What was an abductor in white scrubs is now a big, green and very angry chimpanzee. Screaming, it jumps from bench-top to bench-top scattering everything in its path: other instruments, glassware, and all manner of junk and clutter. Debris is flying everywhere and this rat is scurrying away, trying only to avoid the potshots that keep coming every time it catches sight of me.

Then the floor runs out. One more scurry, one more turn, and the only thing in front of me is the meeting of two walls. Screeching and gibbering, my pursuer perches on the edge of a bench above me. There's something big and heavy in its hand, and there's nowhere left for me to go but to squeeze into that corner. But for some reason my pursuer hesitates. Maybe it's savoring the moment. Somewhere inside the green gunk that is its brain it's probably thinking, *Gotcha! Now let's see what human brains look like.*

Big mistake! The stuttering snake hisses from the far side of the room and my pursuer's head explodes, leaving the rest of it to topple slowly to the floor. It wanted to see red blood splattered across the wall. Instead that blood is green, with some of it once again splattered on me, and here's Ellen standing over me as coolly unemotional as ever. For her it's just another day in the office.

"Are you harmed?"

"Harmed? Am I harmed? Well, let's see, shall we? My heart is running a half marathon, my nerves are looking for the exit, the emotional scars may never heal and I've only been here fifteen minutes."

"So you're not harmed then."

Really! Come on, Ellen, show some empathy. Someone needs a hug and maybe a shoulder to cry on. She's offering neither, which isn't really that much of a surprise. One thing she definitely isn't is a hugger. At least she's taking time out of her busy day of slaughtering aliens to ask.

"No, I'm not harmed. It was pretty close though."

"I got here as soon as I could. Now we seriously need to find the bridge. That thing has had more than enough time to send out a distress call. So come on. Get up. Sitting there isn't getting us anywhere."

And that's it. A helping hand hauls me to my feet and there isn't even time to find something to wipe the gunk away. She's in too much of a hurry and apparently not in the least bit concerned that this stuff might be full of who knows what diseases. After a couple of dabs at it and watching it ooze between my finger and thumb, that certainly concerns me.

"So how come you can go wandering around the universe without any kind of protection—y'know, hazmat suits and the like?"

"I don't know. I can't remember."

That figures. I could already be dying here. Bacteria could

be hacking their way through my skin with machetes and standing in awe at the new world they've found to conquer. They could be setting up base camps, founding colonies like pimples on a Petri dish or invading my internal organs in search of natural resources. But never mind. We have to get to the bridge, and this time I'm sticking close by my new best friend. I might drop dead at any moment but at least it won't be an enraged chimpanzee that kills me.

We go along the passageway and climb up stairwells to higher decks. This ship isn't simply a maze. It's a maze on top of a maze, and then another maze on top of that one. The occasional alien corpse suggests Ellen knows where she's going but it would have been so much easier and quicker if that glowing doorway had worked.

"So how come that thing back there didn't take us straight to the bridge? It worked for one of them after all."

"I don't know. Maybe you're right and it's voice-activated. It worked for one of them because it understands their language. It didn't work for us because it didn't understand your language or mine."

"Your language? I'm pretty sure you're speaking the same language as me. Otherwise how could I understand you?"

"That's not possible. I've never been to Earth and you've never been to my home world. We can't be speaking the same language."

"And yet here we are, and you're speaking English. Are you sure you're not from Earth? Like maybe you're another abductee and you just forgot?"

"Forgot. How would I forget something like that?"

"They memory-blocked you, didn't they? So what if you didn't escape like you think you did? What if they were about to release you? What if you watched too many science fiction movies as a kid and all that stuff you think you remember is nothing more than a fantasy you've created out of all the bits of memory you have left? What if—?"

"Me fantasizing! You're the one creating entire narratives out of next to nothing. First I'm some kind of spy. Then I'm another abductee. Just quit with it, will you? We have more important things to deal with."

Oops. Looks like somebody might have a little bit of a temper after all. Best keep quiet then, for now at least, especially since she's the one with the gun.

Fortunately this ever-so-slightly awkward silence doesn't last too long. One more stairway takes us into a chamber that looks more like a hacker's basement than a bridge. Behind us is a straight wall with another of those blue panels in its center, the doorway we would've stepped through if we had been able to make it work. Directly in front of us is a console. It's filled with open windows and gently slopes toward the chair behind it. "Chair" is a rather loose description. It looks more like a big egg with the front sliced off. There are more consoles and chairs around a semicircular wall, all rooted to the floor by thick stems.

Then there are the screens, hanging in mid-air like movies being projected onto diaphanous curtains. There are small ones on both sides of us, all of them alive with graphics that flash and pulse and scroll. They're quite fascinating to watch but totally unintelligible, at least to me. At the very front of the bridge is a screen so big it fills the wall from floor to ceiling. In its bottom third is the blue curve of Earth, with nothing but the blackness of space above. Of course I've seen the photographs and watched the videos, but still, this is a moment that should take anyone's breath away.

"Wow. It's beautiful, and you really can't see any stars."

"That's right. This close to one, you can only see the rest of the universe in the shadow of a planet. Why? Did you think it had all suddenly disappeared?"

"No. I've never been in space before, that's all. Seeing it first-hand is a whole different experience."

Ellen almost smiles, and then sits in the egg before the central console. That must be the captain's console. After a moment, she very deliberately sits forward to begin tapping and sliding on the console with her finger, scrolling through windows and muttering as she pours over them. "Now. Can I remember how to do this?"

That's not so good. All those graphics and pictographs and streams of text might be as meaningless to her as they are to me.

"It's a pity you can't talk to it. You could do that, couldn't you? If you weren't stuck speaking English."

"I would if I could but I can't so I'm not. Now shush. I need to find us a destination."

Looking at Earth, so serenely blue and beautiful down there below us, suddenly I'm having second thoughts. "Are you sure about this? I mean, it's this ship they'll be looking for, isn't it? What if we just went down there and forgot about it? Maybe they would too. I could go back to my life, and you could hide out in our basement until you've learned how everything works on Earth. You could have a good life: get married, settle down, have some kids. How would they ever find us? How would they even know it was us who did it?"

"Because this ship would still be here. To have abducted that many people, they must have been here for quite some time. They know your capabilities, or lack of them. If this ship is still here with no one on board, they'll know the only place we could be is down there. As to knowing who it was, they'll certainly know it was you. They keep records, y'know. If this ship is still here, the first place they'll go looking is the coordinates you were abducted from. If this ship is gone, they'll likely think we took it and probably not bother going down there at all."

"Likely? Probably? Is that the best you've got?"

"Would you prefer the alternative, which is pretty much a certainty?"

"Not when you put it like that, no."

"Good. Then let's stop wasting time and find somewhere to go." She taps something on the console and all the lights go out. An instant later they come back on again. It could be my imagination, but is that just a hint of embarrassment I see on her face? Probably best not to say anything. She taps something else and that faint hum that I'd never noticed before whines down to nothing. Nope, still not saying anything.

Restoring the hum, she sits back for a moment to think. Then she starts moving windows around until she finds one that's a list, each item contained within its own little rectangle. They could be anything. The one thing they definitely aren't is in English. Her finger scrolls and hovers, then scrolls and hovers again, every item on that list indistinguishable from all the others except for their different but unreadable text. At last, with a little shrug—because what the hell?—she stabs at one. The item lights up, flashing red. More importantly, Earth disappears from the main screen. In its place is the image of some other planet.

"Whoa! Where did that come from?"

Ellen is just as mystified as me. "I don't know. It must be how the system works. So what do you think? It's as good as anywhere."

Possibly, but neither of us can know since the text running

down either side of the planet is unreadable. The photographs embedded in the text are clear enough though, each of them linked to a different region. There's a band of mottled yellow-brown-ocher extending some way out from the equator, with photographs of desert landscapes attached. A band of greens and blues then extends all the way to the white barrenness of the poles. Within it are thick forests, plains and farmland, great lakes and even greater cities, each one highlighted with a photograph of some local landmark. It looks an awful lot like a travel brochure, tempting us with all the interesting places we might visit.

While I'm still taking that in, the ship shudders. It's weird, rather like an earth tremor that fills the air with a frisson of static. It's vaguely orgasmic, as if the great whale that is our ship just had a wet dream, if great whales have wet dreams. I don't know, but who's to say they don't?

When it's all over, Ellen is sitting back in the captain's egg with a tiny grin creeping up the corners of her mouth. "There. We've arrived."

CHAPTER TWO

"**A**rrived? How did that happen? Where are we?"

The blackness in front of us now has a big yellow-orange sun in the top left corner. One tiny pinprick of light sits in the center and a larger, almost disk-like spot sits in the bottom right corner. Earth is nowhere to be seen.

"We jumped. Don't worry. This ship will take us anywhere it has coordinates for. But that's a problem for later. Our problem right now is how long it will take them to arrive at Earth and then figure out where we've gone. So let's use our time wisely and find out what the locals are like. Maybe they can help fill in some of the blanks too, like, for instance, why I'm speaking a language from a planet I've never set foot on."

No sooner has she spoken than the locals turn up, the blackness of the universe and the yellow-orangeness of that big sun replaced on our main screen by another kind of alien. This one is gray and hairless with big red saucer eyes, hardly anything by way of a nose and sharp little teeth inside a wide, lipless mouth. It looks decidedly demonic. It's also staring at us open-mouthed as if it's been caught doing something its mom wouldn't approve of.

"Why's it looking at us like that?"

Silently staring back, Ellen shakes her head.

Somebody has to break the ice here so I give it a big smile and a wave. "Hi. We thought we'd come visit you, if that's okay."

Apparently it isn't. Some people don't like being dropped in on, and this demon is one of them. It's jolted out of its trance, its stare becoming a glare, and now it's barking at us in a language that sounds pretty demonic too.

"What's it saying?"

"I don't know. I can't understand it any more than you can. At a guess I'd say it recognizes this ship and it doesn't like the green aliens either. Maybe they've been abducting people on this planet too. We're probably lucky it isn't shooting at us already."

"Shooting at us! Whoa!" This time, both my hands are waving. "Hey, hold up. We're not them. You can see us, right? We're not them, okay?"

It leans forward, looming as it gazes out of our main screen at me. If it was possible to recognize an expression on its face, that expression would probably be saying, *Who is this mad woman who keeps waving at me?*

Then it disappears, our screen filled once more with the blackness of space and those three heavenly bodies.

"Oh. So what's this then: the brush off? Goodbye and don't come back."

"More likely it's talking to a superior. This has to be some kind of immigration control, and no matter where you go immigration doesn't like anyone, anywhere, anytime. On the plus side, that means they're civilized. On the minus side, that means bureaucracy and bureaucracy means no one is responsible for anything if there's someone else to dump it on. They still haven't fired on us, so I guess we wait and see."

That leads to a tense few minutes. They still haven't fired on us which isn't exactly putting my mind at ease, but there it is. Moment follows moment and they still haven't fired on us. Somewhere down there someone is asking a superior for guidance. That superior is probably watching a recording of us and then asking another superior for guidance. And so it goes on until somewhere along the line of superiors, someone decides whether to let us in or seriously discourage us from ever coming back. Like I said, it's a tense few minutes.

At last the alien reappears. Raising a bony finger, it gives us what it probably thinks is a meaningful gaze but to me looks more like a murderous glare. They still haven't fired on us, although it's anybody's guess as to what that bony finger is about to do.

It points at us, following up with a series of exaggerated tapping motions. The last of them lands on something below the bottom of our screen. It must have a console of its own down there. Immediately a window opens on Ellen's console and we both look down at it.

"Is that a text message?"

"If that's what you call it."

"Wow. You guys are really up to speed with all this tech stuff, aren't you? So what does it say?"

"I have no idea, but it looks like we're about to be boarded."

There's a bright blob in the center of our main screen. It quickly grows into a ship: small and sleek, thick in the middle but flattening out around the edges, with two tailfins rising above its bulbous rear. It's colored yellow and black like a wasp, with big red lettering that probably says coastguard or spaceguard or whatever it is these aliens call it.

Closer and closer it comes, or at least bigger and bigger on our main screen it becomes. Right about when it looks like it's coming through that screen it stops. Another text arrives. It consists of nothing more than a big red flashing button. This is usually when someone says, "Whatever happens, do not touch that." Since there's no one here to say it, Ellen gives it a tap. The big red button is replaced with scrolling code and, for several moments, that's it.

"What's that doing?"

"At a guess, I'd say they're figuring out how to operate that doorway behind us."

Sure enough, even as Ellen finishes speaking, the blue panel disappears. From a gray chamber beyond, six figures step through onto the bridge. All of them are dressed in shiny black one-piece suits and helmets with big visors. Five of them are also carrying very big weapons that say be afraid, be very afraid, except Ellen isn't. She stands to face them as calmly and as level-eyed as a lioness wondering whether or not they might be edible. Yeah, you go get 'em, girl. You'll find me hiding behind the console when it's all over.

Four of them immediately exit the bridge. While the fifth one roots itself at a safe distance, the sixth one steps forward, producing something that looks an awful lot like a smartphone. Maybe it's going to phone home. Aww, that's so sweet. Even aliens have mommies. Then again, maybe not. Choosing Ellen first, it runs the device over her like one of those detector things they use at security points. So this must be the immigration officer who checks your passport then, the one who looks at all those photos without ever cracking a smile. At a beep over the back of Ellen's neck the officer pauses, tapping several times on the device. There's another beep over her left forearm, with another pause and more tapping, followed by several intercom-y sounding barks as, for the first time, the officer speaks.

And, oh my God, Ellen is answering it. "Really? Thank you."

More barking.

"I know. Apparently it's called English."

There's nothing quite as annoying as listening in to half a conversation and not having a clue what the other half is about.

Some more barking.

"Well, okay. And thanks again for that."

Some final barking and now it's my turn. This time there are no beeps anywhere. Oops. Houston, we have a problem. The alien taps the device some more and tries again. Still there's nothing. It holds the device up, giving it a couple of good whacks because that always works. Finally, it shakes it and tries again. Still nothing, and once more it barks at Ellen.

"No, she wouldn't. This is her first time off-world."

Another quick bark.

"You'd have to ask them—except they're all dead, or at least we think they're all dead. We don't know what happened. They did something to our minds. We can remember some things, like waking up on this ship, but it's mostly a blank. Honestly, that's all we know."

"Ellen. What's happening?"

"You're not chipped. Everyone in the civilized universe is, according to this one. That means I'm cleared for entry but you're not. I don't know what their protocol for that is. I don't think he does either."

"What do you mean I'm not chipped?"

"I mean you're not documented: no ID, no medical

record, and no credit score. Officially you don't exist."

"Don't exist!"

Really? This is not how first contact is supposed to be. We're all supposed to be jumping up and down and shouting, "Yay, the aliens have come to save us," or running for the hills while our cities burn. Either of those would at least be some sort of validation: We like you so we came to help you, or we hate you so we came to destroy you. Being declared an undocumented alien and someone who doesn't officially exist is just so bureaucratic. This should be a great moment for all of us, a historic meeting—hands across the universe and all that. The guy on the door says otherwise. No ID, no entry. Then it gets worse. After some more tapping on the smartphone, the doorway opens again and two more of them appear, carrying something between them that looks an awful lot like a hazmat suit, and they're walking straight toward me.

"No way am I wearing that!"

"Unfortunately, yes way. You're also a potential biohazard."

"A potential biohazard! How do you figure that? And why aren't you one too? You've been exposed to me for almost an hour."

"I don't know. Look, it's not my protocol, it's theirs. I'd just put it on if I were you. I think this one's getting a little impatient."

Right on cue, the one with the smartphone barks some more and Ellen translates. "It says you put on the suit or you get thrown out of an airlock."

"Well, this is really civilized, isn't it? Put that thing on or we throw you out of an airlock."

"To them it probably is. You're something he's never seen before: an unchipped alien with no ID and no medical record. Now put the suit on or they might very well throw you out of an airlock. It is their planet after all. They're just trying to protect it."

"Not out here it isn't. We can go somewhere else, can't we, somewhere a little more friendly?"

"No, we can't. Anywhere else we go with you in your condition, we'll probably run into the same problem."

"Oh, so now I've got a condition, have I?"

"Yes. Now put the suit on. We don't have time for this, or have you forgotten about our friends?"

Thank you, Ellen. The fearless alien fighter who was not so long ago blowing the heads off green chimps isn't a lioness anymore. Now she's a lamb, and it's me against the universe, and the universe is winning because I'd really rather not be thrown out of an airlock.

"Okay, fine, but you better not think we're done with this."

By the time they've finished wrapping me up in a cellophane onesie, because that's what this suit feels like, the other four have returned. They report in, with Ellen translating their muffled barkings for me.

"They've done a preliminary search of the ship. They haven't found any of them, not alive anyway, so we're cleared to proceed."

That's wonderful. Excuse me for not saying so out loud, only trying to hold a conversation through this candy wrapper isn't exactly my thing.

The officer puts the smartphone away and heads for the captain's egg. Also sitting forward in it, he or she starts tapping on the console. It's impossible to tell what it is with that suit and visor on, and maybe without it too. Either way, he taps and scrolls for maybe a minute. There's even the occasional shake of his or her head. Then, as if by magic, all the squiggly green script changes to another kind of squiggly script and we're on our way.

The sun slowly slides off the top left corner of our main screen. The blob in the bottom right moves to the center and grows to become the planet Ellen chose before we jumped. It's exactly as we saw it on our main screen except on this, the real thing, there are also bands and stacks of clouds that cast shadows onto the greens and browns and whites.

This will be my first alien world, my first alien civilization. Even wrapped up in this suit, there's a growing sense of anticipation. Except we're not going down to the surface. As we maneuver so that the planet fills the bottom third of our screen, far in front of us and floating high above it is a spot of light. It grows as we approach, becoming a space station: a big, fat ball of a thing with antennae and who knows what else protruding from its top and bottom. Its light gray surface is dotted with points of light and, here and there, more red text. As we come to a halt some way from it, our escort gives the console another tap and the doorway opens again.

Without even so much as an "excuse me," the two who brought the hazmat suit seize me by an arm each and march me through to a gray passageway with low-level lighting and no doorways or exits anywhere to be seen. All there is along both sides of the passageway are widely spaced lights: small, waist-high, and flashing green. One of my escorts passes a hand over one of those lights and an opening appears. What lies beyond is a rectangular box, gray and bare. There's a bench for sitting and sleeping on. There's what must be a toilet. There's no window to glimpse any kind of sky through. There's not even any graffiti to pass a few minutes reading.

With the suit removed, I'm thrust through. The opening behind me is replaced with a solid wall, and that's it: no cell block noise, no pipes to tap on and no neighbors to talk to as we hang out through the bars. For all I know, Ellen might be next door. That's not very likely though. No one called her an undocumented biohazard. She's probably kicking back on a sofa watching TV with a nice bottle of wine. She's probably ordering room service and a masseuse and generally having a high old time of it.

An hour out from Earth, and maybe a million light years away, and this is my welcome. "Hey, nice to see you. Thanks for dropping by. We've reserved this cell especially for you. Enjoy!" Once I've established that it's just over four steps long and barely two steps wide, there's nothing left to do but figure out how exactly anyone's supposed to sleep on a bed made of rock, and if that is a toilet in the corner, how the hell does it work? There's nothing to do but stare at the wall and notice a certain lightness of feeling. What could be causing that is a mystery. Maybe they're pumping something in with the air to keep the inmates happy, a bit like giving chimps in a zoo some old tires to play on. If so it's not working. My thoughts turn to home and I wonder if anyone has noticed my disappearance yet. It's not very likely. They'll all still be asleep. My husband might call in a couple of hours but all he'll hear is a phone ringing forlornly through an empty house. He'll probably think I haven't crawled out of bed yet and hang up. And so it will go for the rest of the day until at last he starts to wonder.

My heart sinks at the thought of it, dragged further down by the likelihood that there's worse to come. Nor is there anything to take my mind off it until Ellen reappears. She's looking terribly serious, not at all like someone who's been living it up in the lap of luxury.

"So when do I get out of here?"

"Yeah, that's what I've come to talk to you about. This civilization calls itself the Nosundomi and they're quite amenable really. They bought our story so stick to it from now on, okay? To be honest I think they were way more interested in the contents of our hold and all that Green tech we unexpectedly landed in their laps. Apparently, thanks to the Greens, we're seriously wealthy. So I cut a deal with them and they've agreed to integrate you. As soon as that's done, we're back on board and a long way from here."

"Integrate me. What does that mean?"

"It means they're going to chip you. The ULD goes in at the base of your skull. That's the Universal Language Database. Once it's installed you'll be able to understand every language recorded on it. The other goes in your forearm. It'll contain your ID, medical record, and credit score. They'll also inject you with nanotech that'll hunt down anything that isn't your DNA and destroy it."

"The hell they will. Nobody's sticking any of that stuff into me."

"Yes, I thought you might say that. So here's the thing. As I said before, every planet we visit, we're going to run into the same problem. Look at it from their side. They can't have just anybody dropping by, bringing who knows what potential threats with them. They're gonna want to know who you are, where you're from and whether you're a danger to them. The alternative is you probably spend the rest of your life in this cell, at least until the Greens turn up, and then they'll likely accuse you of starting a war. Is that what you want?"

"No! Obviously. So why don't you just bust me out? You could do that, right?"

"I could, but that doesn't solve the problem. Besides, then you'd probably have more than just the Greens after you. Do you want to be labeled an intergalactic bioterrorist and have bounty hunters from across the entire known universe after you as well?"

"An intergalactic bioterrorist! Are you kidding? I was abducted from my bed. I've been dragged halfway across the universe and locked up in this cell, all of it by aliens who aren't even supposed to exist and now I'm an intergalactic—why are you calling them the Greens all of a sudden?"

"Everybody does, apparently. That's what the Nosundomi say anyway. They've been quite helpful really, explaining things like the ULD and the ID chip and those blue shimmering doors that are called portal tech. It seems they work the same way as the main engine but on a much smaller scale—something to do with bending space-time, whatever that means. Anyway, not much is known about the Greens apart from they're green, they're nomads and opportunists and they're banned from just about every civilized planet in the known universe. No one even knows if they have a home world."

"So basically they're pirates, taking whatever they want wherever they can find it. Why were they so interested in me?"

"I don't know. Maybe they just didn't like you. That's one of the things we're going to find out. That and why I was on their ship. There is good news though. I've read my ID. I know who I am and where I'm from. My name is very long and unpronounceable so you probably best keep calling me Ellen, and I'm from a planet called Veniramat. And the lesson you should take from that is that you should be chipped too. That way, even if the Greens memory-block you, you'll still know who you are because it'll be right there in your arm. That alone is reason enough to say yes, don't you think? So what do you say? The sooner it's done, the sooner we're out of here."

Talk about a rock and a hard place. She's got me both ways. Do as I say or the green nasties are coming to get you.

What a revelation this would be for the folks back home. Hey, guys, look at this. The universe is just as full of control freaks running around with tablets in their hands as Earth. It's just as full of people willingly accepting it as well, including Ellen. At least she has an excuse: Her memory's blocked. Mine isn't, and the passive aggressiveness isn't going to end until I say yes.

"Debbie. You need to decide. It really is for everyone's good: yours, mine, the Nosundomi's and every other race we might visit."

Yeah, it's for everyone's good. It's only a couple of little chips. You won't even know they're there. I swear it's like talking to a charity worker. The guilt tripping doesn't stop until you've given them what they want, and maybe not even then.

"Okay, okay. My God, just quit with the emotional blackmail, will you? I swear I'd throw up if I could figure out how the toilet worked."

She walks over to it, lifts the lid, and drops it down again. By the time she's walked back, it's flushed all on its own. Okay. Good to know, and very hygienic too. Now all we have to do is teach men how to put the lid down.

The door opens and two of them are waiting outside. This time they're not dressed in black or wearing visors. They're wearing full-face respirators, with those big red saucer eyes peering out over the top of their chunkiness. They're also dressed in pale blue gowns, a nice soothing color because we wouldn't want the biohazard to think something bad was about to happen. At least dogs have tails to curl between their legs when they're taken to the vet.

The portal tech I entered by opens onto a very functional-looking room: bright, white, and spotless. Off to one side is a big laid-back chair with the wall behind it a bank of machines, all blinking lights and screens with oscillating graphics. Suspended above it is a big, flat thing, rather like one of those kinky mirrors except this one is black. Standing in front of all of this is the demon vet, wearing a deeply scarlet gown, the exact same shade as splattered blood. My imaginary tail is now curling all the way up to my stomach.

The portal tech closes behind us. There's no escape, and the demon vet is already breaking out into a big lipless smile behind that mask. There's a lot of barking too, probably intended to set me at ease. It's not working.

Ellen translates. "This is Doctor Splog. He says welcome to Nosundomi. Now, this is a very simple procedure, absolutely nothing to worry about. It will all be over in no time at all. So if you'd like to make yourself comfortable, we can begin."

All that's missing is a few calming strokes from a gentle hand and lots of reassuring cooing. Not that any of that will be coming from Ellen. She's standing there like a nurse, all but saying *Doctor knows best.*

My heart is pumping; my nerves are becoming jittery. At least the chair is comfortable, until it proves itself to be a liar. No sooner am I lying on it than the screen above changes to a deep blue, and it's the Green ship all over again. Some great invisible hand is pressing down on me. At least this time I can still talk. "Ellen. What's happening?"

"Don't worry. It'll all be over in a matter of moments."

Somehow that isn't making me feel any better.

Then it gets worse. Doctor Splog disappears for a few moments. When he returns there's a tablet in his hand. After a few taps, needles appear from somewhere behind me. They hover like the heads of snakes, a big, thick one sniffing at my left forearm and a thinner one sniffing at my right. I am absolutely not feeling better anymore. In fact, my heart is pounding, and I'm ready to be anywhere but here.

"What the hell! What is it with you people and needles? Get me off this thing, or I swear to God—"

"Relax. We can't have those needles going in all the wrong places. That wouldn't do at all." So much for Ellen's bedside manner.

Doctor Splog's isn't any better. He's standing over me entirely engrossed with the tablet in his hand, tapping and nodding, nodding and tapping, and then, with a flourish, tapping one last time. Instantly those needles lunge, stabbing into my flesh like hungry predators, and they're not the only ones. Another one has been lurking behind me, waiting for its moment to stab at the base of my skull. Ow! Ow! Ow!

Really? This is the best they can do? They can cross intergalactic space but they can't come up with anything better than blunt needles?

A moment later, it's all over. Doctor Splog removes his mask, looking down at me with a very pleased smile on his face. I'm glad he's so happy. Now how about some sympathy and concern? How about at the very least letting me out of this chair? There's not even a thought of it. Instead he looks over at Ellen, and she's not exactly showing any sympathy either.

He barks, and together they wander over to a corner. What!

"Get back over here. Get me out of this chair. You are so going to regret this, the both of you. Get me out of here!"

They're not listening. They're too busy having a conversation of their own. It better not involve any more medieval forms of torture or there will be blood on the walls. And if it's payment they're talking about, it better include a discount for all the care I didn't receive, like anesthetic.

Once they're done they wander back, Doctor Splog looking even more pleased with himself. Well, his bank balance did probably just grow considerably. "There now, all done. That wasn't so bad, was it?"

"Wasn't so bad! You just wait 'til I get out of this chair. You just . . . wait a minute. I can understand you. You're speaking English. How can that be?"

"Yes. That'll be your ULD coming online. Good. I think we'll run another scan while we wait for your vital signs to calm down and then I'll let you up. After all, we can't have the patient attacking the doctor, can we?"

Of course not. We wouldn't want that, would we? The very idea.

If the price of release from this chair is calming down it's probably best not to say anything. He's still getting glowered at though, for all the good that does. He's entirely engrossed in that tablet and tapping it again. There's a white bar moving back and forth through the deep blue above me and he's reading the results with a series of satisfied nods.

"Yes. Yes. Everything appears to be working perfectly. Short-range, bio-powered, not quite state of the art but it should give you years of trouble-free service. The ULD has connected with your inner ear and speech center. It's reading your language and creating a downloadable file. Anyone you come into range of now will automatically receive a copy and then they'll be able to understand you too. Within a few days the entirety of any planet you visit will be able to understand English. Your ID chip is also functioning perfectly and you've received the nanotech inoculation. You are now immune to everything that doesn't match at least 45 percent of your DNA. Excellent. I think you're good to go."

"45 percent? Why 45 percent?"

"Oh, that's to protect any unborn child. It wouldn't do very well for the future of the species if expectant mothers were having miscarriages all over the place because the nanotech thought the fetus was some sort of parasite. How silly would it be if we caused our own demise by killing the next generation before they were even born?"

That's pretty hard to argue against, and probably a good reason why some people should stop hoping aliens drop by for a visit. They might view us the same way the conquistadors viewed the Aztecs and that didn't end very well for the Aztecs. Time to change the subject. "So everyone I meet from now on will be able to understand English?"

"That is correct. Why? Is that a problem?"

"Only for the guys at NASA. Every planet we visit can already speak English. How the hell did that happen? Must've been Voyager—and they said we were wasting all those tax dollars. Well, who's laughing now, suckers?"

"Indeed. Is laughing at suckers something you do a lot of where you come from? Never mind. The important thing is you'll be fine. You're certified safe and you're free to go."

The slab above me turns black and my feet hit the floor before he can change his mind or mine.

"Excellent. Is there anything else I can do for you while you're here? A few nips and tucks maybe, or how about some DNA therapy to help keep that aging at bay? You are looking a little frayed around the edges, if you don't mind me saying so."

"Well, I do mind you saying so, and not even imminent death could persuade me to sit in that chair again."

"Ah well. If imminent death does show up, you'll know where to find me. It's our mission statement, you see. As long as you can pay, we'll keep death at bay. And if you should happen to lose a limb along the way, remember to bring it with you. We offer a full body service."

This is beginning to feel more like a motor shop than a

doctor's surgery. Before he can offer me a couple of cans of blood to go, Ellen takes me firmly by the arm. "Good to know but we best be on our way. We have a long way to go after all, and I'm sure we've inconvenienced you enough."

She's dragging me toward the portal tech like I'm a kid in the candy aisle, and it wouldn't surprise me at all if she said, *No, you can't have any. Now stop causing a scene.* That's usually my role, but now I'm the kid asking for candy.

"Do we have to leave so fast? You said it would take the Greens a while to figure out where we went. This is the first alien world I've ever been to. This is the first alien world anyone from Earth has ever been to and here I am, the mom who just left NASA in the dust. Oh, come on. Couldn't we at least take one hour to look around?"

"No. We need to get out of here while they're still being friendly. If another Green ship turns up that could change real fast."

That proves to be easier said than done. Knowing it's called portal tech is one thing. Knowing how to use it is quite another, and neither of us do. So here we are, the fearless hijackers of a Green ship, something no one has ever done before, and we're both standing in front of this portal looking like a pair of fools. If this were a normal door, there would likely be a sign on it saying pull and we'd both have failed to notice it.

After a couple of useless stabs at it, Ellen turns to Doctor Splog for help. "How do we get back to our ship?"

Rather unhelpfully, he merely grins at us. Rather suspiciously, the portal tech opens and there's our bridge on the other side. Someone somewhere has pushed a button. Someone somewhere has been listening. They may have been listening all along, including when I was in that cell. Did either of us say anything that might set alarm bells ringing? I can't remember. Perhaps it is for the best that we leave while they're still being nice.

As soon as we're back on the bridge Ellen sets about scrolling through destinations on the console. It doesn't take her long to find one that doesn't bring up the image of a planet on our main screen. "That's empty space. We should be safe enough there."

Another stab, the ship shudders and we've jumped. Now the main screen is filled with a star field, an endless depth of blue, yellow, and red pinpricks. It's the kind of thing you'd have to be in the middle of a desert to see on Earth. As beautiful and surprisingly soothing as it is, and as safe as she says it is, Ellen is still scrolling.

"What are you doing? Are we going to jump again?"

"No. I'm looking for Veniramat. I asked the Nosundomi to check their database but they have no record of it. The Greens ought to. They're wanderers, vagabonds. There's probably nowhere in the known universe they don't know about, and some places outside of it too. They know where your Earth is, after all. Trouble is I can't read this script. I was hoping I might recognize something but there's nothing."

"Maybe it doesn't exist then. Maybe you are a spy and your ID is fake too."

Abandoning her scrolling, she sits back, fixing me with a level gaze. The silly Earthling is fantasizing again.

"Well, why not? You don't know. It's a universal database, isn't it? Everyone must have the same one so maybe, if the Nosundomi haven't heard of it, the Greens haven't either. Where did it come from anyway? Who created it to begin with?"

"I don't know. Probably no one does. It just is and always

has been. And not everyone's database is identical. It is universal but that doesn't mean everyone shares when they discover a new world. There's the universal database and then there's everyone's private database. That's what the Nosundomi said anyway. They have no record of Veniramat, but somebody else might. We just have to find the right database and gain access. Fortunately this ship's hold is stuffed with valuables so credit is one thing we don't have to worry about. That's good because we're also going to need a different ship before somebody does start shooting at us. Now, I'm going to take a little rest time. Do not touch anything while I'm gone."

CHAPTER THREE

She leaves and the bridge is mine, acting captain in all but name. So it's third star to the left and onwards 'til dawn, except the acting captain isn't allowed to touch anything. Inspecting all these screens will have to do instead. They're filled with oscillating graphs and scrolling data and bar charts moving up and down as they all keep track of something or other. It's fascinating to watch, totally unintelligible but fascinating, until it isn't. What to do, what to do. The bridge is ticking along nicely all on its own. There are no alarms going off or anything blinking wildly because somebody needs to do something. The floor could do with a good sweep, especially in the corners. At least there are no cobwebs, but then spaceships probably don't have spiders, or any flies for them to eat.

Oh, look. Ellen's left the destinations window open. Scrolling through it and seeing what planets appear on the main screen can't do any harm. Sitting in the captain's egg, I immediately find out why Ellen sat forward. There are two big knob things on either side of my head, trying to take hold of it. They might even be trying to get inside. That's interesting. These Greens have memory-blocking technology. Is it possible they pilot their ships through some sort of mind control too? If so these consoles would be merely backup systems. Maybe they do, maybe they don't. Either way they can stay out of my head, so it's back to the destinations window.

The variety is incredible. There are red worlds like Mars, white ice worlds scored all over with cracks, blue worlds with rings, and giants like Saturn and Jupiter. There are lots of deserts. There are zones of green and purple and orange, which must be some pretty weird vegetation. There are even some worlds that are deeply ocean blue, like the one—oh. Oh hell! Selecting when you meant to scroll is so annoying. That's not a problem on a dating website. Just move on. When you've accidentally jumped an entire spaceship to who knows where, it could well be a being-thrown-out-of-an-airlock offense, and there's no way Ellen won't have noticed that.

Worse still, there's no planet. Instead there are two stars: a large bluish one and a much smaller white one, the two connected by an arc of wispy vapor. They are breathtaking, jaw-droppingly beautiful, until they are replaced by another kind of alien. It's pale blue-skinned, thin and elongated, rather like a human who's been stretched out an extra foot or two. Liquid-blue eyes gaze at me over a small thin-lipped mouth, from out of which come high, reedy whistling sounds. Inside my head I hear, "Green ship. You have entered the Demaroven system. You are ordered to leave immediately or you will be fired upon."

"Sorry, my mistake. I'll jump us somewhere else. Sorry."

Like the Nosundomi immigration officer, it leans forward to peer at me through our main screen. "You are not Green. Who are you? And what language are you speaking?"

"I'm speaking English. My name is Debbie and I'm from Earth. But you can't understand a word I'm saying, can you? Please don't fire on us. We're harmless, really. It's all just a big mistake and—"

Blue Eyes disappears, our screen filled once again with those two stars. There's that bureaucracy again, a chain of superiority looking for someone to take responsibility. At least they haven't fired on us yet.

As Ellen bustles back onto the bridge, she might be about to fire on me. "What did you do?"

"I was scrolling through the destinations, that's all, and I accidentally—"

"Didn't I tell you not to touch anything? Where are we anyway?"

"The big blue alien said it's called Demaroven. I don't think they're going to fire on us, not yet anyway."

Not good. The very mention of the possibility that we might be fired upon has Ellen looking exasperated.

Before she can say anything, as if she needed to, Demaroven immigration fills our screen again. "Green ship. You are ordered to leave this system. If you do not understand this instruction we will fire one warning shot. Fail to heed it and we will—"

"I can understand you."

We both can, not that it matters. What does matter is that it can understand Ellen.

"Very well. Who are you and how do you come to be in possession of a Green ship?"

"We are traveling companions from a planet called Veniramat. Our names are very long and complicated, as you'll see when you check our IDs. As to why we're in possession of a Green ship, we're not entirely sure ourselves."

"This does not sound at all convincing. You can prove there are no Greens aboard?"

"If there were any living Greens aboard this ship, do you think you'd be sitting there talking to us? We do have rather a lot of dead ones though. Come and see for yourself if you don't believe us."

Our screen returns to a view of the binary system. Either it didn't like that answer or the buck is being passed again. We could still be fired upon at any moment. In what little time we might have left, just to get things straight in my head before we die, there are a couple of questions it would be nice to know the answer to.

"If everybody hates the Greens so much, why is this ship visible when we jump into their systems? Shouldn't we be hiding behind another planet or something like that?"

"I don't know. I haven't figured that one out yet. It's possible they might have some sort of masking ability but I don't know where to find it. I don't know what the voice command for it is. I don't know what the access command for the ship's computer is either."

"Because you can't read their script. The ULD only allows you to understand the spoken word. You'd have to learn the language to be able to read it. If you are some kind of spy, why didn't whoever sent you have you learn the Greens' language? And why didn't you find out all those commands before they memory-blocked you? Oh. Sorry. Dumb question."

"Just a little, but don't give up on figuring things out. You might even be good at it one day. Quite apart from which, it's Nosundomi script now."

That sounds suspiciously like sarcasm—from Ellen. Before an equally sarcastic reply can be delivered, or any more questions asked, we're looking at Demaroven immigration again.

"You are cleared to approach. Follow the exact orbital insertion trajectory we have sent you or you will be terminated. If any living Greens are found aboard your ship after orbital insertion, you will be terminated. If any other infringements of Demaroven law occur while in orbit, you—"

"Will be terminated. Yeah, we understand. Initiating orbital insertion."

This time there's a big green flashing symbol in the middle of the console. Ellen taps it, more code scrolls, and the two stars slowly drift outward to disappear off the left-hand side of our main screen. Moments later a planet drifts in from the right-hand side. Growing slowly larger, it becomes exactly as it appeared on screen before we jumped: a great orb of deep ocean blueness interrupted at first only by clouds, high stacks of them casting long shadows on the waters below. There's even the great wheel of a hurricane coming over the horizon toward us. Then we begin to see islands: a mottling of greens, yellows, browns, and grays standing alone or arranged in archipelagos. There are no continents or ice-bound poles. With those two suns blazing down on it, this must be quite a hot planet. Hope they've got some nice beaches.

No sooner has the great blue rim filled the bottom third of our screen than our immigration officer returns. "Inspection."

The portal tech opens. Three of them step through, or it might be more accurate to say float through. Dressed in long, flowing pastel blue robes of slightly different shades, they move with a fluid grace that's so effortless they might not be walking at all. This time there are no armed guards, but all three of them are wearing big bubble helmets over their long, noseless, earless and entirely hairless heads.

Two of them immediately leave the bridge. They'll be looking for Greens. Knock yourselves out, guys. There's nobody here but us. That's what the Nosundomi said anyway. If they got it wrong this is going to be a very short visit.

The third one glides toward us, producing a long, thin instrument with a large, bulbous end. It's rather like a TV remote with a doorknob attached. Turns out it's the Demaroven version of a Nosundomi smartphone.

After beeping both our forearms, it removes its mask and carefully inspects the readout. "Veniramat. We do not know this Veniramat. You can enlighten us?"

For some reason it's looking at me. Well, I guess we might as well find out now if Splog's downloadable file has downloaded. "Yes. It's rather awkward really. We've sort of lost the coordinates of our home world. That's partly why we're here. We were hoping you might know them."

If it had a nose it would be looking down it at me from a very great height. At least we know it's learned to understand English. Way to go, Splog. You've turned English into an intergalactic virus.

"Such a thing would not be tolerated on Demaroven. To have lost the coordinates of one's home world is a serious matter, perhaps sufficient to warrant referral to the Ministry of Goodness. Nevertheless, the Ministry of Inclusiveness has cleared you for entry for one day. If you remain beyond that, you and your ship will be terminated. While on the surface, you are required to obey the law. Be polite. Be respectful. Be mindful. Hurtful actions or language will not be tolerated. You may not, for instance, comment upon anyone's dress, appearance, gender, place of origin, status, employment, taste, aesthetics, spiritual beliefs, medical condition, disability, age, innate characteristics, skills—"

"Oh my God, what do you people even talk about? How do you hook up or have children?" My blurting isn't improving the situation.

"Have? We do not *have* children. That is a primitive process practiced by selfish species, and a means of procreation all too often abused for the indoctrination of new associates into the misguided beliefs of their progenitors. The Ministry of Productiveness is responsible for population replenishment. The Ministry of Correctness is then responsible for guiding new associates onto the path of enlightenment."

"Oh, right. I'll have to tell my husband that the next time he wants sex. You're selfish, you only want someone to indoctrinate and you're giving me a headache."

That produces a general stiffening of the body, a raising of the head, and an intake of breath that can only be described as disdain. At least the Nosundomi, for all that they looked like demons, were affable and bribable. These Demaroven sound like they'd find having fun on a bouncy castle problematic.

As disdainful as our immigration officer might be, all the hoops have been jumped through, all the boxes ticked and all the forms and procedures satisfied. This alien world is ready to let me walk among it. Humanity's second—or is it fourth?—contact with an alien civilization is about to happen, even if these aliens don't seem all that excited about it or even very interested.

On the other side of the portal tech our immigration officer floats away, rather like a goldfish that's forgotten what it was doing a few seconds ago. There are two more still on board our ship. Maybe they've forgotten why they're there and how to leave. Maybe, before we do whatever Ellen wants to do here, we should go find them and lead them home. Nah, they're snotty enough to fend for themselves.

Besides, we've been left on one side of a plaza. Elegant buildings soar all around: white, smoothly uncluttered, and gently curving inwards like they're the teeth of some long-dead, sun-bleached dinosaur and we're standing within its partially buried lower jaw. There are planters scattered around filled with weird-looking plants, thick-stemmed with pulpy leaves, or thin and wispy, or wrinkled and gnarly and tortuously bent, all of them bearing huge blooms, reds and purples and blues and oranges. There are trees as well, or at least they look like trees to me. Spindly and warty or thick and mossy, they all reach upward to plate-like heads basking in the warmth of the two suns, blue and white, frozen in their dance above us.

There are benches too, but no one is using them. Instead all these willowy, float-y aliens are wafting by, their attention only briefly caught by us, just quick little glances because staring is probably a crime here. No one hurries. It's almost as if no one has anything particular to do or anywhere particular to be and everyone spends their time being laid-back and in touch with their inner serenity. There are people on Earth who would be delighted at the thought of all this. There are others who would be jumping off the top of those buildings out of sheer boredom. But then boredom is probably a crime here too. After all, admitting to being bored is the same as saying you don't find the people around you interesting, and that might hurt their feelings.

Fortunately we do have something to do and somewhere to be, and Ellen is keen to get on with it. "Okay. We have one day, but we should probably be out of here in less. I'm going to see what I can find. Somebody who has heard of Veniramat hopefully, and a new ship."

"A new ship? What? We're going to find a used spaceship lot and cut a deal?"

"We have to. That Green ship is like a big red light flashing over our heads. You've seen how two worlds have reacted to it.

We've been lucky so far but that luck won't last forever. Why don't you look around and see what you can find? You have something that measures time?"

"I've got pajama bottoms, a t-shirt and somebody else's sneakers. Some real clothes would be good: a cool jacket, tight pants and killer boots. Everything you're wearing, in fact."

"Maybe later. Why don't you just hang out here then? I'm sure you can find something to do, and I'll catch up with you later."

"So you're just going to leave me here then. What if somebody turns off my ULD or memory-blocks me like the Greens did to you? I could end up wandering around an alien world without a clue, rather like you on that ship. How do they do that anyway, mess with your head like that?"

"I don't know. I told you the Greens are largely a mystery. Doctor Splog was fascinated to hear about it. He ran some tests but he couldn't figure out how they did it or how to undo it. The Nosundomi had a good look around the ship too, even took a couple of bodies with them. We've probably advanced the universe's knowledge of the Greens from next to zero to not quite next to zero—if the Nosundomi choose to share of course. Now that they know the Greens can mess with people's heads, that's another reason for keeping them at arm's length. These Demaroven don't know that yet so don't you go telling them. As for the rest, you'll be fine. Just be careful what you say."

Being careful what I say has never been one of my strong points, and now that I've infected this entire planet with a virus called English it's not going to get any better. I'm not an intergalactic bioterrorist anymore. I'm a language terrorist. Let's hope the Ministry of Inclusiveness doesn't consider that a terminatable offense.

Ellen has gone, leaving me all on my lonesome like a stray mutt that's wandered into a pedigree dog show. Okay. So it's stand here being not so politely sneak-peeked by every Demaroven who passes by until she returns, or check out the local scene and maybe find out what they do for entertainment on this planet, if that's not a crime too.

Crime or not, my first step feels like I'm wearing lead boots. On the Nosundomi space station there was that feeling of lightness. Here it's heaviness. The answer, of course, is obvious. It's gravity doing its thing. Nosundomi was smaller than Earth. Demaroven is somewhat larger. I hadn't even thought about that on the Green ship. Whatever planet they come from, it must be about the same size as Earth. The difference must also be why these Demaroven are all so float-y and wispy. This is how you overcome heavier gravity, unless it's the other way around and everyone ought to be galumphing around on tree-trunk legs. But then how would I know? I'm no astrophysicist. It's easy enough to get used to though, and with a few more steps, I've all but forgotten about it.

Now for the dinosaur-teeth buildings. All of them have glassed-in open areas at ground level. Many of them appear to be stores, with all manner of goods inside. Most of it is either unrecognizable to me or looks like nothing more than a collection of spheres and cubes, all of different colors. The clothing stores are more interesting, all of them filled with long, float-y pastel-colored gowns. They're way too long for little me though. Some serious hem work would be needed. Not that it matters. The locals aren't buying anything, and they're not the only ones. According to Ellen we're rather well off as far as credits are concerned, but since she didn't see fit to give me any, there isn't going to be any shopping on this world.

The next glassed-in area I come to looks an awful lot like an art gallery. There's a crowd of Demaroven standing around admiring weird-shaped objects or staring transfixed at big screens where splatters of color writhe and pulsate. They're also eating and drinking, which reminds me: I haven't had any breakfast. All this jumping around the universe first-contacting all sorts of aliens is hungry work. My stomach could definitely do with some TLC. A little gentle gate-crashing should take care of that. After all, no one's going to object. That would be so elitist.

Oh dear. No one's going to object, but that doesn't stop them all casting glances in my direction like the stray mutt just found its way into the VIP area. Worse still, it's almost drooling as it eyes up all that food and drink. And, wow, what a selection there is too. The drinks are red or blue or yellow, and the food looks like sushi: delicate little morsels of fishy flesh, or at least that's my best guess. Any of this could likely kill me but, hey, the Greens are already out to get me. Besides, there's something very squid-like over there that is so talking to me.

With a full plate and sticky fingers, it's time to pay my dues by admiring some of the artwork. For the first two, a little circle of emptiness quickly develops around me. Well, that's not very inclusive. This alien is perfectly legal, y'know, with all the paperwork properly filled in. Or maybe it's the smell from all that green gunk that's dried up and possibly stained all over me. It's not my fault the Greens can cross intergalactic space but have never heard of a shower or a laundry.

At the third, one of the Demaroven remains, gazing down at me from its lofty height with those liquid blue eyes. It might have mistaken me for another exhibit, one that moves, a sort of automaton laid on by the host to heighten the experience.

Or maybe not. Its gaze turns back to the artwork: something completely impenetrable that's long, thick, gently curved, black and marked all over with different-colored hieroglyphs.

Whatever the artwork is meant to be, it definitely has this alien's rapt attention. "Is it not exquisite? I think the memory of it may haunt me in my dreams." The words are delivered dreamily, like some airhead dilettante wearing a two-thousand-dollar dress at the Guggenheim.

My reply is more down to earth. "Yeah, I could get pretty wet dreaming about it myself."

And it lands like the Hindenburg. Okay, so maybe this one isn't female. Of course we're not allowed to ask so it might be anything. The laugh's on me though because these Demaroven don't appear to have a sense of humor either. Instead of bonding us, my risqué all-girls-together and now rather regretted attempt at humor has it looking down at me, magisterially godlike in its failure to be amused. "You're not very sophisticated, are you?"

"Not very sophisticated?" Okay, sweetie. If that's how you want to play it. "Are you calling me ignorant?"

"Beneath the two suns, no. My sincere apologies if I have given offense. Ignorant is such a pejorative word. Perhaps I should have said unattuned to the finer nuances of the work. For instance note the gentle curve of the shaft as it rises, reminding us that, while we might strive to be the best we can be, we should nevertheless be prepared to bend a little to accommodate others. Then there is the blackness of the object with the randomly colored hieroglyphs etched upon it. This surely is meant to remind us that confusion lies all around and we must strive to bring order for the benefit of all."

If you say so. As another morsel of squid-like flesh pops into my mouth, perhaps it's time to try something different.

"Hi. My name's Debbie, by the way. It's really good to meet you."

My held-out hand is viewed like it's a piece of yesterday's squid.

"I am seventh assessor in the third office of the twelfth district of the Ministry of Cooperativeness. Meeting you has also been . . . good."

"Okay. So that's your job title. But what do people call you? Y'know, like a name?"

"Seventh assessor in the third office of the twelfth district of the Ministry of Cooperativeness. The use of personal appellations is not considered beneficial to the greater good. It might lead us into vanity, and to the scorning of others and the forgetting that we are all members of a community larger than our oneness."

Right now I'm dying a little inside. Stultifying doesn't even begin to cover it. At times like this, it's best to simply look on the bright side and move on. "So do you know who the artist is?"

"We do not. Creatives never put themselves forward. That would be insulting to those who are not creative. All works are commissioned anonymously by the Ministry of Creativeness for the better education and edification, and for the general improvement in the attitudes and awareness, of the populace."

"The general improvement of the attitudes and awareness of the populace, huh? Well, who wouldn't want that? So do the creatives get paid for their work?"

With a second Hindenburg looming on the horizon, it looks like these guys don't do sarcasm either.

"Paid? No one is paid to work. Think how that might disadvantage the less able or those who, through no fault of their own, cannot work. No, we are all provided with the means to obtain that which is necessary to our continued well-being, leaving us free to devote ourselves to the better fulfillment of our roles within society. Is this not how things are done in your world?"

"Not really, no. We tried it a couple of times and an awful lot of people ended up dead."

"Indeed. No wonder the Ministry of Safeness advises that only those with the requisite training should consider travel off-world. But then who would want to when the rest of the universe is so unattuned?"

"You have a lot of Ministries, don't you?"

"We have precisely the number of Ministries as is necessary to maintain a well-ordered society. All things must be properly administered for the common good."

It all sounds wonderful and wonderfully seductive too, the perfect society, except for that small herd of elephants that followed me in here. Each of them has their trunk raised and a question they're begging to ask, like, for instance, how did you ever crawl out of the sea and learn how to make fire? Surely there was a Ministry to tell you how dangerous that was. Setting fire to things is bad. Someone might get hurt.

"And what about those who don't want to be administered, or don't you have any alternative voices?"

"If by alternative voices you mean those who will not understand that their purpose is to serve the greater good, the Ministry of Wellness deals with mental health issues."

"Yeah. Where've I heard that before?"

"I cannot imagine. Off-worlders can be very confusing, perhaps because they are so confused themselves. Now, if you will excuse me. It has been a delight conversing with you but there are others I must now engage with."

Seventh floats away, leaving me isolated again. Obsessive

politeness has its limits apparently. No one else wants to be confused by an off-worlder so it's probably time to let them all off the hook by leaving. My plate is empty anyway. The food hasn't killed me yet, and the elephants can decide what they want to do for themselves.

Outside in the plaza, nothing has changed. Demarovens are still wafting by, with the two suns looking down on them like a god with a squint. It's hot, very hot. My stomach is full, and all this excitement is catching up with me. It's been some hours since the Greens abducted me. That would have been in the middle of the night. It might not even be dawn on Earth, not my part of it anyway. It's dawn for somebody, obviously, because it's always dawn somewhere. Precious little sleep was had on that rock-hard bed in the Nosundomi cell either, so it's hardly surprising if my eyelids are feeling a little heavy.

There's no sign of Ellen yet so chilling on a bench for a while seems like a good idea, if that's even possible beneath those burning eyes. There are other eyes too, the ones peeking as they pass by, possibly wondering who this vagrant is cluttering up the place, sitting there in all her alien shabbiness and ruining the perfection they have created.

Not that they're going to say anything. That might cause a scene and the Ministry of Something-or-Other wouldn't like that at all. There's only so much passing disapproval a person can be bothered with though, and then boredom sets in. Ellen still hasn't returned, but then she did say there was a lot to do. She could have given some of it to me, apart from the fact that I wouldn't know where to begin. Maybe she's dumped me, gone off to discover herself all on her own. No, she wouldn't do that. We're in this together. We've committed grand theft spaceship and multiple counts of Greenicide together. Besides, it would also be a really horrible thing to do, like dumping that Christmas puppy by the side of the road because it's grown too big. Think of it sitting there watching the traffic go by, its sad, droopy face just hoping that someone will stop. Honestly, my tail will wag so madly with joy if you do.

No one stops, and still Ellen doesn't appear. My God, it's hot beneath those two suns. It's also quiet. All those gowns floating by are hardly swishing at all. In this almost paradise, apart from and in spite of the hardness of this bench, my eyelids are slowly becoming heavier and heavier. Lying back isn't just an option anymore. It's a necessity, with a forearm thrown over my eyes to shield them from those suns. This isn't about going to sleep though. This is about quietly drowsing the time away until Ellen . . .

CHAPTER FOUR

"**S**leeping in a public place is a crime against the common good. You are required to donate one day's community service. Please report to your nearest Ministry of Goodness outlet for assignment."

"What?" My eyes have snapped open. All the Demaroven are still wandering by, but they're now at an even greater distance. It takes me a few moments of peering to realize why. Floating a couple of feet distant and several feet off the ground is a silver sphere. It's the size of a basketball with no obvious means by which to be hanging there. Nor are there any features, especially not anything to see or speak with, and yet its thin, reedy Demaroven voice is clearly talking to me.

"Sleeping in a public place is a crime against the common good. You are required to donate one day's community service. Please report to your nearest Ministry of Goodness outlet for assignment. Loitering is also a crime against the common good. Move along, please, or you may be required to donate another day's community service."

"What?"

Repeating myself isn't helping, not least reason because it doesn't appear to be listening.

"Failure to comply with a helper from the Ministry of Goodness is a crime against the common good. You are required to donate one day's community service."

"What are you, a policeman or a machine? Or is there some jerk sitting in a control center somewhere, making this stuff up as you go along?"

And the list of my offenses continues to grow steadily longer. "Policeman is a gender-specific term. The use of gender-specific terms is a crime against the common good. You are required to donate one day's community service. You have now committed three crimes against the common good. You are required to donate a further thirty days of community service. Please report to your nearest Ministry of Goodness outlet for assignment. Failure to do so will result in a further donation of one hundred days of community service and referral to the Ministry of Wellness for psychological examination."

"I'd stop talking if I were you."

It's Ellen. She's come back. My imaginary tail is beating back and forth like a beached salmon, which would probably be classed as cruelty to animals around here and that's another crime against the common good.

"Please forgive my friend's ignorance. She is not familiar with your laws."

"Ignorance is a pejorative term. The use of pejorative terms is a crime against the common good. You are required to donate one day's community service. Please report to your nearest Ministry of Wellness outlet to—"

While the Ministry of Goodness' little helper continues to blather on, Ellen takes me firmly by the arm and leads me away. "Don't say another word, okay, or they may declare you mentally ill."

"Mentally ill! I was lying on a bench having a nap. My God, what kind of a universe is this? If I'm not being abducted I'm being declared mentally ill, and let's not forget the intergalactic bioterrorist bit either. And what do they mean by community service? They can't make me work for them. It's illegal. Seventh just told me that."

"Don't worry about it. We aren't going to be here long enough for them to enforce it."

"You found something, right? Please tell me you found something."

"I did. Not Veniramat, I'm afraid, but there's a spaceport for off-worlders on another island. The Demaroven gave me the address so we'll head on over there now before your mouth gets us both declared insane."

"My mouth! You left me here all alone with nothing to do, remember? I could've been helping. I could've been shopping if you'd given me anything to shop with."

"Shopping is hardly a priority right now, don't you think? Well, not here anyway. There'll be plenty of shopping at the spaceport—for instance, for a new ship, after we've emptied the Green ship's hold. There's a portal over there so let's get busy. We need to get all this stuff done and be gone before they terminate the Green ship or the Greens themselves turn up or you talk us into a mental institution."

What a difference a moment can make. We were in paradise, pure and pristine, with exactly as many Ministries as required to maintain a well-ordered society. Now, as the portal closes behind us, we're standing on the edge of chaos. There are the same dinosaur-teeth buildings but they're coarser, weathered and unkept, blotched with areas of bare concrete where the facings have fallen away and rust-stained from seasons of rain. Many of the ground-floor open areas don't have frontages at all, and the wares being hawked in front of them have spilled out into the plaza. There's a crowd too—so many different kinds of aliens that this must be the strangest marketplace any human has ever set eyes on. In among them are a few Nosundomi and the occasional Demaroven. The Ministry of Safeness must have cleared them fit for alien contact, with an extensive training program that included how to elbow people out of the way because these Demaroven are not taking any prisoners in this jostling mass.

It's hot and noisy, and it's rich with all manner of strange smells. There are the stalls of food vendors billowing steam into the air. There are censers hanging from poles and the occasional stove adding strange and strangely beguiling scents to it all. There are also other odors but it's probably best not to think about what might be causing those.

Seventh said off-worlders are confused. I certainly am, but Ellen is heroic. She charges straight in, dragging me behind her like a piece of baggage on wheels. To my left and my right green, yellow, purple and multicolored beings are pushed aside, but no one complains. It's all perfectly normal, the survival of the fittest, and the fittest are shoving things at us: weird-looking fruits, gnarly roots and fistfuls of leafiness. *Best quality, cheapest prices, one-time deal only for you!*

Ignoring them all, Ellen drags me on toward a high, circular wall with occasional towers, all of it as blotched and stained as the buildings. It could be a football stadium large enough to hold the entire population of a medium-sized city. Aliens probably don't play football, but it's an interesting thought. Maybe they have an intergalactic league, planet versus planet. The Nosundomi would probably be quite good at it, the Demaroven very bad. The Greens would cheat, of course, messing with all their opponents' heads to make them think they lost. As interesting as that might be, Ellen explains, "That's the spaceport. We should be able to find something there. Just let me do the talking, okay?"

We approach a great arch with a red flag hanging limply across it, with a yellow diamond filled in with squiggly writing. There are sledges going in and out, all of them floating about a foot off the ground, some piled high with containers, others empty. There are also half a dozen guards. They're Nosundomi. In spite of being heavily armed, they don't look terribly threatening as they casually wave through all the comings and goings. Give them some garden furniture and a cooler full of beer and they might simply be catching some rays, until they catch sight of us. Then it's weapons at the ready and beady red-eyed stares with one of them stepping purposefully forward, at the sight of which Ellen feels the need to remind me: "Don't say anything, okay, but, if the urge to blurt something out is too much for you, just remember this one is female."

"Female. How can you tell?"

She doesn't answer.

The Nosundomi is in front of us, very officiously holding out an expectant hand. "Passes, please."

Ellen replies, "We don't have passes."

"You don't have passes? How did you leave the spaceport without passes?"

"We didn't land at the spaceport. We came here in a Green ship. It's in orbit."

There's a pause, with the Nosundomi gazing first at Ellen and then at me. Her expression is near impossible to read but what might have been disbelief turns out to be props to the both of us. "A Green ship, eh! You're lucky the locals didn't terminate you on sight. So how did you come by a Green ship? They don't exactly give them away."

"It's not entirely clear. Let's just say we got lucky, but it has a hold full of valuables we'd like to offload. We might be interested in another ship too, if anyone has one to sell."

The Nosundomi casts a quick glance around. Satisfied that no one is near enough to overhear, she takes a step forward anyway. "I might be able to help you with that. Shall we say two hundred credits? That'll get you through the arch and an introduction to some friends of mine. Nice creatures. You'll like them."

Now that we're horse trading, Ellen is coolly calculating. "I'm sure we will. Two hundred credits is a bit much though, wouldn't you say?"

"Not really. If you've got a Green ship with a stuffed hold up there you can afford it. Hey, there are just as many cutthroats in there as there are honest traders, but be my guest if you think you can tell the difference."

You've got to admire a people who maintain their cultural purity and this Nosundomi is certainly doing that. The locals would probably be horrified but since no little helpers from the Ministry of Goodness are swooping in to hand out some more community service, it looks like this is the best deal we're going to get.

"We accept."

Ellen throws me a hard glance, a reminder that someone was told to keep her mouth shut. I could give her an answer along the lines of, *We're in a hurry, aren't we? Because the Greens might turn up at any moment?* But it's done now.

At least the Nosundomi is happy, giving us a needle-toothed smile as she says, "Good. We'll just take care of the formalities and be on our way then."

She produces a card, sort of like a credit card with a digital display. Turns out it's a reader and two hundred credits pass through it from Ellen to her. I'd like one of those please, and so would Ellen. The Nosundomi is happy to oblige, dropping us by an office under the arch where we're each given one free of charge, which is to say we're not charged anything extra on top of the two hundred credits we've already handed over.

On the other side of the arch, we enter the spaceport proper. It's huge, with half a dozen or more ships of all shapes and sizes loading and unloading cargo. There are sleek ships with fins; there are big, boxy ones; there are ones shaped like blimps; and there are bulbous disks. Black and yellow, red and white, silver or shining chrome, all of them with lettering on their sides. Each one is in a different script and indecipherable to me, and they beg the question, "Are these ships from all over the universe?"

Our new best friend proves to be quite talkative. "That's right. There are all kinds from all over: Quarnivari, Bidelon, Chood. You can usually tell how advanced their civilization is from their ships. That big, unwieldy, boxy thing over there, for instance, is Ostralon. They only turned up a short while ago. They tend to get into fights a lot, which is good for us because if they do it on our watch, we get to keep the fines. If it's not on our watch, they tend to get drunk a lot, which is also good if your other business happens to be running a bar. We always look forward to one of their ships arriving.

"We look forward to any ship arriving, really. Most of them ply between the major trading hubs like this place, but some prefer to go rummage about in deep space. It can be fascinating what some of them come back with and it's very lucrative too, but also very risky. Some of them are never seen again. They seem to think it's worth it though. Rather them than me, I say. Why put my ass on the line when I can profit from it just by . . ."

As she blathers on, my mind begins to wander. So do my eyes. Beneath some ships there are crews loading or unloading cargo. Beneath others the crews are lounging around watching everybody else's busyness. None of them pays us any attention as we walk by. We're merely another kind of alien in a different port, which is a little disappointing. There are all those people on Earth asking, "Why won't they talk to us?" and there they are lounging around beneath their ships ignoring us, and each and every one of them might as well answer, "Why should we? What's so interesting about you?" Except for the Greens, of course, and whatever their interest is, it doesn't extend to talking to us either.

We're heading for the far side of the spaceport. It's a very long walk, with Ellen saying nothing. Let's hope it's not the silent treatment because somebody's been a naughty girl. No, she wouldn't do that. Something else must be on her mind, something important enough for her to be paying no attention to our Nosundomi escort, who's still talking.

"That way everybody knows where they stand. No cheating, no thieving, no fixing weights, no—"

"So how come you guys are the security around here? It's not like this is your world, after all."

"There's a rota. The locals insisted on it. When this place was first set up, ooh, a long time ago now, there was some unpleasantness, which is to say some full-on turf wars. Not good for business, and definitely not good for all those Demaroven hurty feelings. Story is they nearly shut the whole thing down and told us to take a long jump to somewhere else. Word is the only thing that stopped them was a particular delicacy they could only get from Quarnivari. Couldn't live without it apparently.

"So they laid down the law and now we all just get along, sort of, and this just happens to be our turn. Lucky for you, eh? Some of the others might have charged you ten times as much and then sold you on as cargo. Hey, don't look so worried. You're with me, and we at least know the value of return business. This place is about commerce first and last. If you've got the money we've got the merchandise, and if we haven't got it we'll find it, whatever it might be. A phial of koodlis from the marshes of Sootrax? We can get it. A bud from the senaphid flower? We can get it, and you won't need a spaceship to jump anywhere after one of those, I can tell you . . ."

My mind wanders again, this time toward another ship that's coming in to land. It glides down silently over the spaceport wall, hovers for a moment above a column of shimmering air, and then gently settles onto the ground. It's graceful as a swan and poised as a ballerina, and yet at the same time thick and black as a submarine. It's also the bringer of more commerce and that makes me interrupt with another question.

"Why don't you use portals to transfer cargo? It's got to be easier than landing a ship and then having to blast off into space again."

Our escort casts a glance at the newly landed ship. "It's complicated. I'm a part-time security guard and bar owner, not an engineer, but if you like, I'll give it my best shot."

"Oh, please. As one part-timer to another, I'd love to hear your best shot."

"Okay then. Well, it's something to do with energy busing. Portals are great in short bursts, like zapping a ship around the universe or stepping from one location to another. Keep one open for too long though, and it becomes unstable. It's something to do with self-reinforcing loops and energy cascades and all stuff like that. Basically, if you forget to turn the stove off when you leave home, it might not be there when you come back. That's why they all have automatic cut-offs. There's always someone who's gonna forget and then it's *kerboom*, no more ship."

Well, we've all done that, right? Gone out for a nice sit-down meal and halfway through wondered if you've left the iron on. And would you believe it? Aliens do it too.

Apart from that, it makes about as much sense to me as quantum mechanics, with all those particles whizzing around that are also waves and can be in two places at the same time. It does wake Ellen up though. "So if you leave a portal open for too long, the reactor is likely to explode."

"That's about the size of it. It's nothing to worry about. The automatic cut-off has backup systems, alarms, proximity sensors, and all stuff like that. Or, at least, that's what they tell us. But then, like I said, I'm a part-time security guard and bar owner. What do I know?"

Ellen nods slowly, because apparently this is a really important piece of information.

While she's busy processing it, the Nosundomi brings us to a halt in front of a ship, beyond which there's nothing but the great gray towering cliff of the spaceport wall. "Here we are then. This lot should be able to help you."

This ship is sleek and silvery but at the same time fat and tubular, with big fins and short, stubby legs. Lounging around at the bottom of its loading ramp are some new aliens, half a dozen of them. They're wearing rust-colored suits, one-piece and padded at the shoulders, elbows and knees. Their bare skin is covered in short, downy fur, each one with a different coloration: mottled white and brown, black with a white throat, or plain brown all over. Their faces are long, with nostrils low down above their small mouths, their eyes are large and brown and short and highly mobile ears sprout from the tops of their heads. They could be very hairy seventh-graders all wearing bunny ears, or they could be real bunnies that got bigger as they got smarter. Either way they are so adorably cute that my heart melts at the sight of them. No one on Earth could possibly be afraid of first contact if it was with little guys like these.

With a raised hand, our Nosundomi calls out to them as we approach. "Hey, guys. How're my favorite Lepoorunt doing today? You up for some business?"

They rise as one, a movement so fluid and uniform that a flock of starlings might be proud of it. The tallest of them barely makes it to the height of my shoulder, and I'm not exactly big. They're also all carrying weapons, with every paw-like hand halfway toward their grips. They're alert, like a troop of meerkats, but then who's to say there's not a fox out there waiting to pounce?

The white-and-brown mottled one appears to be in charge, replying in a high, sibilant voice, "Hey, missy red eyes. You know Lepoorunts. We always ready for business. So what you want? You want to sell this pair baldies for big credits?"

"Big credits, yes; baldies, no. They have a big cargo to sell and I immediately thought of my good friend Captain Glurt."

"Ah." Captain Glurt gives us both the once-over, his nose twitching and his gaze greedy with possibilities. They seemed so cute and cuddly less than a minute ago. Now this one is calling us baldies and weighing up the chances of selling us into slavery. "Big cargo, huh. How big?"

Ellen turns hard-nosed businesswoman again. "Very big. We have a Green ship in orbit with its hold stuffed full of loot so you might want to think twice about the name-calling, fur face."

Now there's a glint of steel I wasn't expecting. She doesn't like being called names.

Captain Glurt laughs, not nearly as taken aback as he might have been, and his crew all laugh with him. "Fur face! You baldies, we fur face. We like this. So you have Green ship, eh. You pirates? You pirates with very many offspring if you take Green ship. Captain Glurt apologizes. Lepoorunts make big mistake. Come, we make friends, then make very big credits together. Huggy hugs!"

Like a flock they all rush forward, surrounding us before either Ellen or I can react. Some might call what happens next a family hug. Others might call it love-bombing, what with all those furry little bodies pressed against us and those little furry paw-like hands caressing us all over. A little too much all over in fact. Okay, guys, enough. We're all besties now. Really, just quit with it.

Right about when this is becoming seriously embarrassing, missy red eyes steps in. "Guys. Business."

"Business." Captain Glurt speaks and all his little bunny people step back. This really is beginning to look like a flock of starlings. "Yes, we do business. So big, bad pirate ladies, you got Green ship. We very interested. You offer deal."

Free of them, Ellen might be even more relieved than me. "Yes. We're offering a deal. Ten percent off the top for the contents of the hold before the locals destroy it all. And if you can find us another ship as well, that'll be worth another ten percent."

"Twenty percent, eh."

Captain Glurt thinks about it. All the rest of them appear to be thinking along with him, every nose among them twitching as one. Curiouser and curiouser, as someone who once fell down a rabbit hole said.

"Good. We have deal. My cousins make ready. Then we do this quick. And no more baldies or fur face. We all good friends now. So by what you called, pirate ladies?"

Ellen takes the paw he's offering, which seals the deal. "You can call me Ellen, and she's Debbie."

Already Glurt's crew are busying themselves, with some of them rushing up the loading ramp to do things inside the ship while others are doing things outside. All these things must be some sort of pre-flight checks. While all this is happening, Glurt wanders over to have a word with missy red eyes, and Ellen steps close enough to me so that we can have a private word too.

"What do you think?"

"About what?"

She nods in the general direction of Glurt's crew. "About them. You've noticed how they all move as one, yes? Maybe they all think that way too."

"Maybe they do, but they seem friendly enough. Why? You think they're setting us up for something?"

"I don't know. I don't remember meeting any Lepoorunts before."

"It's for sure I haven't, but look at them. They're like little kids: small and cuddly and cute and furry. Maybe they're just being careful."

"And that's what you're going to base your decision on, is it? They're small and cuddly and cute and furry."

"And careful. They did apologize for the misunderstanding, y'know. I say we give them the benefit of the doubt. Besides, we need to get this done and get out of here, don't we?"

As true as that is, Ellen remains unconvinced, but now we're being called aboard and she isn't backing out. Captain Glurt leads us up the ramp and into the bowels of his ship. On the other side of a spacious hold are two passageways. We enter the one with the hull on our right, doorways to our left and all sorts of service ducts that run above us. It's all very bright and white, and so much pleasanter than the Green ship. Stairs then take us up to the bridge, again so much cleaner than the Green bridge. This one is trapezoid, with the front and rear walls parallel and the two side walls closing in, wide at the rear and narrower at the front. The ceiling slopes downward too, and the floor has two levels. The captain's chair—a proper one this time—and its console sit in the middle of the higher level. Two more consoles sit in front on the lower level. All of them slope slightly upward to a bank of small screens. As we enter only the captain's console is active. The main screen, filling the whole of the front wall, is also live, currently showing us a view of the spaceport.

Glurt wastes no time taking the captain's chair, leaving the other two consoles blank as he says, "Okay. We make quick there and back. No danger. Demaroven space safe for Lepoorunts. No need for weapons or scanners. Everybody ready now?"

We are. Which is to say Ellen and I, along with the rest of the Lepoorunts, are strapped into seats lining the rear wall on either side of the portal tech. The reason why becomes obvious as Glurt presses something on his console and the g-forces kick in. While my intestines are left behind on the planet and portal tech becomes the only way to travel, the main screen slowly changes from pale blue to the blackness of space.

Fortunately it only lasts a few seconds. Then the deep blueness of Demaroven fills the bottom third of our screen, dotted with little islands and scudded with clouds. Slowly they grow thicker and more solid until we're passing over a storm. It's a great white whorl, sparkling with tiny flashes of lightning. Nature can be quite beautiful unless you're on the receiving end, and down there quite a lot of Demaroven must be having a really bad day. All the little helpers from the Ministry of Something-or-Other are going to have their hands full clearing up that mess.

Beyond the storm, with the night side bearing down on us, the Green ship looms into view. Aliens are supposed to make a nuisance of themselves in sleek flying saucers. This is nothing like that. This looks like something someone cobbled together in a wrecking yard, a confusion of banged-together bits and pieces bristling with spines. It's a giant porcupine, and it's getting bigger and bigger. It's filling the entire screen. Those spines are reaching out to grab us. Beyond them is perfect blackness, but really it's a solid wall. This is getting a little worrisome, like reaching the highest point on a rollercoaster ride. There's nowhere to go but down, and it's all held together by thousands of bolts, any one of which might be loose. At any moment the cars might fly free. Those screams of delight will become screams of terror and the ground will be rushing up to meet us. On this particular rollercoaster it's a very big alien spaceship, but the end result will be much the same.

No one else on the bridge seems at all concerned. Glurt is busy guiding us in, his fingers poised over the captain's console. This is probably not a good time to be having a panic attack then. No one will notice if I have a little quiet one all on my own though.

It all ends as Glurt stabs at something on the captain's

console. We've docked, all safe and sound and gentle as a feather. Nothing to worry about—unless you're Glurt, who is in need of a little reassurance. "No Greens, yes? You sure? This ship safe?"

Ellen nods. "No Greens. The Nosundomi searched it before we came here. It's safe."

"Good. Red eyes always thorough. We enter." Glurt stabs at something else. "Docking bay doors open. We go."

He and his crew spring into action, and we follow them down from the bridge and into the passageway. There, four of his crew head off toward the rear of the ship. The rest of us go forward to the docking bay. Through a large round opening is the interior of the Green ship: dim, grungy and silent. So far, so good—except for Ellen. Now she's the one who's looking troubled.

"What's wrong?"

"I'm not sure. Stay alert, okay. If you do want something to worry about, worry about whether Glurt has been keeping up on his routine maintenance. As far as I can see the only thing between us and deep space is a rubber seal."

Thanks, Ellen. I wasn't particularly looking for something to worry about but now that you've mentioned it . . .

Meanwhile, the rest of Glurt's crew has returned, bringing with them hovering sleds, and his crew becomes a well-oiled machine. Empty sleds go in and sleds piled high with containers come out, some of them opened so that Glurt can inspect their contents. It takes a while, but finally the last container comes through. Seems to me it would have been a whole lot quicker if somebody had thought about putting the docking bay in the hold. Somebody messed up, but at least that rubber seal is holding.

As we all head back up to the bridge, Glurt is sounding

very pleased with himself. "We do good, yes? Very big cargo. Very big credits. Now I do math. Math hard. You wait, please."

And that's exactly what he does, totting up on his fat, furry little fingers everything we've brought him. It's fascinating to watch, or at least it is to me. Ellen still has something else on her mind. As we enter the bridge, she nods me over to stand by the captain's console. It's as good a place as any to wait for Glurt to finish. She stands next to the captain's chair. Glurt continues number-crunching on his fingers. That must be some serious math he's doing.

Not until all his crew has arrived does he finish, and then he looks Ellen squarely in the eye. "We offer . . . nothing."

No sooner has he said it than every bunny on the bridge has a weapon leveled at us.

CHAPTER FIVE

Well, this universe just keeps getting better and better. As if being an intergalactic bioterrorist wasn't bad enough, with potential lunatic heaped on top, now we're being mugged by a bunch of bunnies. They seemed so cute and cuddly as well.

Unsurprisingly Ellen isn't surprised at all. "So you were setting us up all along. That's how you could open the Green ship's docking bay door, because you work for them."

"No. We do business with them. This good business. We take Green cargo for ourselves. We tell Greens you sold it somewhere else. Then we sell you to Greens. Good deal for us. Bad deal for you."

"What if we could offer you a better deal?"

"How you do that? You sell cargo for credits, quick deal before Greens turn up. We know. Greens told us. They banned from all civilized worlds. We make trade for them. They tell us to watch for you. Big reward. When you come to us, we know we luckiest Lepoorunts ever. We take cargo. We sell you. We go home. We become big, important Lepoorunts, make many offspring. We make so many offspring we have army. Then we take over government. We become—"

Ellen leaps, seizing his weapon even as she floors him. The surprise of it has everyone else frozen for a moment. Then every Lepoorunt still standing is opening fire. Electric blue bolts spark off every surface, pinging and zinging and pinging again. The bridge becomes a light show, and not a pleasant one. Even huddling as small as possible behind the captain's console isn't safe. Ricochets come from every direction, almost all of them with my name on them. This is no place for a mom from Earth to be. I'm supposed to be cuddled up in a nice cozy bed having sweet dreams. At least those ricochets must mean Ellen is still alive. She needs help though. She needs saving. We both need saving, and there's no one else here but me. At least take a peek.

This is insane. Ellen is huddled in a corner at the back of the bridge. Her only cover is Glurt, and he's soaking up a lot of fire. He must be very dead by now. Two of his crew are also dead. That leaves three of them, all so busily splattering Ellen with fire it's a miracle she isn't dead too. It's enough to keep her pinned though, only firing sporadically and indiscriminately. She definitely needs saving and the only card we have to play is that, so far, the remaining bunnies are too busy to pay any mind to me.

One of the dead Lepoorunts is close by, its weapon lying almost within my reach. This is it then. This is when the tough get going. This is when a mom does what a mom's gotta do. This is when the girls are separated from the women. This is when . . . oh, just do something, will you?

Okay. The weapon's in my hand. That was easy enough. Now stand up and start firing. Electric blue bolts are still flying everywhere. Standing up is suicide. Stay safe. Fire over the top of the console. Can't see what I'm firing at but never mind. Splatter the place and I'm bound to hit something.

"Stop!"

That's Ellen. She's alive. So am I. All the Lepoorunts must be dead. Peering over the top of the console reveals the extent of the carnage. We have seriously made a mess of this bridge. Its walls, floor and ceiling are pockmarked with little scorch marks. So is the main screen, with each scorch mark surrounded by a little area of shadow that distorts the image it's showing. If the fight had lasted much longer we might not be seeing anything on it at all.

That's the least of my concerns though. I mean, look at all these poor little Lepoorunt guys.

"Oh my God. I'm a bunny killer, a serial bunny killer."

Crawling out from beneath Glurt's dead weight, Ellen isn't even trying to feel horrified. "Don't worry about it. They were going to sell us out to the Greens, remember?"

"Maybe, but doesn't it bother you at all that we killed them all, and that you killed I don't know how many Greens before that? Doesn't that make you feel anything?"

"No. And why are you calling them bunnies? Whatever one of those is, these were not small, furry, cute and cuddly. These were sly, lying and greedy. They would've been just as happy to sell us dead as alive. Now, come on. We'll dump their bodies in the Green ship and get out of here before anyone notices."

"Anyone being their relatives. You heard what he said about breeding lots of offspring. How many bunnies d'you suppose will be coming after us?"

"None. He also said they would go home. Chances are they haven't been there in a long time, and like missy red eyes said, people disappear out here all the time. Besides, it's not going to matter how many offspring they've got. As far as everybody down there knows, Glurt came up here to dock with this ship. Maybe he didn't leave before the Demaroven terminated it. Maybe his ship was terminated too."

"But the Demaroven will see us leave, won't they? And then there's missy red eyes. She knows we came up here with him. She was probably in on it from the start."

"All the more reason to get going then. I'll find a sled to load the bodies onto. You start dragging them down."

And that's it. Ellen is already leaving the bridge. I know she's lacking in the emotional department but, wow: no remorse, no guilt, just dump the bodies and move on. If everyone else on Veniramat is like this, it must be a very cold place.

That the answers we're looking for might only be found in a place like that is not a pleasant thought, but then so far space has turned out to be pretty unpleasant anyway. First contact isn't supposed to be like this. It's supposed to be about discovering new worlds and new civilizations and experiencing their foods, their cultures and their history. This is more like a military intervention, discovering new worlds and new civilizations and then killing everyone. Well, maybe not everyone, but the bodies are piling up and we're no closer to where we need to be. One thing is for certain. Standing here worrying about it isn't going to get us anywhere so, as Ellen commanded, we need to dump the bodies and get out of here, and Glurt is as good a place as any to start.

He's heavier than he looks and it's a bit of a struggle. The trail of smeared blood he's leaving behind is pretty yucky too. It's just as red as mine, and it's going to need some serious swabbing. There are pools of it everywhere, filling the bridge with that metallic smell, and there's the smell of other things that don't bear thinking about as well. A bucket and mop are the very least that's called for, if they even have such things on alien spaceships.

By the time Glurt's dead weight has bumpily reached the bottom of the stairs, Ellen has returned with a sled. With two of us on the job, loading the rest of them doesn't take too much time at all, and pushing the sled into the Greens' docking bay is as easy as pie. Then it's back to the bridge, with Ellen only noticing the pools of blood so that she can avoid stepping in them. That might be acceptable to her but it isn't to me.

"We should clean this up before it turns nasty."

"Later. Right now we have more important things to worry about."

"Okay. So while you're worrying about more important things, do you know where the cleaning cupboard is?"

"The cleaning cupboard? Are you serious?"

"Yes, unless this ship has some robots to do the cleaning for us. Seriously, look at it. Ignoring the smell and the general ickiness of it, all these bodily fluids all over the floor are a breeding ground for disease."

"Which you're protected from, remember?"

"That's no excuse for living in squalor like the Greens." Okay, that was a little snappy, but why not? At least it produces a glimmer of a response even if it is only the merest hint of irritation.

"No, I don't know where the cleaning cupboard is. We'll be somewhere else soon enough. We can figure out having the ship cleaned then, if that's okay with you?"

"Fine. I'm just trying to help, y'know. It's not as if there's anything else I know how to do around here."

"And that's what all this is about, is it? You feeling unappreciated."

"Well, yeah. It was me who brought us here to Demaroven, wasn't it?"

"By accident. Okay, okay, you're not entirely useless. You helped deal with Glurt and his crew. Now, if you're done with your hurt feelings, we need to figure out how to undock this ship."

No, I'm not done with my hurt feelings.

Not that it matters. Ellen's taken the captain's chair and is inspecting the window that's filling the center of the console. "This is all in Lepoorunt. Maybe we shouldn't have killed them all, after all."

"Oh, so now you're agreeing with me."

No. Now she's ignoring me, well almost.

"I'm trying to figure this out, if it's all the same to you."

"What's to figure out? That window has some big red lettering flashing at us. That has to be warning us we're docked, right?"

"And you know that because you can read Lepoorunt?"

"No. But it's either a big red flashing thing warning us not to press it because something bad will happen, or it's a big red flashing thing warning us something bad will happen if we don't press it. We're stuck like a limpet to the Green ship. Something bad is going to happen anyway when the Demaroven terminate it, so I say press it. Besides, Glurt left it there and the last thing he did was dock us, so what else could it be?"

She sits back, fixing me with a cool deliberation that might be more than irritation. Come on, Ellen, you must have a button somewhere that can be pushed. Snap back at me. Show some real emotion. Give me some fireworks. Give me passion and outrage, a good old-fashioned hissy fit.

"Well? Do you have a better suggestion?"

What she has is a slow and ever so slightly condescending shake of her head. "This is how you make decisions on Earth, is it, by trying to provoke a fight? Well, fine. If you have a deity, I suggest you start getting your excuses in order."

Sitting forward again, she stabs at the big red flashing thing. It turns green with different text, and in among all the scorch marks we're moving away from the Green ship which puts a smile on my face.

"There you are then. I'm not entirely useless, am I?"

Now she is ignoring me, completely. When we're far enough away from the Green ship, she opens up the destinations window. Planet after planet appears on our main screen as she scrolls through, with the occasional view of empty space in between. But it's becoming ordinary, dull even, like looking at the destinations board in an airport lounge. Then one appears without all the text and pretty pictures on either side of the planet. Instead there are bouncy cartoons with all kinds of multicolored text popping up to fly around the main screen before exploding in showers of sparks and bubbles. It's all unreadable, of course, but then neither of us really needs to read it. We can both recognize a hard sell when we see one. The planet itself is richly umber, a desert world that turns slowly darker toward the poles which are white and speckled with green, and Ellen nods approvingly as she views it.

"This looks promising. We should be able to unload our cargo here without any awkward questions being asked—so long as somebody doesn't accidentally mention the Greens of course."

"Hey, no problem. I'll just keep my mouth shut until I have to save your ass again."

"My ass is fine, thank you very much."

"Says the one who can't remember anything."

An instant later we've jumped, and a large orange star is in the center of our main screen. Then it's gone, replaced by another bouncy cartoon. This one fills the entire screen with big, bouncy stores and big, bouncy smiling aliens, all of it unashamedly in your face while a big, booming voice sells it like it's the best thing since whatever the universe calls sliced bread.

"Welcome to Adestoria, your commerce world. If you've got the moola, we've got the merch, so come on down. Simply choose your landing zone and experience a big Adestoria welcome. All transactions are binding. Adestoria operates a no refunds policy. All spaceports are landed on at the owner's risk. The use of fake credits is punishable by summary execution. So don't be shy, come on by."

A window opens on the captain's console. There are more cartoons, a grid of eight small ones, each with the grinning face of a different alien species—the ones that can grin anyway. There's a Lepoorunt, a Nosundomi, a human, and five others we haven't come across yet. Each one speaks to us as Ellen's finger pauses over it. We can understand them, which is something of a mixed blessing. The messages they deliver are pretty much all the same, each one promising the biggest welcome and the best prices. The only real thing to choose between them is the pole. Four of them are at the north pole and four of them are at the south pole.

The Lepoorunt is at the north pole and Ellen is quick to dismiss it. "We certainly won't be going there. That zone could be full of Glurt's relatives. They're bound to recognize his ship."

"They'll see us coming in to land though, won't they?"

"Not if we land at the opposite pole. How about this one?"

One of the south pole spaceports has the human face, a young woman with a pretty smile and one of those really bright, happy and friendly voices. "Hey, thank you for considerin' spaceport six. We're all just dyin' to meet y'all so why don't you come on down?"

The southern belle act is a bit weird considering how far we must be from Earth, unless, of course, they were abducted too, which would be a pretty amazing discovery.

"Is it possible, d'you think, that these people might be from Earth too?"

"Highly unlikely. The Greens aren't exactly known for seeding the universe and, even if they were, why would they seed you instead of themselves? It is possible they could be from Veniramat though. I guess we'll find out soon enough."

Hopefully we'll find out more than that because the amazingness of it might go even further. Like, for instance, ancient aliens abducting some of our early ancestors and seeding outer space with them, or our early ancestors being ancient aliens who settled on Earth. I could be looking at a bestseller here, maybe even some honorary degrees and a Nobel Prize: the woman who finally answered the big question, with the evidence to back it up. I'll dine with princes and presidents. Hollywood will make a movie. Actresses will fight each other to play me, and audiences will sit transfixed. *Hey, this ain't no sci-fi flick some dude dreamed up in his mom's basement. This is the real deal, bro.*

While my brilliant future is being imagined, Ellen selects that spaceport for our destination, and the girl with the bright and breezy voice tells us to follow the landing trajectory that pops onto our console. The orange star leaves our screen, to be replaced by the rapidly growing planet. It looks exactly the same as its screenshot, which is hardly surprising. What is surprising is the way we barrel in toward it so that the southern pole might just as easily be the northern pole.

As it grows bigger and bigger, Ellen is concerned for my more immediate future. "You might want to consider saving your own ass for the next couple of minutes."

Ooh! The late comeback. Props to you, girl.

She's not a moment too soon either. The atmosphere welcomes us like a skier who's just hit a patch where there isn't any snow. With the ship bucking and rumbling around us, my ass'll be bouncing all over the floor if something isn't done to save it. Both of the forward consoles have a chair. They're bolted to the floor and, soon enough, my ass is bolted to one of them. As the blackness of space gives way to an orange sky, the ship stops bucking. We're on a slow glide toward a landscape of scrubby green interspersed with frozen lakes. Directly in front of us is a large, high-walled enclosure. There are more on the horizon, each one standing well back from the others. If they had pincers, they could be giant crabs beadily watching out for their neighbors in case one of them should try to invade their territory. Earth isn't the only planet with cold wars apparently.

We come in to land, skating over low buildings until we gently settle into a large open area. There are other ships parked around us, all different shapes and sizes. There's also a welcoming party, three of them. Two men and a woman. They're dressed aggressively, an opening statement that says don't mess with us. There are heavy coats, heavy weaponry and belts and bandoliers bristling with knives and machetes. How much of it is for show is an open question, but there are enough scars between them to suggest that disagreements around here usually end up ugly.

Their leader, a small man but solidly built, looks us over. In between grinning a lot, he opens with, "Well, this is interesting. A furry ship being piloted by you two. I can't wait to hear the skinny on this." He spits a lot as well which is rather gross.

Ellen is as upfront and in your face as he is. "We picked it up along the way. You know how that works, right?"

"Yeah, we know. We sorta picked our ship up along the way too. The original owners had some objections to that, but then our philosophy is losers deserve to lose. You're not gonna give us any objections, are you?"

"Wasn't planning to, unless you're thinking of upgrading. We might have to object to that, quite vigorously in fact."

"No, we're good, thanks. So I'm thinking you got a cargo to unload, right? Why don't we take a look, see what you got?"

"Just you and me."

"Sure, as long as your friend stays right where she is."

Ellen throws me a glance. It's not very reassuring. Somebody just got elected hostage, and my vote must have been postal.

With a nod, she leads boss man up the ramp into our ship, leaving me to stand shivering in the blackish-red dirt with his two goons. That's right. It's really cold down here and a t-shirt and pajama bottoms aren't cutting it. Some shopping is required before bits of me start falling off. That's going to require a friend, a female friend who's going to know where all the best stuff is and won't follow me around looking bored.

"Hey. I'm Debbie. You wouldn't happen to know where a girl could get some warmer clothes, would you?"

She looks at me, standing before her with my arms firmly crossed in an effort not to shiver so much. "Yeah, you look like you could use some. You got credits?"

"Some."

Ellen finally remembered to give me some credits. They're good, or at least they better be. The terms and conditions were pretty clear about what will happen if they aren't, and this enforcer looks like she wouldn't hesitate. Taking me on trust, which I'm guessing doesn't happen very often, she shouts over to the male goon, "I'm taking her into the market. You okay here on your own?"

He nods disinterestedly. All that's missing is a big screen showing sports, a cooler full of beer, and one of those big recliner chairs to lounge in, and he'd be set for the rest of his life.

We walk side by side across the landing area, passing by ships with crews lazily hanging out or busy loading and unloading. It could be Demaroven all over again, except I'm not wearing lead boots, but this time my fascination is with what might be in those containers. I wonder what kind of trade goes on between the far ends of the known universe. Maybe there are spices that can only be found on this planet or a fine cloth that can only be found on that planet. Maybe there's exotic booze or rare delicacies. That's not such a good thought. Some of those containers might contain actual wildlife to be delivered alive to a zoo or a gourmet kitchen or, worst of all, a fight club. That's awful. That's terrible. All those poor little creatures being transported halfway across the universe so that . . .

It's none of my business. Discovering new worlds and new civilizations isn't about telling them what they're doing wrong. It's about making new friends, and it's about time one of us broke the ice with their new friend.

"So what should I call you?"

She casts me a glance through strikingly blue eyes. In spite of the scar on her cheek and the other one above an eye, she's really rather pretty. High cheekbones, a full mouth, and almost blonde hair tied up in braids that make her look like some kind of Viking princess. "Everyone calls me Fist-in-the-Face on account of my unfortunate tendency."

"Fist-in-the-Face, huh? Mind if I call you Fist for short?"

"I'll think about it. Depends on whether I decide to like you or not."

"Because if you don't I'll be getting a fist in the face, right?"

"That's how it usually works."

"And is that how you got those scars, if you don't mind me asking?"

"These?" She runs her fingers along the one on her cheek. "No. This one was from some bitch who thought she could take me. Last I heard they were calling her One Ear. As for the other one, well, let's just say his manhood isn't quite what it used to be."

"Well, okay then. Good to know. So you gotta be tough to grow up on this world. Or is this where you ended up?"

"Anyone who grew up on this world has either left or is too dumb to leave. Me and mine, we were all born ship-side. The universe is our home. We're here because this place is easy money with no outstanding warrants."

"No outstanding warrants. What are you, pirates?"

That touches a nerve, with the temperature dropping momentarily by at least a degree. "We're not pirates. We're salvagers, although there are some parts of the universe where they might see it differently."

"So you've been around the universe a few times then. Maybe you've heard of a planet called Veniramat?"

"Can't say as I have. Why? Is that your home world?"

"So I'm told."

Oops. That slip of the tongue has her throwing me a doubtful glance. "So you're told. What, you don't know where you're from?"

Of course I do but I can hardly own up to my ID being fake, not when I'm being escorted by a Viking princess with a very big gun, a very bad attitude, and a level of trust that's only skin deep.

"No, of course we know where we're from. What I meant to say is, well, we're a bit lost. All we've got is a name and we can't seem to find it."

Now she smiles. It would be a really pretty smile if it wasn't for that vague hint of scorn. "Yeah, that sounds about right. Like I said, never heard of a place called Veniramat, but our people are originally from clear across the other side of the universe. Maybe you should try looking there."

"Okay. Thanks for the heads up. The other side of the universe it is then."

"No problem. Now, since I don't like time wasters any more than I like people who try to mess with me, I hope you're good and ready for some shopping because here we are."

CHAPTER SIX

The "here" we've come to is an opening between low adobe-like buildings. The lane beyond is narrow, and made narrower still by stalls in front of the buildings so that only two people can pass easily. Above are awnings reaching out almost far enough to touch, with only the lamplight flooding out from the open frontages keeping the gloom at bay. In between it's a warren, with dark side alleys and spots of deep shadow. Some might think it's cozy and exotic, like a Middle Eastern bazaar, with stallholders hopefully thrusting their goods at the thin drift of passersby. I'm glad Fist is here. This is not the kind of place a tourist should be walking into alone.

Whoever runs security would appear to agree with me. At every other intersection, there's a man or woman cradling a weapon in their arms and looking just as mean as Fist. She greets each of them with a nod; they nod back, and everybody else hurries on by without even giving them the once-over.

"I guess you don't have much trouble with thieves around here."

Fist chortles. It's almost as good as saying keep your hands in your pockets or you might lose them. "Not much, although we do give the grave diggers some steady work. Everybody's gotta make a living, right, except for the thieves and the pickpockets and the shell game artists and, occasionally, anyone we just don't like. If you can't find this Veniramat and you're looking for steady work and you're desperate enough, you might consider grave digging. It would put food on the table and leave you with enough free time to branch out into other areas."

"It's something to think about, I guess."

"It's just a suggestion. You'll want to fit in though, look like you belong. The clothing quarter is up ahead. So what were you thinking? A little salvager chic perhaps, or maybe something more upmarket?"

"I don't know. I was thinking something like Ellen's outfit, but if salvager chic is what you're wearing I could go with that."

We pass through another intersection with another sentry standing guard. He answers Fist with a nod but this nod is a little more than just, "Hey, how you doin'?" This one has Fist stiffening up and placing her finger over her trigger guard. "Don't look now but we're being followed."

"Followed? Who would be following us?"

"Beats me. Probably some spy from one of the other ports wondering who you are. Just be cool. We're here to shop. Whoever it is will probably get bored and wander off."

"And if they don't?"

"Then we'll give him or her a good beating. Don't worry about it. This sort of thing happens all the time. They beat one of ours, we beat one of theirs. The trick is not to kill 'em because that's what usually starts a war. Anyway, here we are. Take a look around. See what takes your fancy. I'll keep an eye out in case our friend gets a little too nosy."

It's not exactly Rodeo Drive. There are too many adobe buildings and too much dirt beneath my feet for that. There's no limo waiting to take me home either, but I do have my own personal bodyguard to keep the common herd from getting in my way. There's plenty to choose from too, store after store to rummage through, with all species catered for. Some of it is so outlandish I can't even begin to imagine how to wear it. But slowly, with store owners hanging over my shoulder because they don't have any other customers, my outfit comes together. It's not exactly like Ellen's but it's pretty good. There's a pair of loose pants with lots of pockets, sturdy boots, a vest to go over my t-shirt and a big warm coat like Fist's to go over that. All that's missing are some bandoliers, some weapons to stick into them and a snake-eyed stare because there's nothing scarier than being armed to the teeth with a snake-eyed stare.

Fist nods approvingly when she sees me, adding the final touch by handing me a sidearm that she produces from inside her coat. "You know how to use one of these?"

"Pretty much. Just point and fire, right?"

"Yeah, just make sure you're not pointing it at me when you do. Now, come on. We'll take the long way back. That'll give us plenty of time to maybe ambush our friend and find out why he's so interested."

We walk on, nice and slow, checking out stalls and disappointing their owners as we go. Who our friend might be seems pretty clear to me, but Ellen made it pretty clear too: Don't mention the Greens.

Another intersection and Fist and the sentry exchange another nod, with some quick hand signals thrown in as well. Things are starting to move, and not just on our side. At the next intersection we turn sharply left. Up ahead there's a man leaning against the corner of a building. He looks entirely ordinary to me, just some guy in nondescript clothing with too much time on his hands. Fist sees something different, and her wariness is putting me on edge too.

The lanes are beginning to fill, not enough to be an inconvenience but business is picking up. Behind us, the sentry has disappeared. If Fist was counting on his support, he'll likely be getting a fist in the face in the not-too-distant future. The guy following us has become bolder too. There's no mistaking his intentions. We were going to ambush him. Now we're the ones being ambushed.

Fist makes her decision: safety off and finger on the trigger. "Come on. These idiots want a war, they can have one."

The guy in front of us must've made a decision too. He's stepping forward. That's enough for Fist. She fires off a burst. He ducks. All the stallholders and the growing drift of shoppers in the lanes duck too. Everyone here has seen a war before, everyone except me. The crack of gunfire sounds from behind, but that guy's not shooting at us. He must have other business to attend to. Fist grabs me by the arm, drags me into the doorway of the nearest store. We crouch down. The sound of gunfire is growing all around us. There were two of them and three of us, assuming that the sentry didn't abandon us. Now there's a whole load of other people getting in on the act. At least the gravediggers will be doing a brisk trade for the rest of today.

Good for them; not so good for us. Bullets are chipping chunks out of the adobe walls and showering them upon us. That doesn't seem right somehow. This is outer space. These guys should be using ray guns or blasters or pulse cannons, not shooting bullets at each other. Not that it matters. Dead is dead however they get you, and we might well be got soon if Fist doesn't do something.

When at last she does, she grabs my arm and drags me into the store behind us. Out back there's a courtyard with neat stacks of stock piled around the walls. On the other side we duck through another store and out into the lane beyond. There's a guy crouching at an intersection, gun in hand. He sees us but doesn't open fire. Maybe he's taken by surprise. Fist isn't. As she fires a burst, he ducks out of sight, crying out, "Here! They're over here."

Through the store opposite and across another courtyard, then we come out into the lane beyond. There's no one waiting for us, but Fist isn't about to relax because of that. "We need to get out of these lanes. Stay close, okay?"

"Fine by me."

She leads, taking us through intersection after intersection and turning this way and that. It feels like we're going round in circles but maybe that's her plan, to confuse whoever these guys are. She's certainly confusing me. Every lane we hurry along is empty, every stall deserted, until we round another intersection. There's a guy. He's crouched in the middle of the lane, covering it with a heavy weapon. When he hears us coming he spins round but he doesn't open fire. Neither does Fist. It looks like they know each other, which is fortunate for all of us.

Fist pulls me down to crouch beside him. "You got any idea who these guys are?"

He shakes his head. "No. Never seen them before, and they don't look like any port crew I know of. Could be anybody. Skulking around another port's turf is one thing but who just walks in and starts a firefight without even so much as a hello? You got any idea what this is about?"

Fist shrugs. We both know who fired the first shot but

mentioning that might not be good for my health.

While they continue to talk, something else catches my attention beneath the sound of distant gunfire.

"Hey. Hey. Over here."

He's crouching back at the last intersection, and he's calling to me. Well, this is a new one. I've had my fair share of weird pickups and this guy is trying—what, here, now, in the middle of a firefight with two heavily armed bodyguards at my side?

"Hey. I can help you. I know what Veniramat is. Come on. Quick, before they notice. No, wait!"

Fist takes the guy down with a burst of gunfire that nearly perforates my eardrum. I'm partially deaf in one ear, for now at least, and my grimace of thanks goes entirely unnoticed.

"What was with that guy? Creeping up on us like that. I've stepped on sand crabs smarter than him."

Smart he might not be. Dead he isn't, and the mention of Veniramat has me rushing to his side. "Veniramat? You said 'what.' If it's not a planet, what is it?"

He looks up at me through dying eyes. "It's . . . It's a . . ."

And then he's gone.

Fist arrives, about as concerned for him as she might be for a stepped-on sand crab. "What was that all about?"

"Veniramat. He said he knew what it was. It's not a planet, it's a thing. And then you shot him."

"Well, yeah. But what are you saying? Are you saying you know who these idiots are?"

"No! Of course not. I don't know who they are any more than you do."

"Really? You know what? It seems to me you got some explaining to do." She isn't so friendly anymore. In fact she's turning downright suspicious, and she's not the only one. As we work our way through the lanes, the firefight slowly dies down. All the idiots must have been eliminated. That leaves me and Ellen, and we do have some explaining to do. In front of our ship Fist's boss is waiting for us, and he's a lot less friendly too. In fact we appear to have walked into the middle of something that's just as hot. For now at least it's not as lethal—not yet anyway.

"So explain this to me again, because I'm a little hazy on the details. The pair of you somehow got lost in space. Some furry decides to give you a ride, and somewhere between there and here you're attacked by someone else. You don't know who they are but you manage to fight them off. Then you turn up here wanting to sell a cargo that was already on board, and while we're taking care of that a whole lot of other idiots turn up and start a firefight and you have no idea who they are. That's what you're telling me, right?"

Sounds about right, apart from Ellen not mentioning the Greens. There are a couple of things I could mention, like the fact that at least one of those idiots claimed to know what Veniramat is and that it wasn't them who started the firefight. But once again Fist doesn't own up to it and probably for good reason. Her boss isn't exactly in the mood. Right now he's busy boring holes into Ellen with his eyes. She's answering him in kind, and somebody needs to lighten things up around here before it does turn lethal.

"But we're all good now, aren't we? The firefight's over and all the idiots are dead. Losers deserve to lose and the winners get to share the profit. So how about you take an extra percentage off the top for your trouble?"

All eyes turn on me, not all of them as blistering as those of Fist's boss, but we're not in the clear yet. There's only one answer to that: talk the legs off him. "Did Ellen mention

Veniramat, by the way? That's our home world. Silly of us, I know, but we sort of mislaid the coordinates. You know how it is. You think you've put them somewhere safe and then when you go looking for them they're not there. I swear one or other or both of us would forget our own heads if they weren't screwed on, a bit like Frankenstein's monster, but then you've never heard of Frankenstein's monster, have you? It's a Veniramat thing. You'd probably like it. But then you'd have to know where Veniramat is to find out. You wouldn't, would you? Know where Veniramat is, I mean?"

Fist's boss is looking more confused than dangerous now. "Are you done?"

"Yeah, I think so. So have you heard of Veniramat?"

"No, we haven't. And if I've never heard of it, it must be a very long way from here. Now, before we conclude our business and you disappear, never to be seen or heard of again, are there any other enemies you've picked up along the way that we should know about?"

"Not that I can think of. Even if there were, they wouldn't know about our Lepoorunt ship so they're not going to track us here. But there aren't any so it's not going to happen. We're in the clear, and a lot richer as well. Everyone's a winner."

"I'll be the judge of that. We'll take 20 percent off the top for the pleasure of having met you. Now I strongly suggest—"

One of his crew arrives. There's news, and some very intense whispering.

Fist's boss listens, his eyes down at first but then slowly rising, and it doesn't look like he's about to have a change of heart. "Well, this is interesting. So we've checked their IDs and all but three of them are known to us. The three that aren't don't have readable IDs. You wouldn't happen to know anything about that, would you?"

He pauses but neither of us has an answer.

"I don't like this. I don't like it at all. I've never in this universe come across an unreadable ID before. Whoever they are, they're not after that cargo, are they? They're after you, and you still can't or won't tell me why. Well, fine. I don't really care. What I care about is we got ourselves a good little earner here and I'm not about to risk that for the likes of you. When I come back you better not be here or maybe I'll throw the both of you into a cell and sell you off to whoever comes looking for you next."

"And if nobody comes looking for us?"

Fist's boss gives me a parting glare. "Oh, there'll be somebody. There's always somebody."

Well, okay then. That's the third enemy we've made and two planets we've been told never to come back to, if we include Demaroven. Not bad for barely a full day in outer space. At least the cargo's gone. So is boss man, taking most of his crew with him. If ever a man was stalking away looking for some unlucky thief to take it out on, it's him. That leaves Fist, the gatekeeper he's left behind to make sure we leave. She ought to look stern and uncompromising, ready to live up to her name, but she doesn't.

There's something else on her mind, something that has her blue eyes flicking between the two of us as she strokes the scar on her cheek. "I like the way you handled that. You got room for another pair of hands?"

That's unexpected. Fist the enforcer should be telling us how many different ways she's going to hurt us.

I'm surprised, and so is Ellen. "Why? You tired of this nice little earner you've got?"

"Pretty much. I miss the old days, the hit and run, the take 'em for everything they've got and the laughing in their faces as they try to catch us. Yeah, we've got it easy here but where's the fun in that? We haven't had a really good war around here for quite some time, and you just reminded me of how alive a war makes me feel. Truth is I'm bored. The boss just wants to put his feet up and watch the credits roll in. He's getting lazy. He's also piling on the weight. Me, I want to get back out there while I still can. It's better to crash and burn than end up smelling of pee, right?"

Ellen's trying not to smile. She's not doing very well at it. "We weren't exactly planning on crashing and burning, or the other thing, but I take your meaning. You need to understand though: We're not salvagers and we are lost."

"Of course you are. But you could still use an extra gun, right, what with those Lepoorunt you've got after you—and I'm guessing they're not the only ones. I got skills, y'know, things you probably never even thought of. You show me a tight spot and I'll show you how to get out of it."

"And your boss won't mind? Because we don't need him after us as well."

"Nah. He probably won't even notice. Give him a jug to sip from and a nice sunset to watch and all he'll be looking for is a blanket. So whaddaya say? Got room for another one?"

"I guess so, although you'll probably never be coming back."

Fist shrugs. "That's okay. I quite fancy seeing the other side of the universe. Like I told Debbie, that's where our people came from originally. There's probably a planet out there where everyone's the same as us. Who knows? Maybe I'll even find some long-lost relatives, and at least there won't be any warrants out on us."

"Warrants? You have warrants out on you?"

"No more than you by the looks of it. Hey, what's to worry? They gotta catch us first, right?"

At this point somebody probably ought to tell Fist about our little green friends, but I'm not putting my foot in it again and Ellen isn't mentioning it either.

"Good. Let's get aboard and take off then. You got any idea which direction we should be heading in?"

"Yeah, I know this part of space pretty well. I know exactly where we should go."

That'll be a first. No more potluck. The universe will open out for us—a grand vista filled with great civilizations—or it might not. Back on the bridge, Ellen takes the captain's chair and we're not going anywhere. On the console she scrolls and taps, taps and scrolls, but not very much happens.

Fist, who's been quietly taking in the bloody mess that is our bridge, watches with a growing frown, until the moment arrives when she can no longer not say anything. "What are you doing?"

"I'm trying to figure out how to reverse the landing trajectory so we can take off."

"Reverse the landing trajectory! Why? Are you telling me you don't how to fly this ship?"

Oops. Barely aboard and Fist is already stepping on toes. Ellen isn't exactly on speaking terms with sarcasm. Looks like her relationship with criticism is pretty distant as well. In fact as she sits back in the captain's chair, there's a steady gaze that suggests she might be thinking of calling it mutiny. They could be about to have their first fight and we haven't even taken off yet.

"I got us this far, didn't I?"

"More by luck than judgment, it looks like. What were you doing? Stabbing randomly at destinations and hoping not to be blown to bits?"

Neither Ellen nor I say anything. That would be way

too embarrassing.

"That's exactly what you were doing, wasn't it? Jumping around the universe without a clue—so little of a clue, in fact, that you haven't even noticed that most of this ship's systems are turned off. Didn't it occur to you at all that all these dead screens and consoles might actually do something? Come on. Get out of the way. Get out of the way!"

Yes, we know about the other consoles. Glurt said we wouldn't need them because we would be safe in Demaroven space. Although that, of course, was before we killed him and all his crew, took his ship and then left Demaroven space.

Again, neither of us mentions that, partly because Fist is busy waving Ellen aside and jumping into the captain's chair herself. One look at the console and she's grinning as everything becomes clear to her. "Oh well, look at this. It's all in furry. Didn't you guys even think to change the text to your language? What is your language anyway?"

"English. It's one of the most widely spoken languages on Earth."

"One? How many languages are there on this Earth of yours?"

"I dunno. A couple of hundred maybe."

"A couple of hundred. One planet and you've got a couple of hundred languages. That's probably more languages than the entire rest of the known universe."

"Yeah, well. We're inventive."

"Inventive! Insane, more like. And this Earth: Since we both know Veniramat doesn't exist, that's where you really come from, isn't it?"

"What!" Ellen's having her own moment of clarity, which is not necessarily a good thing. "What d'you mean, Veniramat doesn't exist?"

Thanks, Fist. Great timing, although Ellen had to know at some point. Now it's down to me to explain.

"Yeah. Sorry about that. I forgot to mention it, but then there wasn't really much of an opportunity until now. Anyway, one of those guys tried to make contact with me. He said Veniramat was a what not a where. Then he died because she shot him, so that's all I know."

"You shot him! Why did you do that?"

Again, oops. Maybe I shouldn't have said that last bit. Ellen's moment of clarity is clouding over. At least the threatened squall is headed in Fist's direction, where it's greeted with a smirk.

"Well, isn't this great? You two really are clueless, aren't you?"

That's hardly fair. Like Ellen said: We've got this far. But Fist doesn't care. She hasn't finished picking through our incompetence yet, and now she's talking to herself as if we weren't even there.

"They don't know where they came from. They don't know where they're going. They don't know what they're doing when they get there. They don't even know how to pilot this ship. In fact, the only thing they seem to be any good at is pissing people off. And there was me thinking this was a good idea. I should leave. I should get off this clown ship and go back to my nice, comfortable life beating up the occasional spy. So why don't I? Because I'm bored? Because I want to go places I've never been before? Because these two are going to get themselves killed without me? Not my problem. Not my problem at all, really. On the other hand . . ."

Nice of her to be so concerned about us, when she's not simply bored. This is not a very promising beginning, but then Fist hasn't finished yet. "Well, okay then. If it's dumb enough to have a sane person running for cover it's dumb enough for me. Let's do this."

She lifts an amulet from around her neck. It's black and oblong, about the size of a finger. As she places it in the center of the console a little green light comes on, and I just have to ask: "What is that?"

"This? This is my magic bullet. It's a hack-anything key. All salvagers have one just in case we come across a ship we like the look of, or at least we used to . . ."

"You are pirates then, like the Greens."

Fist turns instantly steely and it looks like that's something else I shouldn't have said. "Didn't I already tell you? We are not pirates. We are salvagers. And what do you know about the Greens?"

"Not much. We've heard people talking, that's all."

Fortunately that seems to satisfy her. "Good, because they are pirates. We're salvagers. Remember that. You run around the universe calling salvagers pirates and you're going to end up in a whole lot of trouble. And here we are. It's done. We now have full access to this ship's computer."

While she's been speaking, a window has opened and a waterfall of code has scrolled by faster than any eye could follow. Once it's done, she sits forward to read the text that's appeared in another window. The hieroglyphics of the Lepoorunt script have changed into something more squiggly and flowing but it still makes no sense to me.

"Okay. We have full access to the computer. Voice control is offline. I'll deal with that later." A few stabs of her finger and all the dead screens on the other two consoles come to life, with Fist pointing first left and then right. "That's weapons control. That's the sensor array. Can either of you read any of this?"

Ellen shakes her head for the both of us, which doesn't surprise Fist at all.

"Of course not. Silly of me to ask. And that's why mixed crews are such a pain in the ass. Never mind. I'll run everything from here then. Now, before we dust off this rock or my ex-boss comes back, is there anything else we need to take care of like, for instance, visiting the little girls' room?"

"You could clean up this bridge, if that's possible."

Fist grins at me. "I was beginning to think you'd never ask. How about I change this ship's ID as well, in case we run into any more Lepoorunt? Okay then. First stop: empty space. We'll sort this ship out and then we'll go visit some old friends of mine. While I'm about it, I'll reset gravity too. This is a little on the heavy side for me."

CHAPTER SEVEN

Our main screen is filled with a planet. It's an awful lot like Jupiter so really, really big. Its atmosphere is made up of strips, each one a different color, with occasional angry-looking spots interspersed between them. Its sun is big too, blue and way too close for any sensible person to be messing with. Only people with nowhere else to go would choose to live here: misfits, outcasts, people with serious relationship problems . . . People like Fist, in fact.

In empty space she first of all worked the captain's console, stabbing her way through windows like a Viking in a monastery. "Optimizing the ship's systems," she called it. The monks would've probably called it something else.

Then she made some rat-sized robots appear that made quick work of hoovering up all the blood, which was quite fascinating to watch. Now she's made a joystick appear—who knew?—and while she's guiding us in, she explains, "The planet's uninhabitable, but its largest moon is home to a salvager colony so remember what I said. Call them pirates and they're likely to get real mad real fast, and a salvager with hurt feelings is just as likely—"

"Fist? We thought you were holed up on some commerce planet just sitting back and watching the credits roll in."

He's human, larger than life on our main screen, and Fist knows him too.

"Hey, Scowler. So how's it going with you? Still running fast and light?"

"Everything's good. Everything's tight. But what about you? What brings you out here, apart from looking for trouble of course?"

"You know how it is. I got bored. Same old same old every day, and I got some new friends here who needed a helping hand."

He grins broadly. "Yeah, I know how it is. We could likely put some business your way, if you're interested."

"We could be. So are we good to land?"

"Sure. Just follow the beacon."

It's nice to be so openly welcomed for once, or at least it is for Fist. Ellen is tight-lipped, maybe even a little broody, and it certainly hasn't gone unnoticed by me how Fist appears to have appointed herself captain, even going so far as accepting an offer of possible work without so much as a nod from the two of us. Neither of us is going to say anything though, not while the only person who knows how to fly this ship is guiding us in toward a large and gibbous moon. Just within the dark side there appears a ring of lights. The light side— what we can see of it—is gray and rocky, scarred with craters, and very much like Earth's moon. Unlike Earth's moon, this one's surface is also dotted with installations, towers, domes and squat rectangular blocks. Or maybe that is like Earth's moon, if you believe the conspiracy theorists.

As we close in nose-first on that ring of lights, more light appears within it. Some sort of aperture has opened in front of us like the petals of a flower, revealing within a grayness dotted with little stacks of darker gray and tiny black things moving around like ants. It's not the black hull of a Green ship but . . .

"Oh my God! That's a floor. We're heading straight into a floor."

Fist grins, and then stabs at something on the captain's console. As our ship's attitude changes, there might also be the threat of a grin on Ellen's face. Well, I'm glad they both think it's so funny.

Now we're descending through the aperture, floating downward into what looks like a large hanger. There are walkways, pipe runs, conduits and large, red faded lettering in a script I've never seen before, probably saying things like Authorized Entry Only and No Littering. Those little gray stacks turn out to be containers, and there are two other ships parked up outside of the landing zone. Since pirates—sorry, salvagers—aren't exactly known for building things, I have to wonder, "Who built this place?"

"A species called the Formalax. They're giant bugs with colonies hidden away all across the universe. Mostly they keep themselves to themselves unless one of their own turns against them which doesn't happen very often. About seventy years ago one of them did. Zubalix the Insane, they called her. She put together a small army of salvagers—no mean feat in itself—smashed through the Formalax's defenses and then overran the place. They used to come sneaking around every once in a while. Maybe they still do. It happened once when I was here but we messed them up with their own artillery and then got very drunk. Happy days."

Maybe for her. If the Formalax have a warrant out on her

and this entire base, simply by turning up here Ellen and me might have accidentally saddled ourselves with more enemies. More importantly a species of giant bugs with bases hidden away all over the universe might not be good for Earth. What if the conspiracy theorists are right and there's a Formalax colony on the moon? What if our only protection is the fact that they keep themselves to themselves and are simply not interested in us? Let's hope Ellen is right and only the Greens know the location of Earth, as if that isn't bad enough.

But now we've landed and there's a welcoming committee at the bottom of our ramp to worry about. Two of them are human, one is Nosundomi, and the fourth must be Formalax. It's about a foot taller than the rest and bluish-black all over except where the light gives it tinges of red and green. Two small antennae twitch above big button eyes with mandibles beneath that clack as it speaks. Its thorax is about half as long as a torso, with an abdomen beneath that's twice that, and it stands on two long, spindly legs. It also has four shorter arms which must come in useful for all sorts of things, like carrying a round of drinks and being able to scratch an itch at the same time.

There are other species wandering around in the background as well, but that's becoming commonplace now. Aliens, schmaliens. Been there, seen it, done it. Not so the folks back home. What a pity the Greens didn't think to grab my smartphone as they manhandled me out the door. It would have been some exhibition: a boutique New York art gallery with champagne and nibbles, and crowds of well-heeled sophisticates lining up around the block. *"Do you think she really did this or is this something they dreamed up in Hollywood?" "Sweetie, it doesn't matter. What matters is that everyone who does matter is here."*

One of the humans steps forward. He stands almost as high as the Formalax's shoulder, with tattoos instead of hair, and a big friendly grin on his long face. "Hey, Fist. Good to see you. It's been a while. How about we go get smashed and catch up along the way?"

"Sounds good to me. These two are my crew by the way. Debbie and Ellen."

Crew! When did that happen? Oh, I forgot. My postal vote hasn't made it out of the solar system yet. Ellen's hasn't made it out of her system either, which might explain her reticence. She does manage a brief smile though, as our host holds out a welcoming hand.

"Good to meet you. You can call me Grinder. It would be best not to get on my wrong side, if you take my meaning."

Nice welcome, and as if to prove it, when he shakes my hand he has a grip that could crush steel. Then we're on our way across the hanger. Gravity is a little lower here than on Earth. It puts a very noticeable spring in my step. Fortunately, while I learn to control it, there are no low doorways for me to be hitting my head on.

Beyond the rectangular opening that we pass through is a passageway. It runs so far ahead of us that we can't see its end. There are side passages and what appear to be storage rooms and maintenance shops. Not that there's any sign of much maintenance. I don't know about the Formalax but ants and bees usually like to keep their nests clean and tidy. This place is anything but. In fact it's almost as bad as the Green ship. The walls are scrawled with graffiti in as many different scripts as there are colors. There are piles of garbage here and there and, in between them, the occasional sprawled drunk. Hopefully that's what they are, anyway. If they aren't, somebody really ought to come and take the bodies away. It's not made any better by the number of lights flickering as they say their last goodbyes. Now if I was house mother around here . . .

Grinder turns into a long, low-ceilinged hall. Beneath dimmed lights the floor is filled with what must be the strangest array of furniture ever assembled: low tables with big cushions to slob out on, regular tables with chairs of every imaginable kind and high tables with high stools to perch on. The furniture must have been looted from a dozen or more planets, with just as many different kinds of aliens sitting or sprawling around them.

There's a low swell of conversation except in a far corner where a pale, rubbery-faced group is being very loud. With a nod Grinder sends some people over to deal with them. That doesn't go so well. Harsh words quickly turn into thrown fists and there's a short-lived brawl that everyone else ignores. While that's happening we arrive at Grinder's special table, complete with the strangest chair of all. It's big and covered in reptilian hide, with two great reptilian heads looking left and right for its back and two smaller reptilian heads looking straight ahead for its armrests. It's the kind of chair a velociraptor might have chosen to sit in, made up entirely of what was left of its kills, if a velociraptor had been capable of making such a thing.

Perching on the edge of it, the king on his throne, Grinder orders a round of drinks with a wave of his hand. "So, Fist, what brings you back to us?"

"We're heading back across the universe to find out where we came from. Y'know, looking for our roots, that sort of thing."

While she's speaking, we all sit around a circular table and another kind of alien arrives with seven shot glasses all filled with a blood-red liquid. Downing hers in one gulp, Fist grimaces as she slams the empty glass back down on the table.

It sits there, filled with a residue that looks an awful lot like motor oil. Everyone else does the same. Their glasses all look the same. Only mine remains, looking decidedly unappetizing as it sits there staring up at me. Fortunately no one notices as Grinder continues, "Your roots? You were born ship-side, weren't you, the same as the rest of us?"

"Yeah, but somewhere way back we've all got ancestors who weren't. It's just something to do really, while I've got no other commitments. There's nothing wrong with a little self-discovery, is there? Maybe you should try it. Who knows, we might all have families out there we don't know about."

Another round of drinks arrives and now everyone notices, including the alien server. There must be some rule that the next round can't be drunk until the last one is finished. No wonder there are so many drunks lying around all over the place. Oh well, here goes nothing. The glass is barely empty before my mouth and throat are on fire. Oh my God! This stuff must be made from scotch bonnets. The rest of it is spluttered all over the table, much to everyone else's amusement, and no one is more amused than the Nosundomi. "Whoa! Somebody's never had Bedralian blood wine before. Don't worry, sweets. It'll either kill you or make you insane drunk."

While I'm still gagging too much to answer, Grinder looks up at the alien server. "We got any of that Xlechlis piss water left? Bring a glass over for my guest."

My drink quickly arrives in an elegant stem, and it looks exactly like piss water. It tastes faintly of oranges though, and doesn't instantly set about dissolving the lining of my mouth and throat.

Meanwhile Fist is admiring Grinder's throne. "That's a real fancy chair you got there. Where'd you find that?"

"This?" Grinder pats an armrest like it's his favorite hound.

"We got this from some pissant planet we just happened to stumble across. We came down on them in the middle of the night, made them think they were being attacked by an army of demons, and then took whatever we wanted."

"So you screwed them up real good then."

"Nah. We made them believe their gods are real is all. Their emperor's probably looking forward to sitting on this again when the great bird comes to take him away to the afterlife. Maybe we'll visit with them again from time to time, until they develop something more deadly than spears and bows and arrows. There's no sense in getting your ass shot off, is there? In the meantime, that was a good haul. You happen across any more planets like that in your travels, be sure and let us know, yes?"

"Will do. So what's this bit of business you were wanting to put our way?"

Grinder laughs. "Yeah, that's our Fist: always straight to the point. So we came by this artifact. Turns out the race we took it from has sworn eternal vengeance on us if we don't give it back. Not good for business, that. So we opened up a line of communications with them and did a deal. Seems they'll pay handsomely to get it back. We need someone to deliver it and pick up the ransom, someone who can enter their space without immediately being blown to smithereens 'cos they're a trigger-happy bunch of bastards. Shouldn't be a problem since we've already made the arrangements, but you never know. There'll be a handsome payment in it for you, and Blut here will be coming along to do all the talking."

The Nosundomi raises a hand. "That'll be me. Should be a simple there and back. No trouble. No problem."

Now that we're getting into it, Fist is a lot more businesslike. "Okay. So how did you come by this artifact and why exactly do you need us? If the arrangements have been made, anyone could do it, couldn't they?"

Grinder is a lot more purposeful too. "True. Except we need someone with a cool head and a steady hand. I can hardly go 'cos I'm running this place, and as I'm sure you'll remember, most of these knuckleheads are one screw short of a reactor core. Not that you aren't yourself when the mood—"

"In other words, we're expendable."

"Expendable! Oh, Fist, would I do that to you?"

"In a heartbeat."

"Take a look around. This lot doesn't know any other way to behave. They're just as likely to steal something else while they're there. But you, you've been collecting dues on a commerce world. That speaks of a certain level of discipline. It's a straightforward in and out, and as to how we came by it, let's just say the crew that took it got lucky. Well, most of them did anyway."

Fist doesn't reply. Ellen remains silent too, although it's pretty obvious there's something she wants to say. It's one of those not-in-front-of-the-children moments, and Grinder picks up on it too. "Okay. So clearly you want to think about it. That's fine. When you're ready, let me know your decision."

He rises. The others follow, all of them wearing big smiles except for the Formalax, who can't. As Grinder passes Fist, he pats her on the shoulder. "Don't go running off without saying goodbye now. I might feel insulted."

Once we're alone there's a brief silence. It's made of eggshells and issues, of expectant glances and the lull before the storm, and it's Fist who lights the blue touch paper. "Well, what d'you think?"

Ellen's coolness is growing thin. Fist might not have even noticed but I'm finding it increasingly easy to recognize the changes in her moods. "What do I think? I think that sounded an awful lot like a threat. You trust these people?"

I'm staying well out of this.

"Why wouldn't I? I've known them for a long time, or at least I used to know them."

"Exactly. You don't know what they're into now."

"They're into salvaging, the same as they always were, and they're plain-speaking people. You think that was a threat? What have they got to threaten us about? You heard him. It's our decision whether we do it or not."

"Yeah, right. It's our decision but don't go running off without saying goodbye. You want to know what I think? I think we've got more than enough credits after selling that cargo. We don't need more, so let's be on our way."

"True, but we could do with friends. Having a bolt-hole to run to is never a bad thing, especially considering the way you collect enemies."

"We were doing fine before you invited yourself aboard and straight into the captain's chair. We'd still be doing fine now if you hadn't brought us here."

"Oh, absolutely! You ripped off the furries. You completely pissed off my boss. And you still haven't got a clue where you came from or where you're going. You're doing real peachy, aren't you?"

"Says the pirate!"

This is starting to get a little heated, an out-of-character display of actual temper from Ellen. But then Blut did say that the liquor would either kill you or make you insane drunk. For Fist, this is probably quite normal and her full name is how it might end. Well, I might not know how to fly a ship or read any languages out here but I do know how to handle sibling rivalries.

"Hey, hey, we're all friends here, aren't we? We're all going in the same direction on the same ship. We—"

"Is that it! Is that all you got to say? You got a voice here too, y'know, so what's it gonna be? Are we staying or are we going?" Now Fist is turning on me, and it looks like staying well out of it was the right choice. Damn the postal service for turning up at precisely the wrong moment.

"Well, I think both arguments have merit. Like Ellen says, we don't need the credits. On the other hand, it's always good to have a friend. So—"

"What are you, a politician?"

"No! I just—"

"You just nothing. Next time I talk to you I want to hear a decision: stay or go. And as for you . . ." Fist turns what is now a demon eye back onto Ellen. ". . . why don't you tell me what this is really all about? Come on, what's really eating you? And don't call me a pirate!"

"What's really eating me? Fine. Who put you in charge? Who made you captain? You come down here like it's your ship and start making deals without even asking us because all of a sudden we're just crew. How did that happen?"

Good questions. She can't walk in on us and start throwing her weight around. She can't hijack the captain's chair like it's her ship. It's our ship, or at least it is since we killed Glurt and his crew.

Then again, maybe she can. "Well, first of all, I know these people. I know how to handle them. Do you? Second of all, I'm not making deals without asking you because that's what we're discussing right now, isn't it? And third, the ship put me in charge because I'm the only one who actually knows how it works. Now is there anything else you wanna get off your chest while we're clearing the air?"

Yeah, this is not so good. Within a few moments of Grinder bringing us here there was a brawl over in the far corner. The same guys he sent over to start it are now eyeing us up. With Fist on the warpath they might want to rethink that, or at least send for some reinforcements. But the storm is already blowing itself out. Ellen falters, deflating as dispiritedly as a wrinkled balloon.

"No. I think that about covers it, for now at least. I still think we should go though. We don't need the credits and we don't need the veiled threats either."

"But we do need the friends. Great! So now we've got that all cleared up, what does the politician think? Do we stay or do we go?"

With those two moments away from tearing chunks out of each other, it has to come down to me eventually. Well, okay then. "We stay."

That's not so much a decision as a means of avoiding another confrontation. At least Fist is happy, a little smirk appearing on her face which means my face is safe.

Ellen is grumpy though. Looks like, for now at least, we're not friends anymore. She'll get over it. They always do.

Right now, though, that still leaves us in the middle of an awkward silence which means it's down to me again. "Okay. Now that's decided let's tell Grinder and then we can get on with it. The sooner it's done, the sooner we're out of here, right?"

Neither of them answers. Looks like this team-building thing is going to require an awful lot of work.

CHAPTER EIGHT

We're in empty space again, a depthless vista of multicolored pinpricks of light. Blut gave us the coordinates and so here we are, waiting. The artifact is in the hold in a small container carried aboard by his two associates, a human called Wallface—best not to ask—and a Formalax called Flaxamax.

Time is dragging by slowly. There's a tension in the air, as if everyone is expecting someone else to make a move. Fist is sat in the captain's chair staring at the main screen. She looks relaxed, bored even, but that could be an act. She must be well versed in the art of striking first. The same could be said of Blut, who is at her shoulder and also staring at the main screen. Flaxamax and Wallface are both standing at the rear of the bridge with, between them, six arms folded. They look super intimidating, or at least Wallface does, cold-eyed and made out of granite. Flaxamax could be asleep for all any of us know. Ellen is sat at the weapons console. Fortunately she can't read it or the Xvr, the ones we're waiting for, might be in for a nasty surprise. I can't read the sensor array either, which leaves all of us studiously avoiding eye contact. This is an awful lot like riding the subway. Just pick a city, anywhere.

Then my console pings, causing me to almost jump out of my skin. Something is out there. A window opens in front of me and more alien ships than anyone on Earth has ever even dreamed of scroll past at lightning speed. While our computer is trying to identify what's approaching, I'm wondering how much NASA or the Air Force would pay to get their hands on this.

As that thought passes into the place where all passing thoughts go, everyone else is perking up, with Blut firmly taking the lead. "Everybody chill. Nobody does anything unless they do."

The main screen flickers, and we're all looking at a new species of alien. This one looks like some kid made a man out of two eggs. Its head is ovoid and pointy, with a larger pointy ovoid for its body. Two long spindly arms with long spindly fingers work at a console in front of it, and the whole thing is cream-colored in front with the beginnings of black and brown mottling along its sides. There are several small black eyes, a large jaw with a fang on either side and no nose. The whole thing looks decidedly squishy. If the Formalax are descended from ants that got smart, this one could be descended from a spider, and that is not an encouraging thought.

When it speaks though, its voice is surprisingly firm. "I Phnmng of Xvr Space Command. You have item?"

Blut's reply is just as firm. "We do. It's in our hold, all safe and sound."

"Very well. We come aboard. We inspect. If all satisfactory, we complete payment. This agreeable to you?"

"It is."

As our main screen returns to the starscape, Blut nods to Wallface and Flaxamax and they leave the bridge. At the same time, something grows in the center of the screen. At first it's just an array of tiny lights, but gradually it transforms into three spheres held together by struts and beams. There are also two long cylinders on either side that run the entire length of the ship, and a communications dish on top of the central sphere. Compared to our bunny ship, and even the Green junkyard ship, even I can see this is primitive, the product of a species that must have only just mastered space flight.

In a low and even voice, Blut confirms it. "Their jump ability is low-grade, limiting their range, and they don't have portal tech so they'll be coming in to dock. Don't anybody get trigger-happy. Those two cylinders are plasma cannons, deadly when fired but they take time to warm up. Nice and easy does it then. We don't want to spook them."

This is my second time docking. The Xvr ship comes closer and closer, getting bigger and bigger. Its docking port comes before it, a short tube like the beak of some ancient galley. Tell the guy on the drum to set ramming speed and it's full steam ahead. Okay, that's a mixed metaphor, but hey, you know what I mean. It's a breeze though, nothing to worry about. Our two ships come together with a judder and we're docked. Now it's down to Wallface and Flaxamax. Some welcome that's gonna be. Everything must be good though because a few minutes later Wallface returns with Phnmng and two other Xvr in tow. Waddling in on long, spindly multi-jointed legs—six each—all three of them are wearing harnesses, each one festooned with pouches and curious bits of equipment, and a chunky-looking sidearm. That doesn't help to lessen the tension at all.

Everyone regards each other with flinty eyes, except for

those who might be descended from spiders. They simply stare while Phnmng opens with, "We inspect now. Soon as good, we pay."

Blut agrees. "Soon as good, you pay."

After that we all stand around silently waiting, like an office party where everyone's trying to avoid talking about work.

After slowly casting all his eyes—or is it her eyes?—over the bridge, Phnmng finally breaks the silence. "Nice ship. You sell?"

This time Blut doesn't agree. "Sorry. We need this ship to get home in."

"Nooo. We give you ship. Part exchange. Very good ship. Get you home real fast."

"No. It's not his ship to sell, and we're not selling either."

In answer to Fist's firmness Phnmng nods slowly, looking over the bridge again. It's hard to tell if he or she is disappointed or slyly figuring the odds. At the same time something on his harness buzzes. It's a communications device. He answers it. Only he can hear what's being said but we can all hear the sound of gunfire. The conversation is short, very short, and he's not figuring the odds anymore. All his eyes are fixed on Blut, and he looks even more like a spider regarding a fly.

"You betray us! You bring others aboard to kill us?"

So much for Blut selling us out, or Fist selling Blut out, or everyone on this bridge selling everybody else out. It's Blut selling the Xvr out, or it might not be because Blut is just as surprised as the rest of us.

"Others? What others? We came here in good faith."

"You lie!" Phnmng and his Xvr all reach for their weapons. Well, Grinder did say they're a trigger-happy bunch.

Blut and Wallface are the first to react, with the bridge exploding into a chaos of gunfire. Ellen and Fist both dive for cover behind their consoles, and then join the fight. That leaves me sat at my console transfixed by the thought, *Would someone care to explain exactly what the hell is going on?*

Fortunately no one thinks to shoot at me and the fight doesn't last long. By the time it's over, Wallface is on the floor surrounded by a growing pool of red blood, Blut is flat out in a pool of blue blood, and the three Xvr have gone down too, their heads exploding like bags of puss, which is possibly even more disgusting. Looks like we'll have to get the cleaning bots out again.

Ellen and Fist rise to their feet. After surveying the mess, they exchange a look that quickly settles something and Fist takes charge. "You two find out who these others are. I'll undock and jump us out of here. And if you come across any more Xvr, kill them too."

"You got it. Come on, Debbie." Ellen isn't waiting for a reply, and I'm not even particularly shocked anymore. This whole blowing aliens' heads off thing is becoming way too normal, which is a little worrying. At some point, if I ever get back to Earth, I'm going to have to explain to NASA and the UN and every government we've got how I made first contact with several different alien species and pretty much declared war on most of them. That should go down well.

For now, we race from the bridge down to the docking level to find Flaxamax crouched at the corner of a passageway. She's taking the occasional potshot around it, with several bolts of blue light flying back in answer. For some reason, when we appear, all those bolts stop flying. That's curious, but not so curious as to be worth wasting time on. We dart across the passageway and crouch behind Flaxamax.

"You know who they are?"

After some serious antenna twitching, Flaxamax answers

Ellen with, "No. They must have hacked their way through a portal just as sneaky as you like. I'm guessing they're some other bunch of salvagers looking for an easy score. Can't hardly blame them. An Xvr ship docked with us makes both of us as good as defenseless. Who wouldn't jump at that?"

"Who wouldn't, and at precisely the wrong moment too. Well, whoever they are, we gotta take this ship back."

"Agreed. I'll stay here and keep them busy. You work your way round to the other side of the ship. That way we can hit them from both sides before they do it to us."

Ellen sets off, with me trailing along behind. Flaxamax lays down a covering fire which keeps the salvagers at the far end of the passageway quiet. At our end, Ellen turns the corner then quickly steps back, holding out an arm to stop me.

"Xvr in the docking bay, five of them. You ready for this?"

No, not really. "Shouldn't we try talking to them first? Y'know, explain it all and then maybe they'll help us? We've still got their artifact, after all."

"Or maybe they'll just start shooting at us. Phnmng wanted this ship as well, remember, and he brought them aboard without us knowing about it."

On second thoughts, now she's put it like that, maybe not.

On Ellen's word we charge the corner. The Xvr are all looking rather lost and leaderless, with one of them rapping its spindly knuckles on the closed docking bay door. It doesn't appear to have dawned on them that there's a firefight going on around the corner. They don't notice us either, and what follows is little more than a turkey shoot. By the time it's over, the docking bay is drenched in puss. The sickly smell of it is not something anybody's stomach should have to deal with. I hold my breath as we hurry on, reaching the next corner. Ellen stops. The only sound is the occasional distant burst from Flaxamax. Whoever our new guests are, that's some of them being kept busy at least.

Ellen raises a finger to her lips and then peers round the corner. Right then the ship shudders. We've jumped. Whoever these intruders are, they're just as trapped as the Xvr, which is all the more reason for them to seize control of our ship. Well, not so fast, suckers. You're up against four females armed with very big guns and invading our space is the wrong move.

At a signal from Ellen, we both advance, weapons raised and ready to fire. The passageway ahead is empty. Maybe Flaxamax is keeping them all busy. Or not, because now two of them appear. They don't look much like pirates, what with those black suits and visors they're wearing. Not very original, but then maybe whoever makes those things has the same business model as Henry Ford: You can have any color you want so long as it's black.

Whoever they are, the leading one holds up a hand. They want to talk. Ellen has other ideas. With two short bursts she takes both of them down. So much for hearing them out, and so much for that body armor too. They must have bought it from the lowest bidder.

After that there's silence. Flaxamax's firefight must have ended as well. If she lost, these guys' friends could be on their way to our bridge right now. That'll be their bad luck because Fist will be waiting to greet them. Hey guys, thanks for dropping by. Now let's parteee.

As she lowers her weapon, Ellen must be thinking the same. "Come on. We'll search the rest of this deck in case there are any more of them and then head back to the bridge."

She leads the way, pausing only to make certain the two in front of us are dead. Carefully moving on, we check out every room and corner as we go. We find no more of them.

Nor do we hear any more firing. Either they've taken out Fist and Flaxamax or our girls have taken them out. It's a long, slow and eerie creep back around to the other side of the ship. But at last we round a corner and there, coming along the passageway toward us with her weapon raised and ready to fire, is Fist. After almost opening up on each other, we all breathe a sigh of relief.

Then Fist is as matter of fact about all this carnage as Ellen. "How many?"

"Two. And you?"

"Four. Flaxamax took down two before they got her. The other two made it to the bridge but I made short work of them. The ship is clear. Let's get back to the bridge. We've got some decisions to make."

I'm apparently the only one with any hint of a conscience left, that nagging feeling that somehow this shouldn't have happened. If this is how business is done out here in the universe, perhaps Earth is better off in its all too often not-so-peaceful isolation. These aliens are even more messed up than we are. Believe me, guys. You don't want these people coming to save you.

The bridge greets us with two more bodies added to the butcher's bill, and that's after passing Flaxamax and another two of them in the passageway. This is one hell of a mess that someone's going to have to clean up, and that's only the bridge. There are also five Xvr in the docking bay and another one with the artifact.

With no one but me noticing the stench—again—Fist heads straight to the sensor array to check for nearby threats. Ellen heads for one of the visors, removing it to reveal the face of a human male beneath. Then she lays both of their forearms bare, checking their details with her reader card. "I can't access their IDs, their medical record or their credits."

"So just like those three guys on Adestoria then. Like my boss said, it's you two they came looking for, isn't it? And you still don't know who they are."

Whatever anyone else might think of her, Fist is no fool. But then she can safely leave that to me as I put my foot right in it. "Probably because you keep shooting them. Well, you do, don't you? You killed the one on Adestoria and you killed the two down there in the passageway. If we'd talked to them instead we might know who they are by now."

Okay. Not good. Both of them are giving me the steely eye, and it's Ellen who weighs in first. "Like you wanted to talk to the Xvr. If another Green ship shows up, do you want to try talking to them too?"

"The Greens. Are you telling me the Greens are after you?"

And so it gets worse. Don't blame me. I didn't mention the Greens. For now at least, Fist's rapidly chilling gaze is fixed firmly on Ellen, and for a moment or two she's struggling for something to say.

"Yeah. Sorry. We . . . Well, that cargo we sold your boss, we took that from a Green ship after we killed all the crew. We were going to sell it to the Lepoorunt, but then they tried to sell us out to the Greens so we killed them and took their ship too."

Fist is going to explode. She's going to go postal, ballistic, full-on T. Rex with a toothache. She might even throw us out of an airlock. We'll be left floating in space, alive just long enough to watch her jump our ship to somewhere a long, long way from here.

Instead she smiles, then chortles, then lets fly with a full-on guffaw. "Wow. You two might be even more insane than Zubalix. You wiped out the entire crew of a Green ship, you wiped out the entire crew of a furry ship and then you walked away with the cargo. I gotta say, I am impressed. And to think you told my boss you were lost, just poor little innocents without a clue."

She's happy. That's a relief, and if she's happy, so am I. Airlock avoided, until Ellen decides to go for full disclosure. "We are lost. We took that cargo from the Greens after I woke up aboard one of their ships. I don't know how I got there or why I was there or where I came from. They memory-blocked me. She was on board because they abducted her. Neither of us knows why. Those are the questions we're trying to find answers to, starting with Veniramat. If you're right, and you probably are, these guys knew what Veniramat is, and yes, Debbie, you're right too. We should have talked to them. But that still leaves the question: Who are they? They're all wearing the same armor and carrying the same weapons. They're all unidentifiable. They must be some kind of assault team, but why would anybody be sending an assault team after us? Unless it is because of that guy you killed on Adestoria."

Just when I thought we were in the clear, now we're back where we started, and Fist might be thinking airlock again.

"Oh, so now it's my fault, is it? Here's me keeping you pair of geniuses alive and only now finding out you've got the Greens on your case. Add to that the furries, Grinder and the Xvr, and now some bunch of mysterious ghost troopers who might be trying to talk to us or they might be trying to kill us."

"And? A few moments ago you were quite impressed with our ability to make enemies. So what's the problem? I thought you wanted some excitement, a last hurrah before your bladder starts leaking."

Yeah. Not helping, Ellen. Fist's fists are twitching. This

time that T. Rex really does have a toothache, and she's the one Grinder thought was disciplined enough to send out here. Not that Ellen is doing much better. There's the look about her of a coiled spring waiting to be released. Not good at all.

"Okay. Let's all just calm down and start over, shall we? The next time someone looks like they want to talk to us, how about we don't shoot them? Can we all agree on that at least?"

The atmosphere remains taut. They might not even be listening to me.

"Oh, come on. We're all adults here. We've all just been through another firefight but that's no reason for us to turn on each other, not when we've got all those other enemies, any one of which might turn up at any moment. These ghost troopers must have come from somewhere. Is there another ship out there? If there is we should get out of here before more of them turn up, shouldn't we?"

We should, and at last Fist relents. "Fine. No shooting unless they shoot first. The sensors are clear so if there is another ship out there we're not picking it up. There shouldn't be, since we've jumped, but another jump will make sure of it. So where do we jump to?"

"Where do we jump to? We're heading for the other side of the known universe, aren't we? You're here because you're supposed to know the database, so pick some coordinates and get us out of here."

Oh dear. Here we were making up and being friends and Ellen has to go all confrontational again. This isn't going to end until one of them comes out on top. Or maybe she isn't. Maybe she's simply being Ellen, with no filter, nothing more than another side of her lack of emotional engagement. She doesn't even realize she's doing it.

The expected explosion doesn't come though. Far from

threatening violence, Fist's reaction is surprisingly sheepish. "I know this part of space but the local database only goes so far. This furry database might go a little further. Once we reach the edge of that, though, we're going to need an update or we'll be stumbling around in the dark, maybe even risking jumping into the center of a star."

That's disappointing, and Ellen doesn't take it well at all. "Really? And you didn't think to tell us that before we left Adestoria?"

"Well, I guess it slipped my mind, a bit like you not mentioning the Greens."

It's been less than ten minutes and we're already ringing the bell for round three. Honestly, these two don't know how lucky they are that I'm here. "We should go back to Demaroven then."

Both of them look at me. The dumb Earthling said something stupid again.

"Well, why not? They gave us one day to leave orbit, didn't they? So the Green ship must still be there. All we gotta do is download its database and then we'll have the entire known universe at our fingertips, including the location of Earth. That might not mean much to you but it does to me, so let's go get it while we can."

At least Fist is thinking about it.

Ellen goes straight for the dumb Earthling option. "Because the Greens might be waiting for us."

"No, they won't be. The Demaroven said they'd terminate any Green ship that enters their space. So long as we jump into their space the Greens won't be able to get near us. And with our new ID the Demaroven won't know we're flying Glurt's ship. A quick in and out and no one will be any the wiser."

Fist nods approvingly. "Sounds like a plan to me. If the

Greens are waiting for us and the two of you managed to wipe out an entire crew, the three of us should have no trouble dealing with them. And we need that database, so I say let's do it."

Ellen is yet to be convinced though. "All well and good, but when the Demaroven read our new ID, how do we explain that? What is our new ID anyway?"

"It's salvager. I've never heard of the Demaroven so it's unlikely they'll have a warrant out on us. Or at least they shouldn't have a warrant out on anyone from Adestoria. I can't speak for what other salvager crews might have been up to."

That's okay. I can put Fist's mind at rest on that score. "The Demaroven told me only properly trained and licensed members of their species are allowed to travel off-world. In fact they don't seem to like off-worlders very much at all. Their spaceport is on an isolated island so all we have to do is come up with a convincing story. They'll recognize Ellen and me but they won't recognize you. How about we mess up the main screen so they can't see us properly? Then we tell them we're having technical difficulties and request permission to land. Instead we head straight for the Green ship. How long will it take to download that database anyway?"

"Bare minutes. We get aboard, I hack the computer, we download the database, and then we're gone while they're still figuring it out. Like you said, it's a quick in and out. So how about you, Ellen? You good with that?"

After a moment's thought Ellen nods and we're on our way.

CHAPTER NINE

Fist is on the bridge. Ellen and I are hiding outside at the top of the stairs. Our main screen is clean, apart from all the old and new scorch marks, but according to Fist, the signal we're sending Demaroven is all messed up. They can barely see anything. Still, not being there seems like a sensible precaution, even if Ellen doesn't like leaving Fist to do all the talking on her own. Trust is a mountain with lots of loose stones, and we've barely even started climbing it.

In reply to Demaroven immigration questioning the quality of our transmission, Fist launches into our grift with, "Yes, we apologize for that. We're experiencing technical difficulties."

"Indeed." That high, reedy, whistling voice makes it impossible to tell if the immigration officer is buying it or not, and our ULDs don't exactly do nuance. Either way, after the briefest of pauses, it continues, "You wish to land and make repairs? That will have to be cleared with the Ministry of Safeness."

There's that bureaucracy again. Nothing gets done on this

planet without some ministry or other giving it the okay.

"There is also the matter of your ID. We do not recognize it. You can explain?"

"Of course. We're from a planet called Adestoria. It's a major trading hub. We came out here looking to make new contacts, if that's something you'd be interested in."

"The matter will be considered. Please hold."

Fist calls us back to the bridge. In the bottom third of our screen is the big blue arc of Demaroven: vast oceans dotted with islands and mottled from above with the shadows of clouds. She isn't seeing any of that though. She's busy working the captain's console.

"Okay. The Green ship isn't too far away. Now's as good a time as any, wouldn't you say?"

Ellen isn't so sure. "Shouldn't we wait, see what they say? We could land at their spaceport, blend in, and then go for the Green ship. Once we've established ourselves, we might even be able to persuade them to give us its bridge portal code."

"You don't know its bridge portal code. Great! Do you at least have the docking bay door code? Because once we start this, we aren't going to have time to hack our way in from outside."

"Yes. Glurt opened it the last time we were here. The window should still be open."

A few moments of searching and Fist has it.

"So we'll be docking then. As for landing, wasn't this Glurt from here? How many eyes will there be down there that'll recognize his ship and wonder why he isn't flying it?"

Good point. Missy red eyes must have been promised a cut from Glurt selling us out. She's probably chaffing right now, thinking that Glurt sold her out too. And she's a part-time security guard, with full authorization to shoot on sight and write anything she wants in her report afterward.

But it's too late now. Fist has already begun our approach.

That brings Demaroven immigration back onto our screen and he or she is not at all happy. "Your ship is performing an unauthorized maneuver. You will return to your previous position and await authorization."

Fist grins. She's enjoying this. "We apologize. Our computer appears to have developed a mind of its own."

"This is unlikely. You are approaching a quarantined Green ship. You will—"

Fist stabs at something on the captain's console. Demaroven immigration disappears. The Green ship is ahead of us and growing fast, way too fast it seems to me, and now it's my trust in her that's being put to the test.

"Fist?"

She's still grinning. "What? You don't like this? Come on, find your inner salvager before their planetary defenses lock on to us. Whatever they are, missiles or cannons, it's unlikely they can fire on us immediately. They'll have to target. They'll have to launch or power up, and there's flight time as well. We've got, say, five minutes to get aboard, hack in, download and then get out."

She's not joking either. The Green ship is looming large, bearing down on us like an asteroid that's not playing chicken. All its spikes and spines reach out for us again and still we hurtle inward. We seriously need to start slowing down. This is my third time docking. It was getting easier, until we handed the controls over to a speed freak. Oh my God. Oh my God. Now it's filling our main screen, a great black windshield that isn't even going to notice the fly that's about to splat into it. Oh my God. There are mere seconds before impact. Oh my God. Fist, do something!

Then the deceleration hits, so hard it almost throws me forward into our main screen like another fly. By the time I've pried my white knuckles loose from the sensor array console, Fist is already on the move. "Ellen, you stay here. That window is the sensor array. That window is weapons control. You see anything coming at us, you open fire. Debbie, grab one of those heavy weapons and start running. We've got maybe four minutes."

And run we do, all the way down to the docking bay and then up through the Green ship to its bridge. That uses up maybe a minute. Fist takes out her hack-anything amulet and places it on the captain's console. A window opens with another cascade of code flowing through it. We're counting down to two minutes, but everything's good. We're doing this. We're going to make it. Nothing could possibly go wrong, until—

"You will cease and desist. This is an unauthorized action. You will be referred to the Ministry of Wellness for psychological examination."

The portal at the back of the bridge winks shut. Before it, floating at head height, is a large silver ball. It's larger than the Ministry of Goodness's little helper and it has a weapon on each side. The Demaroven have drones to do their dirty work for them. Fist does her own dirty work. Muttering something very uncomplimentary about someone's mother, she opens fire. Sputtering and hissing, the drone cracks open, then falls sparking to the floor.

That was easy enough, apart from us having added the Demaroven to our growing list of enemies. Fist can't complain about it this time. In fact she's very much up for it. "You keep an eye on that portal. Anything else tries to come through, you blow it away."

Yes, ma'am.

While I do that she checks the status of our download, and then brings Ellen up on the main screen. "How are things over there? You got anything?"

"No. How about you?"

"We've got drones. Only one so far but I wouldn't be surprised if there were more. As soon as Debbie's back with you, you undock us. And watch your portal. If they know its address you might be having visitors too."

"I'll be ready."

As Ellen disappears, the portal opens. There are three more drones on the other side, all stacked neatly one on top of another. This time they're not talking. Bolts of orange light stream into the bridge, a horizontal rain that hits the back of the captain's chair and streams through all those diaphanous screens to spark and sizzle off the circular wall behind. The couple of shots I get off are enough to warn Fist and by the time the portal closes, we've both taken cover behind the captain's console.

Fist peers over the top of it, partly to check out the progress of our download and partly to see the portal. "Wow. These guys really don't like us being here, do they?"

"Maybe they don't want to share. Ellen said no one has ever gained access to a Green ship before us. Do you think I should tell them the *Nosundomi* got here first?"

The portal opens again. More orange fire hits the back of the captain's chair, the wall and the consoles arranged along it. Some of them are now sparking and hissing, so it looks like no one will be using them again. But then we probably have little more than a minute before no one will be using this entire ship again, or ours either.

Fist returns fire until the portal closes again, then answers with, "You can try, but somehow I don't think they'll be listening. So what is it about this ship that they'd be so interested in keeping to themselves?"

"Probably the mind-blocking tech. Ellen told you about that, how she can't remember anything. From what I've seen of Demaroven society, they'd probably see that as the best thing since sliced bread. There are people on Earth who would too. They'd likely pay a fortune to get their hands on it."

Again the portal opens. This time the three drones are advancing, attempting to enter the bridge. Both of us fire back. I hit one, causing it to veer sideways. Fist hits the other two, taking both of them down. The portal closes, either because it's timed out or because they need more drones.

"A fortune? In sliced bread?"

"No. Sliced bread isn't currency. It's bread that's been sliced before it's sold. You do have bread out here, don't you?"

"Can't say I've ever come across it, but then your planet has two hundred languages so I guess anything is possible."

"Yeah, yeah, yeah. How's our download doing? Can we get out of here yet?"

She peers over the top of the console. The portal hasn't opened so she stands, then she thrusts the amulet at me. "Take this to Ellen. All she has to do is place it on the console and the database will download. Now go."

"What are you going to do?"

"I'll be right behind you until we reach the docking bay. Now get moving."

We're barely halfway toward the exit when the portal opens. There are three more drones, all firing ahead until they realize we're not behind the captain's console. By the time they've turned, Fist has already destroyed one and we're racing down the stairs to the docking bay level.

As we reach the docking bay itself, Fist waves me on. "Go! Get to Ellen."

Leaving her our side of the docking bay doors, it's a race to reach our bridge before those drones arrive, and I'm shouting all the way: "Ellen! Ellen, undock us now!"

There's gunfire behind me. It's over quickly. My God, Fist! If the worst has happened, it's too late to turn back. Reach the bridge. Get us out of here. Worry about her later.

Up on the bridge, the Green ship is receding on our main screen. That must be why the burst of gunfire was so short. Sure enough, Fist arrives. That's a relief, but it only lasts a moment. The sensor array console starts beeping. No one needs to ask why. We've got incoming. Fist almost throws Ellen out of the captain's chair and begins working the console. The weapons array console lights up. Windows pop open and closed on it as if it's being worked by a ghost. We're firing. The Green ship isn't. Things are exploding all over it, with little puffs of debris forming a glittering halo around it. Our weapons console is still firing. Our sensor array is having a panic attack. The quickly disintegrating Green ship disappears from our screen. Fist is scrolling through destinations. As soon as she finds empty space, we jump.

The silent splendor of somebody's galaxy fills our main screen. Peace is with us, already helping to still my pounding heart. Ellen is, as usual, all but emotionless, but Fist is grinning hugely. "Now that's how salvagers do it. There's nothing quite like staring death in the face to prove you're alive."

I'm glad she thinks so. Being alive without staring death in the face will do for me, or it would have done not so very long ago. Now staring death in the face is becoming something of a habit. They say you can get used to anything, but there are some things no one should have to get used to. This is one of them, and it's not over yet. The sensor array kicks off again, demanding attention like an angry toddler. A couple of stabs at the captain's console from Fist, and right there in the middle of our main screen is another Green ship. As it bears down on us, its front end opens up into a great maw. It means to swallow us whole, and Fist isn't grinning anymore. "They followed us? How can they have followed us? How can they have even been there in Demaroven space?"

"Because Ellen was right. They were waiting for us. Think about it. That last Green you killed sent a distress call so they knew we'd taken their ship. Glurt worked for them so they knew that ship was in Demarovan space. They couldn't enter Demaroven space so they came and waited for us just outside it."

Fist isn't buying it. "Why? Why would they wait for us? Why would they even think we might come back?"

"Because of Earth. They know I'm from Earth. They know they're the only ones who know the location of Earth. They know I can't go home without those coordinates."

Ellen isn't fully on board yet either. "Maybe, but that doesn't explain how they followed us."

"It does if they planted something in the database, something that would transmit our jump coordinates to them the instant before we jump."

That causes more bemusement.

"Oh come on, guys. You must have viruses out here. Y'know, a piece of malicious code someone wrote to steal your personal details or mess up your computer so they can hold it to ransom."

Ellen is the first to get it. "A worm. They hid a worm in their database and waited for us to upload it. And if we jump again they'll be right behind us."

Not that we're going to jump because now the lights are flickering and the hum of various systems that no one notices become noticeable by their stuttering absence. Our computer is turning psycho. If it had a voice it would be telling us how this was for the good of the mission and then sing some old vaudeville song. Meanwhile the Green ship continues to bear down on us. It's a great metal basking shark looking for a tasty morsel, and we're it.

"Reboot."

One of these days they're going to stop looking at me like I'm an idiot.

"Reboot the computer with a virus scan. You can do that, can't you?"

Ellen doesn't know, which is to say, thanks to the Greens, she can't remember.

Fist does, but she chooses this moment to ask questions first and shoot later. "We don't have time to reboot the computer. That thing is seconds away from swallowing us."

"We don't have time not to, then. Look, my husband is a techie. He deals with this kind of thing all the time back on Earth. Seriously, if he was here he'd tell you exactly the same, except he's not here because no one abducted him. Now do it, will you, while we still can."

Our lights are all but gone. The bridge is deathly silent. Our systems are being eaten one by one. Even our main screen has started to flicker, which in one way is a relief because the Green ship is filling it. It's almost as if they want us to watch our ship slowly die. That's the kind of aliens they are: vicious, sadistic and probably sitting there on their bridge laughing their little alien socks off.

At last Fist shrugs. "Okay then, but don't blame me if we all end up memory-blocked."

"If we do all end up memory-blocked, we won't be able to remember to blame you, or me for that matter. Now do it."

She works the console, tapping in a number of commands, and everything goes dead. Thankfully there's emergency lighting, a dim red glow that allows us to just about see each other. In that we wait, a long, slow expectancy that at any moment there will be a dull thud that says we've been taken.

It doesn't come. Instead our systems begin to return. First are the lights, then the background hum. After that all our screens come on: first the consoles, all streaming with code, and then finally the main screen. The Green ship isn't bearing down on us anymore. In fact it's backing away and ponderously turning even as its maw is closing. And up there in the top left corner of our main screen is something else. It's too far away to make out any details but it's clearly another ship and it's firing blue pulses on the Green ship.

"What the . . .?" Fist's jaw has dropped, which is something I never expected to see. "Who are they?"

To which Ellen adds, "More importantly, why do they appear to be defending us?"

The Green ship is returning fire with pulses of green light streaming toward our mysterious defenders, if that's who they are. It's all rather pretty really, if you ignore the destruction— the small flashes of light on the Green ship's hull and the little mushroom clouds of debris they're throwing out. A screenshot of it would likely be worth millions back on Earth. That's assuming any of us live long enough to make it back to Earth, or anywhere else for that matter.

"Maybe it's a coincidence. Maybe they just happened to turn up at these coordinates and they don't like the Greens either."

"Coincidence! Are you serious? No one just happens to

turn up at coordinates in empty space. That ship has to have followed us here too."

Okay, so Fist didn't like that suggestion.

Ellen has a different take. "Right now it doesn't matter how it got here. If that ship is following us, it must be where these ghost troopers came from. Since we have two of them lying dead behind us and several more below, I think maybe we ought to get out of here before one of them wins."

Which just made things a whole lot better. At least no one, which mostly means Fist, is arguing. Searching through the database, she quickly finds more empty space. An instant later we've jumped. We ought to be safe. Then again, maybe not.

"Now we wait."

Our captain is pulling rank again, which doesn't go down well with Ellen. "Wait? For what? We have the database. Why exactly are we waiting?"

"To see if they follow us of course."

"But if there's the remotest chance of that happening, shouldn't we jump again? The more coordinates we put between us and them the better."

"Or we find out now, because it won't matter how many times we jump if they can still track our coordinates. I'll run a diagnostic, make sure that worm has been roasted."

That was remarkably easy, except there's one thing they both appear to have overlooked.

"What about that other ship? If it appearing like that wasn't a coincidence, then they must be tracking us as well. Could these ghost troopers have planted a virus too?"

After a few more stabs at the console, Fist confidently replies, "Maybe, but if they did it was roasted along with the Greens' worm."

"So they can't follow us then."

"Well, that's what we're waiting to find out. If they do, then it's likely they planted a transmitter. It would be small and portal-enabled, plugged into our computer and drawing power from our reactor. The diagnostics don't show anything but then it'll probably be short-burst, sending our coordinates to a listening station that then relays them to that ship. We'll give it a few more minutes, I think. Then we'll jump again and search this ship."

CHAPTER TEN

Our search turns up nothing, which isn't all that surprising since we don't really know what we're looking for. An hour later, having exhausted every nook and cranny, every conduit and junction box, we're in the hold. As unlikely as it seems, there's only one place we haven't looked: inside the container Blut brought aboard with the Xvr's mysterious treasure in it.

"All right then. Let's see what the Xvr were willing to pay a ransom for." Fist crouches in front of the container. Before anyone can say anything, like what if it's something really nasty that's going to leap out and do horrible things to us, she's releasing its catches. There's an air of expectancy, a growing tension that might be anticipation, or it might be me preparing to make a run for it. Moment by moment and degree by degree, the container opens to reveal its contents until finally, disgustedly, she throws the lid back.

"It's a rock. Great! That would've been well worth dying for."

"It was for the Xvr. It must be part of their culture, like a cultural artifact or even a religious one. Maybe it was a meteorite and they decided it was a gift from their god. People on Earth used to worship rocks like that."

For a pair of intergalactic adventurers, neither Fist nor Ellen appears to know much about cultural diversity.

While Ellen stands impassively by, Fist snorts loudly. "Of course you did. And did you used to beat each other over the head with them as well? How did a rock worshipper like you ever make it into space?"

"Ellen already told you. The Greens abducted me. And I said used to, not still do. We've moved on since then. We've even landed men on our moon."

"Well, aren't you just the clever ones. Did you *used to* worship that too?" Slamming the container lid shut, she rises to her feet. "So what do we do with this rock then? Stick it in a locker and forget about it, or dump it into space along with all the bodies?"

Or we could do something else. "How about we give it back?"

"Give it back!"

Oh come on, Fist. I'm trying to be constructive here.

"Yes. Well, why not? The Xvr were willing to pay a ransom for it, weren't they? And it would be one less enemy to worry about."

"If they don't shoot us up first. Our last meeting didn't go so well, after all."

"True, but Blut said their technology was short range, so how likely are they to know that? For all we know they're still waiting to hear what happened. Grinder doesn't know yet either since we haven't told him. So why shouldn't we go make our own deal and, if we don't ask for a ransom, maybe even some friends? Wasn't it you who said having a safe haven to run to is always a good idea?"

It was, not that it's cutting any ice with her. I could use an ally right now.

Wake up, Ellen. You must be hearing all of this. Give me a helping hand here. At last she does, saying, "She could be right, y'know. They might not have a clue what just went down."

But Fist still isn't buying it. "They'll know something happened when we turn up. How're you going to explain that?"

"By telling them the truth, or at least part of it. Some other bunch of salvagers turned up and wrecked it. Sorry about your crew but here's your artifact all safe and sound."

"No wonder you two keep collecting enemies. There's a difference between seizing an opportunity and deliberately looking for trouble, y'know. We don't need the credits, that ghost ship is still out there and Grinder must have started wondering why we haven't returned yet. We jump a couple more times and none of them will be able to find us. Well, that ghost ship might be able to, but we'll deal with that later. We'll just have to remember never to cross Grinder's path again. As for that thing: Put it in a locker and keep it safe. Who knows? A rock might come in useful one day, especially if we ever happen to drop by Earth."

Thanks, Fist. I'm really appreciating your sensitivity and consideration for others. Us Neanderthals have feelings too, y'know, when we're not bludgeoning each other to death.

My moderately hurt feelings aside, Ellen is busy considering Fist's words too. This time the big decision is hers. It must be a hard one too since she's staring at the floor, or maybe at that empty sac with arms and legs in a puddle of puss that used to be a Xvr. That should be enough to concentrate anyone's mind. It's certainly concentrating mine. We definitely ought to do something about that before we go looking for the Xvr, if that's what we're doing. They're not going to like us tramping their relatives all over our ship like so much dirt. The carelessness. The disrespect. Execute them all.

It's not happening though. Ellen has made her decision. "Okay, I'm with Fist on this one. We'll keep the rock and jump out of here."

Two jumps later and we're a very long way from Grinder and the Xvr, or at least that's what Fist tells us. There's a very pretty nebula filling our main screen, deep red with filaments of white and clotted with lumps of stars, a great flower unfolding across space in the hope of attracting some bees. There are bees too, but they're more interested in us. There's an entire swarm of them, tiny, glittering, darting, and making it look like the star field on our main screen is suddenly dancing.

While Ellen and I stand transfixed, Fist is stabbing at the captain's console. "I don't know what those things are or how they're doing it but we can't jump. We can't do anything."

The swarm closes in, turning our main screen into a confusion of twinkling pinpricks and then a sea of static. Without that there is no sense of anything. We could be standing still. We could be moving. We might even have jumped, with this swarm taking us halfway across the universe. Fist continues to stab at the captain's console, but it's useless. Somewhere out there someone else is in control and we are mere passengers, helpless and clueless, and this time that includes Fist. She's sitting in the captain's chair with her arms folded, grimly doing the nothing that is all any of us can do. Whoever is controlling these things had better be good people or things could turn ugly real fast—for them, not us.

When our screen returns, the swarm is gone and we're in a docking bay. There has been no dull judder as we made contact. There is only Fist flatly announcing, "Someone just opened our docking bay door."

That someone now appears on our main screen. There are five of them: humanoid, androgynous, gray-skinned and all wearing one-piece gray suits. Beneath black hair that looks like it's been plastered down with way too much gel, their gray faces break out into gray smiles which are strangely lacking in warmth, as is the greeting one of them offers us. "We welcome you. Please. Join us."

Weird, very weird and creepy too, like some maniacal toymaker animated some of his dolls, and now they're inviting us into his murder factory. I'm not sure I'm up for this. Fist appears to be having doubts too as she asks, "What d'you think?"

"Do we have a choice? We didn't ask to come here and we have no idea what else they're capable of." From Ellen, it's hard to know if that's calculation or resignation.

Either way it's pretty hard to argue with, so Fist turns to me. "How about you? What d'you think?"

"I dunno. It all looks a bit cult-y to me, but then, like Ellen said, do we have a choice?"

"A cult? What's a cult?"

"It's usually a tiny group of weirdoes who think someone out there is talking to them and that someone is going to fly by in a spaceship and take them all to a better world. Boy, would they be surprised if they knew the truth—except maybe they do, because it's not unusual for them to all end up committing suicide."

That's enough to make Fist's mind up. "All right then. I guess we better go introduce ourselves before they do all commit suicide. Otherwise we might never get out of here."

We leave through our docking bay door, stepping into

somewhere even weirder. The walls, floor and ceiling are white and bright but somehow insubstantial, as if they are made of pure light. Apart from the three of us and the five of them, this chamber is empty. There ought to be echoes, but there aren't. There's only a sepulchre-like silence: serene, dispassionate, eternal—and them.

Up close, they're a head shorter than me. Their eyes are purple verging on black, their noses thin and sharp and their mouths almost lipless but still wearing those empty smiles. At any moment they might crowd around us and start pawing at us as the Lepoorunt did. That thought only makes this feel a whole lot creepier, so creepy in fact that even Fist and Ellen are watchful, waiting for those masks to be ripped aside to reveal crazed eyes and sharp little teeth perfect for slicing and dicing.

Instead the centermost one of them holds out a hand, directing us to a wall with no door. "Come. We have food prepared. We wish to make you feel at home among us."

"Great." Fist doesn't sound like she thinks it's great at all. "So who are you?"

"We are the Watchers. I am Greeter Prime. These others are greeters also. We are tasked with the performance of first-contact protocols. We have reset gravity to match your ship. Is it to your liking?"

I haven't even thought about it. Nor, it would appear, have Fist or Ellen. It's becoming nothing more than background noise, like living next to a schoolyard.

Without waiting for an answer, Greeter Prime continues, "Very well. You will follow me, please."

He walks away without any thought of a refusal appearing to occur to him. He's not wrong. We're still outnumbered by his happy-dippy mob, and mobs tend to react badly when you say no to them. They follow on behind like ducklings, or should that be baby velociraptors waiting for mommy to give the signal? It's enough to have all three of us exchanging concerned glances. We're armed, of course, but that doesn't seem to bother them at all.

Then Fist decides to start a conversation. Nothing could go wrong with that, right? "So, Greeter Prime. You get a lot of visitors, do you?"

"No. We are assigned daily tasks according to need. Today's need is to welcome you. By this service might we one day aspire to be joined with our gods."

Yep, it's a cult, and we're probably about to be love-bombed, unless Fist turns them into a slice-and-dice mob first.

"Your gods, eh. So who are they?"

"They are the creators. All things are because of them. They are always with us, sleeping now but one day they will awaken. If we have served them well, it is their covenant with us that we shall be rewarded with their love."

"Yeah, haven't heard that one before." That earns her some cautionary looks, which she ignores. "So when do your gods awaken? Because usually it's at the end of time."

Part of the wall Greeter Prime is about to walk into shimmers, dissolving into an opening. Barely noticing, he replies, "Time is an illusion, a false perception based on inadequate input. We have been since the creation and will be until the gods awaken. What passes in between is irrelevant, a mere matter of functionality. If, when the gods awaken, they decide to end the illusion, it will be by their choice and their will. It is not for us to question."

"Even so, it must be pretty boring. What do you do for entertainment around here?"

"Only those who have no faith know boredom because they do not understand the value of service. If we should forget, it is a simple enough matter to reconnect. As for entertainment, the concept is unfamiliar. Our service is sufficient."

Beyond the opening is another chamber. This one has a round table in its center with three chairs arranged evenly around it. Everything is white, thin and spindly, barely looking strong enough to support anything. On the table is a feast fit for many more than the three of us: fruits, vegetables, meats and beverages. Some of it looks vaguely familiar. Most of it could be anything.

Turning to face us, Greeter Prime holds out an inviting hand. "Please. Replenish yourselves. If you should desire anything else, you have but to call and one of my colleagues will assist you."

Not waiting for an answer, he heads toward another wall where another opening magically appears. Without a word being spoken by any of his grinning gaggle, they follow him and we're left alone. Fist's first thought is to follow too, but when she reaches the wall it's solid, far more solid than a veil of light ought to be. Nor is there any sound as she raps her knuckles on it. Her fist follows but it bounces harmlessly off, and now I'm wondering if this place is some kind of intergalactic asylum and we've just voluntarily committed ourselves to one of its rubber rooms. Judging by the worried expressions on Fist's and Ellen's faces, I'm not the only one having such thoughts.

Stepping back, Fist casts her eyes over the entire wall as she looks for something, anything, that might be a way out, but there's nothing. "Well, great. When do they start pumping the gas in, d'you suppose?"

Ellen is a lot more relaxed about it. "I think if they wanted to harm us they would have done it already. I don't know about you two, but after all the excitement we've just had, I could do with some replenishment."

"What?" Fist stares at her in disbelief. "You're not actually going to eat any of that, are you?"

"Why not? Like I said, if they wanted to harm us they would have done it already. Besides, again, what choice do we have? Whatever they're going to do, they're going to do. So if this is our last meal, we might as well enjoy it."

Taking the nearest chair, she looks over the feast for somewhere to begin. Fist stays firmly where she is, and so do I. If Ellen wants to play guinea pig, that's fine by us. She begins by slowly filling her plate: a red mash of something here, green florets of something else there, and a brown stew-looking goo that could pass for chili. It could be, but then again it could be anything.

"Do you know what any of that stuff is?"

Ellen smiles at me, and then leans in to draw a deep breath. "No, but it sure smells good. And if I should suddenly drop dead in the next minute or so, it was nice knowing you."

The red mash is first, spooned in without hesitation. Some determined chewing follows, during which she fails to drop dead. "Mmm." She points at her plate with her spoon. "This is good. You should try some."

Fist is the first to crack, leaving me standing alone eyeing it all from a safe distance. Her plate fills quickly: something yellow that might be giant peas, something else long and thin and purple, and a couple of small haunches of something it's probably best not to ask about. She shovels it in like there's no tomorrow, which there might very well not be, her hamster cheeks on either side of an increasingly satisfied grin.

Between mouthfuls, Ellen looks over at me. "Oh, come on. You don't want to be left standing there all on your own once we've keeled over, do you? Sit down. Eat something before you put us off."

That hardly seems likely. They're both stuffing themselves like beef is about to be declared illegal. Oh well, I did eat that Demaroven sushi. If this feast is poisoned in some way, we might as well all die together, hopefully with enough time before my final breath for me to deliver a big fat *I told you so.*

Even so, turning vegetarian suddenly seems like a good idea. My plate fills with giant yellow peas, the long, thin purple stuff and some of the red mash. Fist isn't at all impressed with that. Picking up another haunch, she tosses it onto my plate. "Go on. Live dangerously."

"Live dangerously! Isn't having half the universe hunting us dangerous enough for you?"

"Exactly. You could walk out of this room and be dead in the next five minutes. You could still be caught by the Greens and then you'll wish you were dead. So what have you got to lose? Maybe you'll be poisoned. Maybe you won't. Whatever happens, at least you'll have filled your belly first."

"Oh, thanks for that. You've just made me feel so much better."

She does have a point though. The Greens are still after us. So are the Lepoorunt, the Demaroven, and probably Grinder, and the Xvr would be if they could. There's that ghost ship as well, and now we have this cult to figure out too. If they're anything like cults on Earth the brainwashing will come next, followed by the giving up of everything we have, including our freedom. Neither Ellen nor Fist are ready to hear any of that though, not while there's still a mountain of food to be gorged on. What the hell then. That leg of something does look rather enticing. And it does taste good, a little bit like lamb in fact.

CHAPTER ELEVEN

"**Y**'know, that was so good I'm almost tempted to stick my fingers down my throat and start again."

That's Fist, and she might not be joking. It's hard to tell with that mischievous little grin she's wearing, a grin that only grows broader as she sees my obvious disgust.

"Please. I don't even want to think about that."

"Relax. Who would do a thing like that? Unless, of course, you're speaking from personal experience. Do people do that where you come from?"

"They used to, supposedly. There might still be some who do, but I've never been invited to a party like that."

"Wow. Your planet really is messed up, isn't it? So what else do they do there apart from using sliced bread as currency and worshipping rocks?"

"I already told you, we don't do any of that. Oh, I see. This is let's all make fun of the dumb Earthling time, like we're all monkeys in a zoo or something."

It must be. Both of them are smiling, Ellen just a little

but Fist with a wicked glee. "Why not? There are a lot of worlds out there, many of them with entertainment executives who'd pay a considerable amount to put that in front of their audience. Maybe they'd even like some specimens to put on display. They could take their kids to look at you and, if you were still alive, maybe feed you as well."

"Don't you dare! Don't you dare even say that. My God. And you're calling us messed up. Well, at least we don't go around stealing other people's . . ."

Maybe not, but then it's too late. My big mouth has already given Fist all the ammunition she needs.

"What were you going to say? You don't go around stealing other people's . . . spaceships, maybe? Or killing them all and then stealing their cargo like . . . pirates, maybe?"

"That's not fair. The Greens abducted me, and they memory-blocked Ellen."

"Oh, well, that's all right then. So long as we've got our excuses ready, we can do anything we want."

"No. Piracy's illegal, or at least it is on Earth."

"It is out here too, and since you're already up for two counts of it, you better hope no one catches you. In fact, come to think of it, that would be a good backup plan. If this all goes down I could sell you out to the Greens or the furries. Well, maybe not to the Greens, but I'm sure the furries would be interested."

"That is not funny, Fist, not funny at all. Ellen, are you just going to sit there and let her say that?"

While Fist is almost openly laughing at me, Ellen at last decides to step in. "Yeah. Perhaps, Fist, instead of roasting Debbie, we'd be better occupied considering our options."

"Options? I thought you said there weren't any options."

"No. I said if they meant to harm us they would have

done it already, and the fact that we're not dead yet would seem to confirm that. I also said whatever they're going to do, they're going to do, and they're going to do it when they come back. So the question is what are we going to do about it? Because I rather doubt they brought us here and fed us out of the goodness of their hearts. Now why don't you tell us more about these cults you have on Earth, Debbie?"

"Well, they usually prey on the lost and lonely, people who are searching for a reason to be. Then they set about convincing them that they're their best friends and that they love them and will always be there for them. And then, once they're inside their heads, they start brainwashing them into believing that the cult leader is some kind of prophet with a hotline to God."

"Brainwashing? You wash people's brains?" Poor Fist. This is getting really confusing for her.

"Not literally, no. It's when they make people believe whatever they want them to believe. And this lot does seem rather obsessed with their gods and how their only purpose is to make sure everything is ready for their return. Sounds like pretty standard cult stuff to me."

"Well, okay then. If that's what they're planning to do it ain't gonna be a problem, because they've picked on the wrong crew this time."

Ellen isn't quite so gung-ho. "Or not. What was that Greeter Prime said? Something about how we might all need to reconnect sometimes. The Greens have memory-blocking technology. Who's to say they didn't get it from this lot? What are you going to do if they plug you in and restructure your brain so you'll believe whatever they tell you to believe with you never even knowing they did it?"

"They'll have to tie me down first, and that wouldn't be so

easy even if they weren't furry-sized."

"And if they've already drugged us?"

"Drugged! I thought you said it was safe to eat this."

"I did, but now I'm rethinking it. I'm not saying it is drugged. I'm just speculating, considering possibilities, and asking what we should do if—"

"I'll show you what I'm going to do." Throwing back her chair, Fist marches determinedly toward a corner of the room.

"Fist! Now just hold on a moment. We need to talk about this before we do anything stupid. That swarm they sent for us took control of our ship without even blinking an eye."

"So we find whatever's controlling them and shut it down. First of all though . . ."

"Fist! Don't—"

Too late. Her fingers are down her throat and, oh my God, we've all been there—the sound and the smell. Ellen and I don't need fingers. We're already running toward our own corners and it's a perfectly delightful end to a lovely meal. It's also when Greeter Prime chooses to reappear. Casting an eye over the mess we've made and the weapon Fist has drawn, his insouciance is so perfect there are butlers on Earth who would kill for it.

"Was the meal not to your liking?"

Without any hint of insouciance, Fist has him firmly fixed in her sights. "It was wonderful, but we have to be careful what we eat, y'know? It's a girl thing. Now take us to your control center."

She might just as well have been asking for coffee and mints.

"I'm afraid I do not know what a 'girl thing' is, but we shall be more considerate of your dietary requirements in the future. Please be so good as to put that weapon away. We should all take the greatest care to prevent avoidable accidents."

"Oh, there'll be nothing accidental about it."

"This facility has internal defense systems. We invited you here in a spirit of friendship. It would be a pity if it were to end otherwise. As for myself, I might require a short period of regeneration, nothing more."

"What does that mean? You'll grow a new head?"

"Fist!" Wow! Who knew Ellen could be so commanding? It takes me by surprise, and it makes Fist think twice.

"What?"

"Put that weapon away. We didn't come here to start a fight."

"We didn't come here at all. We were brought here."

"It doesn't matter. We're here now so let's all just calm down, shall we?"

Fist's determination visibly crumbles. She had been moments away from blowing Greeter Prime's head off, but now her weapon wavers. Then it's holstered, hard and harshly, with something probably very unpleasant muttered just as harshly.

Throughout all this Greeter Prime has been little more than a casual observer. Once it's all over, he continues as if nothing has happened. "If you will follow me, please. Your accommodation has been prepared."

He must really like us, in his subdued way. Throwing up all over the Persian rug doesn't usually get you invited to stay for the night.

Of course that begs the question why, which must have occurred to Ellen too. "That's very good of you, but we'd best be going. It's a big universe and we have things to do. I'm sure you understand."

"You wish to leave? But why? Have we been remiss in

some way?"

"No. You've been very welcoming. We just need to get going, that's all. Thank you for your very generous hospitality but you can take us back to our ship now."

As much as Ellen is trying to let him down easily, Greeter Prime, for all his own lack of emotion, is sounding crestfallen. "We have failed. We will try harder."

This is becoming weird again. Greeter Prime's apology simply doesn't fit with the situation we think we're in. Neither Ellen nor Fist appears to have noticed but there's a feeling creeping over me that we're in the middle of some huge misunderstanding. This is not how cults are supposed to behave. They should be browbeating us, love-bombing us, breaking us down by degrees until we accept their doctrine, not apologizing to us as if we were their gods. Unless . . .

"How long have you been waiting for us?"

While my words mystify Ellen and Fist, Greeter Prime understands perfectly. "Since the gods retired. Before they rested, they commanded us to serve them well and be ready for their return. We have waited. We have prepared. We have served. Now that you come to us, you tell us we have failed. We shall accept this judgment even though it is our end."

"Whoa, hold on a minute." Mass suicide might be the cult-y thing for them to do, but I've just become a god and that most definitely isn't in my game plan. "You say your gods rested. Where? Are they still here?"

"Yes. You wish to see them? But, of course, how foolish of me. You wish to commune with them, to ask them how well or poorly we have served. Please, follow me. The way is being prepared."

As Greeter Prime turns to lead us, Ellen whispers, "The way is being prepared? What does that mean?"

"I don't know. I guess we're about to find out."

I'm the first to follow, which is new. For once the two space girls are following me. Really we're all following Greeter Prime, with me hoping I haven't got this all wrong. Followers who disappoint might choose to kill themselves. Gods who disappoint tend to end up face down in the dirt waiting for an archaeologist to come find them.

From our befouled chamber we step through into another: clean, bright, and empty—except for the large round door on its opposite side. Even as we approach, it swings silently open. There's a passageway beyond, also round and at least three times as high as me, the beginning of a maze that once again we'd be hopelessly lost in without our guide. Unlike the clean, bright emptiness we've seen so far, these are functional, with pipe runs and conduits and lights that flicker on as we approach. There is also a patina on everything, a rime of age that suggests these passageways have not been trodden for centuries, maybe even millennia. It's a bit like walking through a piece of architecture that's at least a thousand years older than my entire country.

"How old is this place?"

"Time has no meaning. All that matters is the faithfulness of our service."

That's dedication. It might be cultish dedication, but the sincerity of it can't be faulted, unless it's something else. The suspicion that it might be something else is slowly growing, unless that's me watching too many sci-fi movies. Best not put it into words yet then, not until I'm sure.

Fist, of course, having no filter that I've seen yet, has no trouble saying what's on her mind. "What? Don't you guys ever get out? Y'know, see the universe, have some fun, get blasted and blow shit up? I know this place is ancient but you can't spend all your time keeping it from falling apart."

"The world our gods endowed us with has everything we need. All systems for production and maintenance are functioning optimally. We need only watch over them so that when the gods awaken, all shall be as they left it. 'Getting blasted' and 'blowing shit up' are not concepts we are familiar with."

"Really? Well, perhaps you should become familiar with them. Everybody needs to get crazy once in a while or what's the point of it all? Come on, man. Lighten up."

"Are you requesting that the lighting level be increased? If so it can easily be arranged."

Yeah. In other words: does not compute. Fist obviously isn't getting it. All she's hearing is a failure to communicate that stops her trying. It's impossible to tell if Ellen has figured it out yet either, and the rest of our walk through the passageways passes in silence.

It ends in front of another huge round door that opens silently in front of us. Lights flicker on to reveal a long, narrow chamber. There are two banks of horizontal cylinders, one set along each of the long walls. They are chest height, white and sleekly featureless, covered in that now familiar patina of age, and all of them are connected to the wall behind by a short, thick umbilical. That'll do it for me. Everything is now crystal clear.

As he steps through into the chamber, Greeter Prime spreads his hands almost like a supplicant. "Behold our gods. They—"

Suddenly he stops, as if those gods are talking to him. "You will excuse me."

And with that he closes down, any suggestion that he might in any way be alive disappearing. He's statuesque and vacant-eyed, and for him we might just as well not be here anymore. It's the weirdest thing yet, at least for anyone who hasn't figured it out.

That includes Fist, who's waving her hand in front of his face. "Hello? Hello?"

It also includes Ellen, who looks to me instead. "Okay. Since you seem to be in the lead here, you want to explain to us exactly what is going on?"

"Sure." My voice drops to a whisper. "But first of all, Greeter Prime might be frozen but that doesn't mean he isn't listening. Come on. Let's move further in."

We all enter the chamber, stopping far enough away from Greeter Prime that we're certain he can't hear.

"So this is how I see it. Greeter Prime and all the rest of them, they're androids—y'know, humanoid robots? Right now he's communing with the rest of them, probably through some sort of Wi-Fi."

Ellen shakes her head. "Wi-Fi?"

"Yeah. Short-range wireless data transfer. That's probably how the gods sustain them as well: some sort of wireless power transfer. We've been experimenting with it on Earth."

"And you know this how? You some sort of big techie genius back there on planet ooh-we're-so-clever-we've-sent-men-to-our-moon?"

"That's right, Fist. You have a good sneer at my expense. Just remember, one of these days I might get to not liking you very much."

"And you'll do what? Kill me? Ooh, I think I need to go change my underwear."

"If you're quite done, Fist, hear her out because she's making sense to me."

Thank you, Ellen.

"These cylinders are some sort of hibernation chambers. Their gods are sleeping inside them. If Greeter Prime and the rest of them think we're gods too, whoever's inside those cylinders must be human. Think about it. We're looking at a race that must be almost as old as the Big Bang, a race that seeded the universe with itself and then, for some reason, decided to go to sleep."

It might make sense to Ellen but Fist is still missing it by a mile. "Okay. So they might be human, and Greeter Prime and the rest of them might be androids who think we're gods too. Exactly how does that help us?"

"Really? You're a pirate"—that earns me a sharp glower—"sorry, salvager, and you can't see the biggest prize that's ever fallen into your lap? This ship must have technology on board that even your most advanced civilization hasn't dreamed of yet. If it's got weaponry too, and if we can keep them believing, we can go wherever we want and not even the Greens'll be able to touch us."

Fist is still giving me the evil eye, which isn't helping anyone. One day I swear she's going to give me some credit, some recognition that this Neanderthal Earthling is making a useful contribution, but it's not today.

In spite of that, and entirely due to me, we have a plan—a very good plan until Ellen starts picking it apart. "*If* we can keep them believing. What happens if we can't? What if they've made a mistake? If you're right, these androids might not have seen a living being in millennia. What if they've forgotten what their gods look like? What if they all need to reconnect and they don't know it because their database is corrupted? Perhaps we ought to open one of these cylinders. That way we'll know for sure."

"Oh, great idea! Let's mess with their gods and see how

pissed they get." That, of course, is Fist. Right now walking away and letting them get on with it until one of them comes out on top is looking very attractive. Greeter Prime and I could go somewhere and have a nice long conversation about all things godly. On the other hand both of them have a point, so what's needed here is a third way, something we can all commit to without the sniping.

"Or we play it by ear and don't look a gift horse in the mouth."

"Don't look a gift horse in the mouth? You know what, I'm not even going to ask."

"What are you not even going to ask?" Greeter Prime has returned, which only gives Fist another target.

"You're back then."

Her sarcasm is lost on him.

"Back? From where might I have returned? It is you who walked away from me."

"Never mind. So what's the buzz? What's happening? Anything interesting?"

"A ship is approaching. It has engaged our outer defenses and seems intent on making contact."

"What kind of ship?" Ellen speaks for all of us, probably with the same alarm bells ringing. Somebody must've won that space battle and somehow followed us. Unaware of all of this, Greeter Prime replies, "We are not concerned with identification. We are only concerned with intent. Whatever its designation, we have determined that the probability of its approach being a coincidence is low. Therefore we conclude this ship is in pursuit of you."

Which tells us nothing. It could be that Green ship or it could be the ghost ship. Not that it really makes that much difference, unless it's somebody else entirely. Fist is in no doubt though.

"It has to be that ghost ship. They must have planted a transmitter on us after all. We need to get rid of that ship. First of all though, we need to get out of here."

"You wish us to relocate? We shall begin powering up immediately."

"Powering up? You mean you can't jump immediately?"

"No. Relocating a planet requires a great deal of power."

"Are you serious? This is a planet?" Fist isn't the only one who's shocked to hear that.

"Of course. When the gods decided to leave their system, they took their planet with them. Its core is sufficient to power our daily needs but relocation requires a great deal more. There will be a short delay but you need not concern yourselves. Our defenses will be sufficient to keep that ship at bay. A moment, please."

Greeter Prime goes into another trance. It must be a safety thing, their version of not using a cell phone when driving. Otherwise there might be androids walking into walls all over the place. Perhaps the gods should've made them female. Multitasking? Not a problem.

A moment later he returns. "They wish to talk with you. Follow me, please."

This is going to be interesting. Not so long ago we were killing them. Well, Fist and Ellen were anyway. We still have the bodies aboard our ship. Maybe they want them back. Maybe they want us handed over to answer for them. Good luck with that because we're gods now.

At the far end of the chamber is an area separated by rimmed glass. As Greeter Prime leads us into it, the lights slowly flicker on to reveal a control room filled with consoles and blank screens. This must be where the sleeping gods are monitored from, although no one has monitored anything from here for centuries. For all Greeter Prime knows, his gods might be dead and he hasn't noticed yet. Well, there's no need to mention that. Mass suicide is still a possibility, if androids can commit suicide.

Once a screen has been activated, we're looking at the head and shoulders of a man, definitely human. He's a jarhead with close-cropped hair, a jaw that might have been hewn from granite, and penetrating eyes that could probably cut through granite. He does have a nice smile though, which he clearly knows how to deploy to devastating effect.

"Captain Travanis Praganathulis. I am Major Amarthin Drovenanthis of the First Security Directorate. May I say what a pleasure it is to finally meet you? We've been trying to answer your call, but unfortunately you kept shooting at us."

A lot of confused glances are exchanged. One of us is a captain for real? Well, it's certainly not Fist, and it's not me either.

That leaves only Ellen. "I'm sorry. I don't . . ."

"You are Captain Travanis Praganathulis of the First Security Directorate. You activated the distress code."

"Distress code? What distress code?"

"Veniramat. It's a fake home world placed in your ID so that no matter what happened, you would be able to call for help. As soon as you searched for it, our agents picked it up and we came for you. You don't remember any of this?"

Ellen shakes her head. "I can hardly remember anything from before I woke up on that Green ship."

"I understand. Thanks to the very bribable Nosundomi we are aware of the Greens' memory-blocking tech. No matter. We can—"

CHAPTER TWELVE

"What! What just happened?"

Ellen is teetering on a cliff edge. She's not the only one. The screen is dead, taking with it the big reveal we must all have been hanging on for. Only Greeter Prime is unaffected by the air of disappointment.

"We have relocated, as you requested."

"Great! Couldn't you have waited until we'd finished talking to him?"

"You requested immediate relocation. No criteria for delay were specified."

As exasperated as Fist might be, there's really no answer to that. Greeter Prime is an android, which is a little like being a lawyer. Everything must be stated in precise terms or the details will trip you up every time. The detail here is a missed opportunity, which is simple enough to put right.

"We can finish talking to him, can't we? All we have to do is go back." I turn to Greeter Prime. "We can go back, right?"

"We can, but you should be aware our power reserves

have been depleted. The star at the center of this system will recharge them. Should we relocate now, it will take some time for our own resources to achieve the same."

"So if we do go back we'll be a sitting target. Does anyone want to take that risk? We don't know for sure they're who they say they are."

While Fist is looking on the dark side, which is not necessarily a bad thing, Ellen is thoughtful and hopeful. "They did explain Veniramat. This might be exactly what we've been looking for."

"Yeah, if you believe them, Captain Travanis Praganathulis of the First Security Directorate, whatever that is. Hasn't it occurred to you they might still be after the Xvr stone? Who's to say they wouldn't say anything to get it? I say we negotiate from a position of strength. We jump to another star and recharge. Then when we go back—if we go back—we'll have the firepower to face them down. What d'you think, Debbie?"

"I agree. We should recharge first. We should also search our ship again. If there is a transmitter on board, we need to find it. Or maybe Greeter Prime could do that for us."

"You wish your ship searched? What would we be looking for?"

"Some kind of transmitter. We don't know what it looks like but we think it'll have portal tech, if that's any help. At the very least we need to deactivate it or that ship will likely follow us. Perhaps you could do some cleaning as well. There are quite a few bodies that need to be taken care of."

"It will be done. Do you have any other instructions?"

"How about you show us to somewhere we can rest up? I don't know about anyone else, but after the last few hours I could do with a nap at the very least."

With neither Ellen nor Fist disagreeing, Greeter Prime

leads us back through the rimed passageways. Lights flicker out behind us, the heavy door we entered by swings silently shut, and once more we are in a white room. Beyond is another with a coffee table in its center. Someone's even thought to place a vase of flowers on it, which is a nice touch. They look a bit like orchids, yellow and red with hints of purple at their extremities. Or they're just a construct, holographic projections, the same as the table and the sofas on either side of it, richly red with deeply plumped seats and cushions. As comfy and laid-back as it all looks, I was hoping for something more, but that's okay. Greeter Prime has it covered.

"This is your communal relaxation area. If you require anything, simply call and it will be delivered. Now, if you will each follow me."

Three exits appear, with mine leading into another white room. This one is tastefully appointed with a very good approximation of Art Deco furniture: a table and chairs, two more sofas on either side of another coffee table and shelves and cabinets around the walls. They're stacked with art, weird statuary that I swear moves when I'm not looking at it and just as weird landscapes that are definitely moving whether I'm looking at them or not. There's also a huge bed, stacked with pillows and coverlets, that might almost be crooking a finger at me as it says, "Come. Let me enfold you in my arms and soothe away your cares." Well, it must be hard work being a god, what with all those worlds and civilizations waiting to be created. And now this mere mortal is about to sleep in a god's bed. Let's hope they're as good at making mattresses.

~

Sometime later a rough shaking awakens me. It's Fist. "Hey,

wake up. Somebody out there doesn't like us again."

"Who?"

Now we're making enemies in our sleep. This universe is like a bad neighborhood. Breathe in the wrong direction and they're coming for you.

"Don't know. Greeter Prime is talking to them. Seems some people don't like other people appearing an entire planet in the middle of their system. Orbital perturbations are a bitch apparently."

Fist heads out, leaving me to crawl out of my nice warm nest and hurry along after her. A new exit from our communal area leads to another white room with another big round door that's already standing open. Beyond is another passageway. This one is not rimed with age, so it must be well used. It's also short. It takes us into a huge control center filled with consoles and diaphanous screens and blinking lights and scrolling graphics. This is clearly the nerve center of everything, with Greeter Prime and his little band of androids running it all.

Ellen is already with him, and together they're looking at a huge screen that fills the entire front wall. Filling it are the head and shoulders of a new kind of alien. This one has big yellow darting eyes and an actual beak for a mouth. Its multihued skin has a sheen to it that suggests scales, and a crest of tall feathers runs all the way over the top of its head. My first thought is turkey, especially with the way its head jerks around or rises and falls on that rubber-chicken neck.

"I repeat: You have entered our system without permission, and now you are threatening its stability. The Great Og, Illustrious Creator and Emperor of Everything, demands compensation, or all the glorious forces of the Empire of Og will be unleashed upon you."

Wow! We've accidentally stumbled into an evil empire. It

must be a very secret evil empire since no one anywhere we've been has ever heard of it. And then there's their god-emperor who claims to have created everything but is keeping awfully quiet about it. Fortunately for him Greeter Prime's gods are asleep or we might be looking at a divine spat, something along the lines of, *"We created the universe and everything in it." "No you didn't. We did."* Except, of course, for now at least we're their new gods, and somebody needs to deal with this before Fist declares war.

"What kind of compensation were you thinking of?"

Its eyes dart toward me. So do Ellen's and Fist's.

After a brief pause, in which it's probably consulting with a higher authority, its idea of compensation surprises us all. "The Great Og likes your planet. It's very big and shiny and powerful. The Great Og could be persuaded to allow the continuation of your insignificant existences in exchange for such a gift."

"Could he? I thought our planet was destabilizing your system. Not that it matters. It's our planet and we're not giving it to you. We do have a very nice artifact though, very valuable if you sell it to the right people."

There's a longer pause. Someone somewhere in the empire of everything is preparing their glorious forces to attack us. Or they're realizing they've had their bluff called.

"You will present yourselves before the Great Og. He will inspect this artifact. It would be unwise to keep him waiting. A flight path is being transmitted to you now."

The alien disappears, and the top left corner of our main screen is now filled with a small red sun. That's it, there's nothing else, so what planets we're supposed to be destabilizing is a mystery.

After a few moments of silence, it's Fist who says what we

all must be thinking. "This is probably the worst scam I've ever seen, and I've seen a few. How dumb do they think we are? I say we tell them to take their empire of everything and squawk off."

Greeter Prime, who may not even know what a scam is, sees it differently. "Inadvisable. We do not know their offensive capabilities. Our defenses are operational but if they attack, it cannot be predicted what damage they might inflict."

To which Ellen adds, "Drovenanthis might appear too. Whether or not he's who he says he is, that could only complicate matters. Can you maneuver to within portal range?"

"Again, inadvisable. If we were to come too close to their home world our gravitational fields might rip both planets apart. Besides, we have not ascertained that they have portal technology. The only way to approach that planet would be in your ship."

Ellen quickly points out the obvious flaw in that. "Yeah. Unfortunately that might result in Drovenanthis being sent our coordinates, which is precisely what we don't want right now. Have you checked our ship for a transmitter?"

"We have. Although we could find nothing hidden aboard, some of the bodies were equipped with micro-burst transmitters. We have disposed of them."

"Micro-burst transmitters!" exclaims Fist. "What? Inside them?" She looks sideways at Ellen. It's the kind of look a lab rat might dread to see. "When was the last time you were scanned?"

"Your people scanned me, remember? So far as I know, I have an ID chip and a ULD. Why? You think they somehow planted a transmitter on me without me noticing? You think they implanted me with portal tech?"

Clearly Fist does, but before scalpels can be reached for,

Greeter Prime comes to Ellen's rescue. "Not inside them. The transmitters were built into their body armor. We are currently investigating the possibility of any transmissions having been made. The likelihood of such a burst being detectable is, however, small."

That's a relief. Having portal tech implanted does not sound like a good idea. Imagine if it failed to turn off. Your intestines could be sucked out and end up on the far side of the universe, an eternal mystery to whoever discovered them. It would be rather like being eaten from the inside out by one of those wasp grubs, only thankfully a lot quicker. And then the transmitter would burst into flames because it didn't shut down and its battery overheated. Ugh.

Time to think about something else, as Fist is already doing. "So we don't know if that ghost ship has our coordinates or not, and if we don't go over there the Great Og might start shooting at us. Talk about being caught between a red giant and a white dwarf. I say we get on over there, get this thing done and get out of here as soon as we can relocate. All we have to do when we get there is convince the emperor of everything that what he really needs more than anything else in the entire universe is a lump of rock."

In the docking bay, our ship is all bright and shiny and new. No officer, nothing happened here. You must be mistaking us for someone else, unless you're Major Amarthin Drovenanthis of course.

With the flight path blinking red on our captain's console, we set out. For a few moments, Fist switches our main screen to a rear view. Who knew? Immediately we understand what the bird was talking about. There is Greeter Prime's god world, a giant mirror ball hanging in the blackness of space, its sunward side glowing red. What must be its entire surface is covered in solar panels, all of them drinking in the energy it needs to recharge.

Looking forward again, we're approaching a purple planet. There are deep purple oceans and lighter purple and rusty red landmasses. The polar ice caps extend halfway toward the equator and even they are tinged with a delicate pastel purple. It doesn't look very enticing at all. Under that red sun this must be a very cold world, so they're probably not big on sunbathing. Fortunately we're heading for the equator so we won't be slipping around on all that ice.

A great city grows beneath us, a perfectly laid-out grid of suburbs with tiny little fires everywhere beneath a partly obscuring shroud of smoke. In its center is a great square surrounded by stepped pyramids, each one with a burning beacon on its summit. It's all disturbingly familiar, except for those beacons. It can't be though. It's just too much of a coincidence unless, a long time ago, Earth was part of this empire of everything and some former Great Og was remembered and worshipped under the name Quetzalcoatl. That's even more disturbing. What the Aztecs used to do on top of their pyramids—well, the Great Og's idea of compensation better not be a little human sacrifice followed by a bang-up meal, or we're in big trouble.

Ellen and I carry the container with the Xvr stone inside down the loading ramp. At the bottom of it, a welcoming committee awaits us, half a dozen of them. They all have big, yellow darting eyes and feathered crests of different sizes and colorations, and they're all wearing feathered cloaks. They're also wearing feathered knee-length pants, or those might be their own feathers. They do seem rather tight-fitting. The length of each cloak matches the size of the wearer's crest so it must be a sign of rank. The biggest crest wears the longest cloak, a multicolored, calf-length affair. Big Crest is also taller than the rest, and it's the one doing the talking. "You are now under the jurisdiction of the Empire of Og. You will surrender your weapons."

That's some achievement, talking through a beak like that. It hadn't occurred to me before but perhaps they're all descended from myna birds or parrots. Perhaps they evolved on Earth and they're the last remnant of some great civilization that rose and fell, and everybody except the Incas and the Aztecs forgot about them. They do say the dinosaurs were starting to get smart before the asteroid took them out. This could even be all that's left of Atlantis, which would be another stunning discovery to take home with me. At this rate I'm going to need a bigger mantelpiece for all those Nobel prizes they'll be showering me with.

Meanwhile Big Crest makes a fluid gesture that ends up pointing at us. All the small crests, with waist-length cloaks, raise their weapons. Some welcoming committee this is. Not that there's any choice. We hand over our weapons and then, surrounded, we set off across the square toward the largest of the pyramids.

Their knees bend backward as they walk, just like birds. Their heads bob slightly back and forth on top of their long, bald necks too, also like birds. For the first half dozen or so steps it's decidedly unsettling. Birds of prey are dangerous enough without giving them military-grade hardware. After that, it's the cold and the dimness that grabs my attention. That sun isn't doing much to lessen either. Nor are all those fires and beacons, which appear to be doing nothing more than filling the air with a sweet-smelling smoke, unless that's what they're there for.

"What's with all these fires? Don't you guys have electricity?"

Tight-lipped glances from Ellen and Fist are warning me to be quiet, but the leader is happy enough to talk. "Of course. Our empire spans the universe. Our battle fleets rove at will, enforcing our dominion. These fires burn to call upon our gods to return. They deserted us, taking with them the power of our sun. Every year the ice creeps a little closer, but our priests assure us that the burning of sweet fires will call them back and they will order the ice to retreat."

"Really? I'm no scientist but I don't think it works like that."

Those glances are becoming glares, and the leader is becoming a little anal too. "Our scientists failed us. They claimed nothing could be done, so the Great Og had them all executed. The Great Og does not tolerate failure. He does not tolerate blasphemy either. Therefore you will stop talking."

Okay. Fair enough. Besides, the greatest of all the pyramids is now towering in front of us, rising like the shoulders of Atlas into the cloud-streaked orange sky. Directly before us is a great, triangular mouth, its height taller by half than its width, with mini-crests standing guard on either side. The lighting beyond is just as dim as outside, red verging on orange. It comes from globes that float above us, just below where the sloping walls meet. Some of the globes are flickering. The odd one or two have failed altogether. Guards stand beneath them at regular intervals, all very rigid and resplendent in their feathery cloaks. They're probably meant to be intimidating. Some of them might be better employed changing a few light bulbs or at the very least turning up the brightness, unless this dimness is all that their great, yellow eyes can stand. Now there's something to think about, that this entire empire of everything might be brought to its knees by nothing more than a few flashlights. Shame we don't have any.

At the end of the passage is a vast chamber, its ceiling so high that the globes lighting it don't even penetrate the abyss above them. There are more braziers too, filling the hugeness with sweet-smelling smoke. There's also music, soft drums and shimmering cymbals and a choir of voices that gently warble and occasionally wail. It's an ocean of sound, rolling and reverberating, with crying swells and lamenting troughs. Someone here wants us to feel an awestruck reverence. Someone here wants us to grovel before his godlike presence. Someone here might be overcompensating just a little bit.

In the center of the chamber is a much smaller pyramid. It rises in a series of high steps to a platform, upon which sits what can only be described as a nest, a carefully constructed mess of purple boughs and foliage. Above that is a layer of down, and nestled into that is a figure wearing a cloak of silver and gold feathers so vast that, where it isn't all piled up around him, it spills out over the edge of the nest to almost touch the top of the platform. This can only be that someone, the Great Og himself. With his crest lying flat and his eyes closed, he appears to be asleep.

The leader of our party bends his knees backward and settles down at the foot of the pyramid. All the others do the same. As we fail to follow suit, the leader hisses at us, "Kneel before the Illustrious One."

Fist stiffens. The very idea of kneeling in front of anyone has her fingers curling. We don't have any weapons so, with the container on the floor between us, she has little choice but to obey. It's either that or insult the Great Og, and insulted Great Ogs probably have all sorts of nasty punishments they can hand out.

We wait. Then we wait some more. The Great Og hasn't moved. He hasn't noticed us at all. He must be asleep. At last the leader of our escort gives a barking cough. Its effect is like an electric shock. The Great Og's eyes spring open, his crest jumps erect and his neck cranes as high as it will go. "Eh, what? Have the gods returned? Has rebellion broken out in the far reaches of my empire? Have my glorious legions brought me new worlds to cower before me? Then what is this perfidy? Cannot a Great Og contemplate for a moment the joys of youth: the loving peck of his mother's beak, a regurgitated bug from his father's, a chick's simple joy at ripping out the succulent entrails of some small furry thing?"

One of his big, yellow roving eyes at last settles on us. "What's this? Have you brought me tributes from a world I have long forgotten? Enlighten me or I shall have your gizzards inflated and sported with within the hour."

That doesn't sound good, but at least I know. Ellen and Fist don't. Somehow they have to be warned but not now, not while the leader of our escort has his head bowed, avoiding that hawk-like gaze for all he's worth.

"My apologies, Illustriousness, but these are the interlopers who have impertinently disturbed your divine order. They have brought with them an offering in the hope you will see fit to exercise your infinite mercy."

The Great Og's unblinking gaze flicks over the three of us. "An offering, you say. I hope it's a very good offering because I do so hate to be disappointed. Well, come along then, come along. I haven't got all day. I have criminals and heretics and deniers to execute." The Great Og's eye becomes even beadier. "I do have criminals and heretics and deniers to execute, don't I? It would be a very slow day if I didn't. I might have to wonder if someone wasn't doing their job properly, like the head of my secret police, for instance. I do hope you're doing your job properly or I might have to execute you too.

What a thing it is, when a Great Og cannot rely on anyone to execute his will. Yes, I remember well what my mother used to tell me as she nursed me under her wing. 'Remember, boy. Either you eat them or they'll eat you.' She was a simple hen, a traditionalist, a firm believer in a firm hand and the rightness of the pecking order. Ah, if she were only here now. If only she hadn't wandered away from that rest home and been eaten by a grunzit, what would she . . . ?"

While the Great Og wanders off into fond reminiscences, the leader of our party is furiously waving at Ellen and me to carry the container to the top of the pyramid. It's done quickly and quietly because it's obvious no one wants to disturb the Great Og while he's in such a good mood. His beady eye sees us anyway as we hurry back to the bottom of the steps. Then, leaning forward, he fixes a single eye on the container, considers it for a moment and then harrumphs. "Am I expected to open this myself when I have so many other matters to deal with?"

"Of course not, Illustriousness. I do most humbly apologize."

The leader waves a commanding hand at one of his lesser crests. The poor thing's head jerks upward, and then nervously from side to side. It must be hoping one of the other lesser crests is being gestured at. But all the rest of them are staring rigidly at the floor. Sorry, pal, nothing to do with us. Oh, and by the way, it was nice knowing you. Left with no choice, it scurries up the pyramid to grovel before the Great Og, desperately fumbling at the container's fastenings before scurrying back down again to hide among his oh-so-faithful companions.

The Great Og leans further forward, his head almost inside the container as he inspects its contents. No one moves. No one breathes. No one makes a sound until he rises to fix that eye on us again.

"It's a rock."

"It's a very valuable rock, if you know who to sell it to." Well, somebody has to say something to sell it to him, even if doing so means his eye comes to rest on me. Here's hoping he's got a full log of executions already lined up for today.

"Is it? Why? Is it a magic rock? Does it confer great power on whoever holds it?"

"I don't know. All I know is the Xvr will pay an awful lot to get it back."

"The Xvr. Who are the Xvr? Why have I not heard of them? Why have we not conquered them? I will not tolerate such defiance in my universe. Send me my generals. Send me my admirals. We shall dispatch a fleet immediately. And execute my head of intelligence. That I should have to rely on creatures such as these to bring me such information is a disgrace, an outrage." He pauses, his big bird brain considering who knows what possibilities. He's not the Great Og for nothing, after all. "Perhaps there is more. I'm always interested in new worlds and new cultures. I think we shall dine together. You shall be dressed as befits my table and we shall delight in the novelty you bring to it."

CHAPTER THIRTEEN

Surrounded by our escort, we're led from the great chamber toward another exit. Ellen and Fist are walking shoulder to shoulder in front of me. Beneath the music, still swelling and falling like waves upon a beach, they are whispering intently to each other. I can't hear them, and nor can our escort. They look like Cinderella's sisters arguing over who gets to wear what at the dinner we've been invited to. They still don't know, and time is rapidly running out for them to be told.

Beyond the exit is another passageway. It slopes gently downward into the bowels of the pyramid. As dim as everywhere else, with orange globes burning or burned out above us, it's also increasingly silent as we leave the music behind. Now is as good a time as any and, catching up with them, I'm just in time to hear Fist finish with, "I'll tell you one thing for sure. That Great Og is barely on speaking terms with reality."

"Yeah, I got that too. He said he wants information from us. What do you think he'll do if we don't give him any?"

Okay. Here goes nothing. "He'll eat us is what he'll do."

Both of them snap searching gazes toward me. Ellen's comes with a frown, Fist's with a mocking grin as she says, "He'll eat us, will he? Oh, I just know there's some quaint Earth thing coming our way. Okay, tell us how you all eat each other on your terribly civilized world, or should I just say terrible?"

"You can laugh all you want, but I'm telling you. I recognize these pyramids. The people who built them on Earth used to declare war on their neighbors so they could take prisoners. Then they'd cut their still-beating hearts out, feed them to their gods and eat the rest themselves. And if you want to talk about civilized, how many species have tried to kill us already, Ellen?"

She doesn't answer but her frown is growing deeper.

As for Fist, well, if you don't understand it, mock it. "Yeah, right. Ooh, the big, bad aliens are going to eat us all. Quick, run and hide. The Great Og said he wanted information from us. How's he going to do that if he eats us?"

"I don't know, but if I were to take a guess, I'd say by eating one of us and then giving the other two a simple choice. He said we'd be dressed for dinner so we could bring novelty to his table. What d'you think he meant by that? You think he's going to give you a feathered cloak and then be dazzled by your sparkling conversation? Look, the point I'm trying to make here is that being dressed could also mean being skinned, boned, spitted, sat on a platter, and served up as the main course."

With her smirk faltering, Fist shakes her head. "Nah. That doesn't make any sense. If we're just meat to them, why didn't they kill us as soon as we landed? Why didn't they kill us as soon as they saw that rock? Whose brilliant idea was that anyway? Oh, that's right. It was yours."

"It was, and I didn't hear you complaining about it overmuch. I was right about Greeter Prime, wasn't I? You can't say for definite I'm not right about this."

"And you can't say for definite you are."

We've come to a crossroad, with all passageways except the one behind us leading further downward into dimness.

Here the leader of our escort raises his hand, bringing us to a halt but still surrounded. "You will now each be taken to a place where you can be prepared. You should know that it is a rare honor to be brought to the Great Og's table. Many dream of it, to honor him and, through him, our gods, but few are called. Do not sour the occasion with ill words and ill thoughts. Do not . . ."

While the leader continues with his little lecture, Ellen throws Fist a glance. She also stealthily points to the right-hand passageway, and Fist understands. They then both throw me glances, with Fist pointing toward the left-hand passageway, and I understand too. Sorry, guys. Thanks for the invitation but we gotta run.

Ellen dashes for the passageway in front of us. Fist makes off to the right and I run to the left. For a few seconds no one follows. That's probably because the leader is still talking. These Ogians do like to talk a lot.

After that there's the shouting of orders, the running of feet, and the beginning of a chase that takes me further and deeper into the pyramid. Other passageways lead off to the left and right. I could lose my pursuers by taking them, but then I'd probably also lose myself. Out of one of them steps another bird. This one is squat, thick-necked, without a cloak and with only a fleshy crest. Narrowly avoiding colliding with me, it looks at me with startled eyes. Deciding it doesn't like what it's seeing, it then squawks and runs away. Some sort of menial, perhaps. It'll be running to find more guards and tell them tonight's main course has escaped. Oh, for a flashlight, just one. That'd take care of them all.

The guards behind me are gaining on me. There's nothing to be done but keep going and hope to work my way back to wherever Ellen and Fist might have ended up. That's a tall order down here in these labyrinthine depths. Then it's not even that: The passageway ends and I've arrived on the threshold of hell. Okay, it's not hell. It's a kitchen, a high chamber filled with long banks of raised hearths that might as well be burning with the fires of hell. Each one has two or more spits over them, some already with turning carcasses. This is not good. The toast always lands butter-side down and I've very nearly put myself into a frying pan, literally.

Behind me two guards and maybe more are still coming. In front of me is a brigade of chefs. There must be at least twenty of them. Beneath a great, gray, seething cloud of fuel and fat, they are all working away: skinning, boning, tenderizing, and skewering. Above them all, like some Renaissance god, is the big guy, the lord of all he surveys, the *eminence terrible*, the Chef with a capital *C*. He's a great, big bird with a great, big crest. Sitting in some kind of hoist, he's coasting around above their heads, stopping regularly to crane his neck downward so that his great yellow eye can twitch back and forth as he inspects every little thing they're doing.

It's for sure there's no turning back. It's almost as for sure there's little chance of going forward either, unless a little mouse can quietly scamper through under their feet.

Then there's no choice. One of them sees me. Its head shoots up, its eye fixed on me, and it squawks very loudly. My ULD doesn't translate. Maybe only the bigger crests can actually talk. Not that it matters. That squawk is understood by the rest of them and every other head shoots up, every other eye fixes on me and an awful lot of cleavers are suddenly looking very interested. The last to see me is Chef. His head shoots up even higher, his gaze even more intent. Behind it he's probably already trying out recipes: what sauce, what garnish, what shape of plate, how best to present this novelty.

As he floats toward me beneath that cloud, behind me come the guards, a whole squad of them. That's it then. There's no choice but to scamper, scurrying on hands and feet between workstations and hearths and a detritus of kitchen waste. There are squawks and screeches all around and stamping feet with white-tipped talons followed by singing blades. Somehow they all miss—miss me, at least. In the spreading confusion, some of their own aren't so lucky. Like big galoots they're getting in each other's way, with all their squawking and screeching growing louder and angrier. Then a hand bounces across the floor in front of me, with a cleaver still attached. That's followed by an arm, and then a head.

This might not be hell but all hell is breaking loose. Bodies are dropping and there's an awful lot of blood. At least as they turn on each other they've lost interest in me. It's a full-on bar room brawl, and just to add to the fun, now the guards have arrived. There's a moment when everything stops, a catching of breath as the guards recognize the mayhem that's broken out and the mayhem recognizes the guards as the enemy they hate even more than each other. Then the guards open fire and it's total chaos. Poor old Great Og. All he wanted was a nice dinner. Then the main course went and started a riot, rather like a butterfly causing a hurricane. Well, that's life: a series of little disappointments, one after another.

Through all this, I still have to find a way out. There is

only one, and working my way back to it is becoming easier. The guard's fire is lessening, and some of the chefs have turned their attention to Chef, jumping up to grab at his feet as they try to drag him down. Squawking loudly, he kicks back at them, but at last they get him. Brought down like a roped heifer, he's still kicking and squawking but only for as long as it takes for all the skinners, boners and tenderizers to get to work. Poor old Chef. It would seem he wasn't all that popular. He'll be popular now, for one night at least, with the new main dish for the Great Og's enjoyment being something of a Chef's surprise.

Before they notice me and consider adding an appetizer, I'm headed straight for the exit. There all the guards are dead, every one of them skewered with at least one sharp instrument. That leaves plenty of weapons scattered around the floor and an empty passageway beyond. So long as it stays that way, retracing my steps in hopes of finding Ellen and Fist is my best course of action. They could be anywhere by now. They could even be dead. That doesn't bear thinking about. They're capable, far more capable than me. Thinking like that isn't good either. I'm a hard-core bunny killer, a dangerous desperado, and I'm packing heavy.

Passageway follows passageway, still empty until some guards appear. Word must be spreading that the kitchen is revolting, which it was but not in that way. They stop when they see me, nonplussed by something. Maybe it's because they've never seen the likes of me before. Or maybe it's because turkeys aren't supposed to fight back. We share a moment, a brief exchange of not quite knowing whether it's fight or flight. Then it's both: a headlong rush and red tracer flying everywhere. By the time it's over they're all down and there's not even a scratch on me. Well, that was easy, and it does my confidence a world of good. This hero stuff is a walk in the park.

Back at the intersection where we parted company, all I know is Fist went that way and Ellen that way. This is not so easy because all three of us could be wandering around this labyrinth until more guards or starvation finds us. It has to be one or the other though. Standing here simply isn't an option. Well, okay then. Fist is as good a choice as any. Wherever she's at, at least she'll be making a noise about it, unless the guards have already taken her. She and Ellen are going to need a hero then, someone like me fearlessly stalking these passageways in search of wherever they've been taken. Holding cells probably, in some dungeon way down deep and dark and full of rats, with skeletons chained to the walls and straw scattered on damp floors. Okay, let's rein the imagination in. This isn't some medieval castle. This is the Great Og's palace, and those holding cells could just as well be his pantry.

Forward and downward it is then, level by level, into an increasingly brooding but not always complete silence. Occasionally there's the skittering of talons on stone, but peering around corners never reveals anything. It's almost as if they're avoiding me, which is a little strange. The Great Og must have an entire army inside this pyramid. One turkey ought to be easy enough for them to deal with, unless starving me out is their plan. Best find that pantry then, and maybe some yummy rats, battered and fried in a bucket. I'll take a large drink with that, please.

Further and deeper through passageways shrouded in a thickening gloom. There are few glowing globes down here, and enough of them are not working for some stretches to be left barely lit at all. Passageways meet and cross at intersections, some of them opening out into large rectangular chambers.

Some of them have sharp turns and switchbacks, but none of them lead anywhere but further into the labyrinth. That's a little unsettling because labyrinths usually have something nasty living in them, and these nasties have talons. They skitter constantly, always just out of sight until at last I see one. It dashes out into the passageway ahead of me, pauses to regard me with an eye far too large for its body, then disappears again. About the size of geese with huge, stabbing beaks and black plumage, these things must live down here like rats in the crawl space. And that is what this place must be, the vaults of the pyramid with hidden chambers everywhere, guarding all manner of secrets. Here's hoping Ellen and Fist haven't been shut up in one of them.

With that not very comforting thought, I move on. Those creatures aren't bothering me so I won't bother them. Then I come to a chamber. In one corner are the remains of something, nothing more than bones and shredded clothing. Oh my God. These creatures must be vultures, or the Ogian version of them. They feed on carrion, and there are no guards chasing us because they are waiting for us to starve to death. It makes sense really. There's no point in risking an army if nature will do the job for you. It settles one thing for me though: I don't like this place. Being here is no fun at all.

The only good thing is that this maze can't be endless. The Great Og's pyramid might be big, but it's only so big. The bad thing is I'm hopelessly lost. A ball of string would've been a good idea, or even a stick of chalk. What a pity none of us thought of it while we were jumping around the universe in other species' spaceships. ID: check. ULD: check. Blaster: check. Ball of string: Say what?

Creeping onward as the vultures continue to circle, there's a growing sense of urgency as I call out, "Ellen. Fist. Are you there?"

After I take a few more turns, more than likely going round in a big fat circle, voices come back to me. They're not echoes and they sound familiar, especially in the way they're carping at each other.

"Ellen. Fist. Is that you?"

There's a moment of silence then one of them, probably Ellen, calls out, "Debbie? Where are you?"

"I'm over here."

"Well, that's a real big help." That has to be Fist.

"Let's everyone keep talking and then we can work our way toward each other."

Which is easier said than done. With all its twists and turns and switchbacks, this place is about as navigable as an insurance agreement. There's an awful lot of calling out: "Where are you now?" and "Can you still hear me?" and "Didn't we already come this way?"

Slowly, sometimes coming closer to each other and sometimes going further away, we work our way through the passageways until turning a corner brings me face-to-face with them. There are smiles all round, and a hug from Ellen. That's unexpected, but rather nice. Maybe she's lightening up at last.

Fist remains Fist though. "We pretty much decided they must've cooked you by now."

"No. Well, I did stumble into their kitchen and sort of start a riot. There were knives and arms and heads flying everywhere. The guards joined in too, shooting anything that moved. I think maybe they cooked Chef instead. But how about you? How did you find each other?"

"The same way we found you: by stumbling around hopelessly lost until we heard each other calling. Fortunately the guards didn't chase after us. That might have something to do with the local wildlife. You've come across them, yes?"

"Yeah, I've met them. They seem harmless enough as long as we keep breathing. So let's hope there's nothing else down here, like a Minotaur."

"A Minotaur?" That's short and sweet, which makes a change for Fist.

"It's mythological: a big male body with a bull's head on top. The king of Crete used to feed tributes to it until a hero called Theseus killed it."

"Great. So a happy ending then. Happy endings are good."

"Not really. When he sailed home Theseus forgot to change the sail on his ship. His father thought he was dead and committed suicide. The people who came up with that story didn't really do happy endings."

"Didn't really do happy endings? Who doesn't like happy endings? Oh, I forgot. This is Earth we're talking about."

"Hey, I've got a gun, y'know. In fact I appear to be the only one who has a gun and I've already shot some of the guards."

There's a broad grin from Fist. Well, that is her kind of happy ending.

Ellen is, as ever, the practical one. "So there's probably no Minotaur then, and those little ones are harmless so far. Maybe the guards aren't coming after us because they've released something else into these passageways. Maybe they haven't. Either way, now that we're back together, we need to find a way out that doesn't include going back up to where they're waiting for us. I say we find an outer wall and follow it. Could be there's a service tunnel they forgot about."

Sounds like a plan to me.

Not so much to Fist. "Seriously? You want to wander around this hole for who knows how long, looking for a way out that might or might not be here? What are we going to do? Shoot critters for food and drink their blood? I say we go back up there and fight our way out. We've got a weapon. So long as she can shoot straight, we'll get more. Better still, why don't you give that weapon to me?"

Well, that's not happening.

"I got this weapon because I *can* shoot straight, thank you very much."

Okay, not entirely true, but Fist doesn't know that.

Neither does Ellen, but then she's not asking me to hand it over. "Calm down the both of you. We've got one weapon and no time for bickering. We've also got two ways to go and it looks like the casting vote is yours. So what do you think, Debbie? What do we do?"

"Why can't we do both? We find the outer wall, walk it, or better still run it, and if we can't find a way out then we go back up there and shoot our way out, maybe, if there's not too many of them, if we can grab more weapons, if—"

"Yeah, yeah, yeah. If, if, if. You see, this is what happens when you overthink things. Better to shoot first and worry about it later. Now are we going to do this or not?"

Overthinking things is something Fist is never going to be accused of, along with subtlety. It's probably best not to mention bulls in China shops then. She'd probably consider that to be another weird Earth thing—and what's a bull or a China shop anyway?

She does have a point though, and Ellen is quick to agree. "Let's get moving then: straight ahead, or as near as we can, until we find an outer wall. You lead, Debbie, since you've got the weapon."

"Yeah. You got the weapon, Debbie. You lead the way."

That's right, Fist, you have a good smirk about it. Me, I have a husband and two kids to get back to. I've completely lost track of time out here. It could be Monday back on Earth. They could be standing in an empty house wondering where Mommy's gone, with 911 called and all the neighbors standing in the street inventing their own versions of what's happened to me. Being a missing person and losing out on all of that is not how this is going to end. So stay out of my way, Fist, because I'm getting my Vasquez on, and I only need to know one thing: where they are.

As we head off through the skittering dimness this place feels like a haunted house, with unseen eyes raising the hairs on the back of our necks. They are on mine anyway. That's an interesting thought, that this labyrinth might be wired for sound and vision, that the Great Og might be sitting up there on his purple nest watching every move we make. Some minions would have brought a screen to hold up in front of him because, of course, he couldn't be expected to exert himself. It would certainly beat the boredom of having to wait and see if anyone comes out alive. Maybe he's even holding a gamepad and using it to move monsters around as he hunts us through these passageways.

My God, concentrate, will you? This is not the time to be indulging in wild fantasies. We don't have health bars, and even if we did, there are no health packs down here to replenish them with.

Through twists and turns and intersections, we trace a hushed and creeping path. We're moving in approximately the same direction, or at least we think we are. Time is meaningless. One minute could be five. Five minutes could be half an hour. Intersection follows intersection, corner follows corner. Everywhere is orange-red dimness, sometimes flickering, sometimes broken by patches of darkness. Nothing is moving except us. Well, nothing we can see anyway. That skittering is still all around. Above us is the entire oppressive weight of the Great Og's pyramid, perhaps with a whole host of beady, darting eyes watching us, all of them waiting for something to happen: a sudden rush, followed by screams and weapon fire and, when the fun's over, some of them will be sent down to collect the mangled corpses. No need for Chef. They're pre-prepared and ready for the spit.

Then something does happen: a muffled boom. We all stop, with Fist whispering, "You hear that? What was that?"

"I don't know. I don't think we want to find out either. The outer wall can't be that much further. So come on. Run!"

There's no need for Ellen to say it twice. A few more turns, another intersection, and at last we come to a blank wall with a passageway stretching away into dimness on both sides. We run to the right: It's as good a choice as any. For a while there's only more skittering. Then we hear something else. Once again we come to a halt. There are scrapes and scratchings, not at all like the vulture skitterings, and they are coming slowly but steadily closer.

Uncertainly, Fist says, "Guards? Have they sent guards down here after us?"

I'm not too certain either.

"Why would they wait this long to send guards down after us?"

"I don't know. Perhaps you should go ask? While you're there, ask them why they're throwing explosives around too."

That'll be a pass, if it's all the same to you. Not that Fist is waiting for a reply. We're already moving, running the length of the passageway, hoping for a corner to appear. It doesn't. Instead some guards do, maybe two hundred feet behind us, and they're not asking questions. Red tracer fills the passageway, ricocheting off the walls and turning the entire width of it into a zinging light show of certain death.

Someone ought to fire back. That'll be me. Before I can though, Fist has grabbed my arm and dragged me into a side passage. Ellen is close behind, and once again we're turning corners and crossing intersections. Where we're going is anybody's guess but somehow we emerge into another long passageway. Fist drags us to a halt. She's seen something, or at least she thinks she has, and this time she's not asking. "The gun. Give me the gun. Sorry, ladies, but we're outta time. We gotta give these bird brains some serious discouragement and maybe grab some of their weapons too. So give. Give me the gun."

At times like this, Fist is not someone you want to pick an argument with.

Okay then. Weapon in hand, she's shooing us into a side passage. She takes a knee and takes aim. She fires, her red tracer answered by sporadic and poorly aimed fire from the guards. It's all very heroic, insane but heroic. Then she stops firing. She looks at the weapon. "I don't believe this. We're out. Couldn't you have picked up a gun with a full mag at least?"

"Oh, I'm so sorry. That was really careless of me in the middle of a riot with cleavers flying everywhere."

Before she can snap back at me, a voice from somewhere behind her shouts, "Down! Get down!"

CHAPTER FOURTEEN

Fist hits the deck. The guards' red tracer instantly increases, but now it's being answered by blue tracer. All we can see is the light show. All we can hear is the zing and ping of ricochets. It doesn't last long. The red tracer slowly lessens until there's only blue tracer left, and then that ceases too.

Feet come running and there they are: black-armored ghost troopers. If nothing else, they're persistent.

One of them raises a clenched fist in salute, speaking through his visor, "Captain Praganathulis, I am Captain Andranalapsis. We're your rescue party. Major Drovenanthis is standing off. We don't know for sure what kind of defenses this planet has. I suggest you come with us, and quickly, before more of them turn up."

Captain Praganathulis, a.k.a. Ellen, nods slowly. "That explosion we heard. That was you?"

"It was. We had to blow out a section of the wall to gain entry. But all of this can be discussed later. We need to move, now."

That's good enough for Ellen. If it's good enough for her, it's also good enough for me. Strangely it's good enough for Fist too, who utters not a single word of protest as she raises herself from the floor.

With a wave of his hand, Captain Andranalapsis moves us out. There are six of them, three in front and three behind.

As we run Fist recovers herself enough to find her voice. "How did you find us down here?"

"We've been tracking you for some time."

"Yeah, we know that. But this is underground with thousands of tons of rock above us."

"We found your ship and sent down some spy drones. They're tiny things, virtually impossible to detect in this gloom. They've been watching you from above the light globes ever since you entered these passageways."

"Great. You couldn't have used them to give us directions and maybe some extra firepower?"

"Like I said, they're very small. They've been relaying your position to us and mapping this place out along the way, enough for us to find you. Isn't that good enough?"

Probably not, but then Fist isn't replying. Even if she was, no one would be listening. Up ahead something is approaching us. All we can see at first is that it's big, very big. Big enough to fill the passageway and have Captain Andranalapsis bring us to a halt. "You know what that is?"

With the rest of us also staring transfixed, there's no answer.

What it is becomes clearer as it ambles toward us, its four feet plodding and the three long and viciously curved talons on each one going *clickety-click* on the hardness of the floor. Above is a barrel of a body, low at the shoulders on short front legs and high at the haunches on thicker, longer legs. All of it is covered in tawny down except for the red racing stripe of long feathers standing up like hackles all the way to its stubby tail. Leading it forward is a bald head and neck with a great hooked beak that's swaying from side to side. If that wasn't threatening enough, there are also two large horns above red eyes that peer into the dimness before it. It doesn't appear to have seen us yet, which is a good thing. Maybe it can't. Maybe that beak is swaying from side to side because it hunts by tasting the air and it hasn't caught our scent yet.

While I'm thinking triceratops with body issues, Fist is thinking something else. "I don't know about the rest of you but it seems to me we should try a different way, and let's all be nice and quiet while we do it."

Sounds like good advice. The last thing we need is a ten-thousand-pound puppy bristling with sabers bounding after us. Nice and quiet isn't good enough, though. As soon as we move, its head shoots up almost to the level of the glowing globes. It's seen us, or at least it's seen something, and that great beak is thrust forward, sniffing like a bloodhound.

"Run. Run!" Captain Andranalapsis hardly needs to say it. We're already pounding for the last intersection, with a loud squeal sounding behind us. That's followed by the clatter of talons and a sort of strangled, whinnying laughter. Somebody is enjoying this. It certainly isn't us.

The intersection comes. We turn, and then turn again. But by now it's got our scent. We can't shake it off. We can't lose it.

As we enter our second chamber Captain Andranalapsis makes a decision. "Firing line. The rest of you get behind us."

While the three of us stand in the mouth of the exit opposite the one we entered by, Captain Andranalapsis and his team form two lines. The front takes a knee, the rear stands, and every weapon is leveled on the entry opposite. We wait for the approaching clatter and that now almost demonic laughter. Somebody really is enjoying this.

It appears at the last intersection. It turns to face us. It shakes its head, lets out a squeal, and then charges. Our rescue party opens up on it, a hail of blue tracer, but the thing keeps coming. It doesn't need acid for blood. It's got Kevlar for skin.

At the last moment Captain Andranalapsis shouts, "Scatter!"

His men spread out around the chamber. He steps backward into our exit. At the same moment, the beast enters. It's surrounded and taking fire from every side, all of it useless. Our rescue party might just as well be using BB guns. The beast turns, charging down one of Captain Andranalapsis' men and smashing him into a wall. Everyone can hear the splintering of bones. It turns again, leaving that trooper to collapse like a rag doll. It sweeps its head and one of its horns connects with another trooper. He flies, crashing into another wall. The beast screams, searching for its next victim. While its beak is wide open, revealing a black and wormlike tongue, Captain Andranalapsis dashes forward, thrusting his weapon into its mouth and opening fire. The beast screeches. Its beak slams shut, ripping the weapon out of Andranalapsis' hand, and then it pancakes onto its belly. There it sits, pole axed, with everyone holding their breath in case it isn't—except for Fist, who simply has to come out with, "Some Minotaur. I thought you said a man's body and the head of some animal."

"Well, I got it half right, didn't I? Hey, different planet, different monster. Fortunately we had a hero with us to kill it so what's with the nitpicking? He could've lost a hand, y'know."

Fist smirks. She might as well be saying, *Lose a hand? He's still got the rest of his arm, hasn't he? Just walk it off.*

Andranalapsis might almost be saying something similar.

Far from being concerned, he has his foot on the beast's beak while he prizes his weapon free of its bite, all the while ordering his men to report. The report from his left isn't so good. "Dead. Crushed like a bug."

The report from the other side of the chamber is better. "He's fine. Maybe some cracked ribs but he'll do."

"Okay. One of you help him. And somebody grab that weapon. We're not leaving that behind."

"What?" The trooper who ought to be doing the grabbing isn't too hot for that. "What about this guy? We're not leaving him behind."

Some of the others aren't either, but Andranalapsis is standing firm. "Yes, we are. Look, if another one of those things turns up the last thing we'll need is to be carrying him. I'm sorry, but that's just the way it is. Now grab his weapon and get ready to move."

Heads are shaken but the captain has already moved on. Raising his left forearm, he starts tapping at some sort of portable console. Everyone else waits, listening to the occasional skitterings that sound both near and far, any one of which might turn into a clatter at any moment. For someone who wants to move fast and light, he's awfully engrossed in sending a text, if that's what he's about.

As the moments drag by, it's Ellen who finally challenges him. "What are you doing? I thought we were supposed to be moving?"

"We are, but we need to know where we're going first. I'm almost done redirecting the spy drones. They'll map out a route for us. All we'll need to do is follow the directions."

He makes one final stab at his forearm and the next thing we hear is a female voice, warm and friendly and ready to tuck us all in for the night. "No threats detected. Please proceed."

We have GPS, a Mommy GPS that's going to keep us safe from all the monsters and have warm milk and cookies waiting for us when we get home. Whose home that might be is open to question. It could be Ellen's friends and relatives throwing a big welcome home party for us or it could be the First Security Directorate throwing us an entirely different kind of party.

However it goes, we still have to escape this place first, and that means more passageways, more intersections, and more chambers. As quiet as mice we go, with Andranalapsis paying little attention to anything outside of his console. This could be the blind leading the blind. This could be us turning a corner and walking straight into an ambush if it wasn't for a rather severe Mommy GPS very abruptly looking out for us.

"Halt! Entities detected."

And take the garbage out too or you're grounded for a week.

Maybe not, but still we stop. We're in the middle of an intersection, Andranalapsis is staring down at the console on his forearm, and Fist is beginning to chafe. "What are we waiting for? If there's something out there the last thing we should be doing is standing around here waiting for it."

"We're waiting for clearance. We can't—"

"Waiting for clearance! Are you—"

"Multiple entities approaching. Turn left. Wait at the next intersection."

Captain Andranalapsis obeys, his faith in Mommy GPS so complete that he might step off the edge of a cliff if she told him to. The rest of us huddle along behind. If we do go over a cliff, at least we'll have someone to grab on to.

At the next intersection Captain Andranalapsis stops again. Orders say wait. Orders must be obeyed. Fist is starting to fidget. Mommy GPS had better come up with a plan real soon or Mommy GPS is going to get very seriously shouted at. As for Ellen, or Captain Praganathulis, there must be some training subconsciously kicking in inside her head because all she's doing is obeying orders too.

"Multiple entities maintaining distance. Return to last intersection and await instructions."

"What?" Fist isn't fidgeting anymore. "This is ridiculous. If we keep listening to that thing we're going to end up going round in circles. We need to find the outer wall is what we need to do. And you can give me that extra weapon too. If another one of those things turns up you're going to need all the firepower you can get."

We might not be able to see his face behind that visor, but it's a fair bet being spoken to like this by damsels in distress is not something Captain Andranalapsis' military training prepared him for. "That is not standard operating procedure. I cannot—"

"Oh, don't give me standard operating procedure! I was fighting my way out of tight corners while you were still learning how to polish your boots. Now give me that weapon before multiple whatevers turn up and attack us from all sides."

"I am not about to put the lives of my men at risk because of your impatience. We will proceed when—"

"Give her the weapon."

"Captain Praganathulis, you know very well—"

"Give her the weapon, will you? Look, I know you're in charge of this squad, Captain, but you came here for me. I might not know why, but someone somewhere thought it was important enough to send you. If we stand around here for too long waiting for a safe path to appear, the Great Og is going to swarm this place with guards and who knows what else and then we may never get out. Therefore I would strongly suggest we make a move, find the outer wall, and make it back to your access tunnel as fast as possible. And if you have any more spare weapons you might like to give them to Debbie and me too. As Fist said, we'll likely need all the firepower we can muster."

Wow. There's Ellen taking command again, and this time Fist approves. While she grins, Andranalapsis hesitates. There's not really very much he can say though. If we stay, we probably die. If we move, we probably die. But if we don't move, that access tunnel isn't going to come looking for us. With a wave of his hand the assault weapon is handed over to Fist, which puts an even bigger grin on her face. For Ellen and me there are sidearms: big, black, chunky things. That puts a bit of a grin on my face too. Ellen's is purely functional, a means to an end, and that end she means to achieve without further delay.

"Good. Now unless I've completely lost my bearings, the side wall is that way. Keep it tight, keep it silent. We stop for nothing, unless it's another one of those things."

She leads with Captain Andranalapsis close behind. The rest of us follow, weapons raised but hearing nothing, not even skitterings.

Unfortunately no one told Mommy GPS and now she's becoming passive-aggressive. "Return to position, please. Unauthorized movement may result in avoidable casualties. Military code subsection three, clause eight clearly states—"

With a stab of his finger Andranalapsis turns Mommy GPS off. That seems a little unfair. She was only looking out for our best interests after all, which no one anywhere has ever said about AI, including my husband and he should know. Maybe I should take one of those consoles home with me. It would be something nice for him to play with.

For now there are more important things to be thinking about. Silently we continue along the passageway, passing through two more intersections before reaching the long passageway of the outer wall. There we hear something. It sounds like distant gunfire.

Someone's got themselves into a fight, and Ellen hardly needs to ask. "Yours?"

Andranalapsis nods. "That's our exit. You were right. We need to get there while we still control it."

That's easier said than done though. We've hardly taken a step before we see something stalk out into the passageway ahead of us. It's not another one of those beasts, but that's hardly an improvement. This one is the size of a staghound, with a long snout lined with dagger teeth, talons, high shoulders like a big cat, and scaly skin. If Mommy GPS was still with us she'd probably be scolding us, "See. I told you so, but you never listen, do you? No, you just go and do whatever you want. I don't know why I bother, I really don't."

As a second one appears behind it, we bunch up to a halt. Big yellow eyes stare greedily at us. Rows of spines rise along the creatures' backs while drool drips, splashing and splattering on the floor, and the creatures are growling. This is not good, and it's Fist who puts into words a thought that must be occurring to the rest of us. Well, it is to me anyway.

"How many pets does the Great Og have?"

"Pets? They look more like a hunting pack to me." Thanks, Andranalapsis. We really needed that.

The troopers in our rear are sounding nervous warnings too. Two more of those creatures are stalking out of the passageway that brought us here and another two are padding along the outer wall passageway. Perhaps we should have listened to Mommy GPS after all, because we've just walked into an ambush.

Then it starts, with all of them coming at us at once. One leaps at me, bowling me over. It's standing over me, lips trembling as it breathes foul breath into my face and shows me the teeth that are about to rip my throat out. Wrong move, doggie. If Captain Andranalapsis can stick a gun in a beast's mouth, so can I. It goes off and the creature collapses, pinning me to the floor. Orange goo dribbles from its mouth like treacle, plop-plopping onto my face. It's disgusting, like being slobbered on by a bloodhound. It's also irritating—not quite acid for blood but there's certainly a dash of chili juice about it.

"Will somebody please get this thing off me?"

No one does, but then they are rather busy. The sound of firing is continuous. There's a lot of shouting too, a confused melee that I'm not seeing any of. There's no choice but to try and wriggle my way out from underneath this dead weight on my own, all the while trying to avoid the dribbling goo.

Then there's a hand grabbing my wrist. Someone is trying to rock the creature off me.

"Debbie! Debbie, are you okay?" It's Ellen. "Hang on. We're getting you out."

The creature rocks some more. Ellen and somebody else are tugging at me. Slowly, by degrees, I'm dragged out from underneath, and not a moment too soon. There's still firing going on. The last of the creatures are busy mauling at two of Andranalapsis' fallen troopers, but somewhere way back in the distant gloom behind us there are more guards and once again they are filling the passageway with red tracer.

"Run! Run like the Greens are here!" Ellen doesn't need to say it twice. She's beside me. Others are behind. The firing is following us. Fist must be back there. I hope so. The same goes for Captain Andranalapsis. The passageway ahead of us disappears into a gloom that might be endless. The firing up there is getting slowly louder, the firing behind never lessening. We might be racing into another trap—until there's something about the air that changes. A large chunk of rock appears, followed by more, a debris field scattered all over the passageway floor that leads to a gaping hole in the side wall. Now there's blue tracer and answering red tracer. Ellen adds her fire to the blue tracer. The two troopers with us join in. After a moment's hesitation, I join in too. None of us can see what we're firing at. It doesn't matter. It's spray and pray again.

We reach the opening. There were four troopers defending it. Two are now dead. One of the remaining two pauses long enough to wave us through. Ellen immediately turns around to take up a position between them and add her fire to theirs. I stand back, wiping orange goo off my face as I look back through the opening at the curtain of red and blue tracer filling it. Somehow Captain Andranalapsis bursts through it to join us. He brings Fist with him. They both look like they've been mauled, Fist with clothing torn and bloodied from ugly-looking gashes. That's not going to stop her though. No sooner is she with us than she's firing too.

So far so good, mostly, but we're not done yet. We're only halfway out, and now Captain Andranalapsis takes charge. "Fall back! Fall back! Two in front, two in the rear. Move."

Two troopers run into the lead. Ellen follows, with Fist and me close behind. Captain Andranalapsis and the other two troopers bring up the rear. We're headed into darkness, the orange-red dimness of the passageways barely reaching beyond a few feet. Fortunately the troopers have their own lights. In those beams we can just about glimpse the walls and ceiling of a tunnel. It's huge and roughly hewn, with outcrops like buttresses in its sides and big bellying clumps hanging down from the roof. It must have been carved out long ago and then forgotten, along with the finished stone blocks we pass, all of them sitting on the crumbling remains of rollers.

At first all we hear is the crunch of sand and gravel beneath our boots. Then we hear something else, faint at first but steadily coming closer. We slow to a halt, listening. It's a kind of rushing sound, like waves on a beach. Above that are squawks and squeals, all of which makes it sound like we're about to be trampled by a stampede.

Unfortunately Fist doesn't appear to know what a stampede is. "What's this? They've sent an entire army after us? Maybe we should wait for them and send what's left scuttling back to their Great Og."

That doesn't sound like such a good idea, especially not to Captain Andranalapsis. "We came here to get you out, not die trying. I've already lost half my squad. We must be nearly halfway through this tunnel. We keep going and fight only if we have to. Captain Praganathulis?"

"I agree. We keep going, and fast. They're getting closer all the time."

They are, and only Fist looks likely to object. If that's what she wants to do, she'll be doing it on her own. The rest of us are already moving, dodging blocks in the bobbing and weaving of the troopers' lights. There are other obstacles too: chunks of rock that have fallen from the ceiling and slides of rubble where the walls have subsided. All the while, the rushing wave and the echoing squawks bear down on us. Then comes the first of the red tracer, zinging through the air and pinging in wild ricochets off the walls. For a short distance we continue to run, but the intensity steadily grows until Captain Andranalapsis is forced to give the order. "Take cover. Return fire."

I dive behind a block. Ellen is there with me. The squealing and squawking are loud now. At the very limit of the troopers' beams of light we can see them, a horde of arms and legs and burning yellow eyes. It's like something out of a zombie movie, a maniacal collective hell-bent on taking down anyone who isn't them. Whatever they're on, right now I could do with some of it.

We return fire but only for a few moments. Our blue tracer can't miss and we hear screams. They might be screams of rage though, because then they reply and the tunnel is filled with red tracer. It's a hailstorm, knocking chips out of the walls and ceiling which rain down on us. Some of them are razor sharp and it's not long before both Ellen and I are cut, larger lumps forcing us to huddle up as we try to protect each other. This is impossible. Only a lunatic would try to move and only a mad person would stay. This might very well be the end.

CHAPTER FIFTEEN

Explosions: one, two, three of them. Screams and squeals, then three more explosions. The shards and lumps stop falling. The red tracer is diminishing. From behind us come three lights. There's blue tracer as well, with Captain Andranalapsis and his three troopers, along with Fist, adding their fire to it. Ellen and I remain down, watching the lights approach as another three explosions boom around us. One more of those and we'll likely be deaf for life. Instead there's a low rumble, growing into a crashing, hissing, sliding. They've brought the roof down, burying the Great Og's army beneath a pile of rubble. That's good, until a thick cloud of dust rushes over us.

All we can see are the beams of troopers' lights. As the reverberations of it all die down, we can just about hear the leader of the newcomers as he brings his men to a halt before Andranalapsis. "Sir. The end of the tunnel is secure. I left three men guarding it and hurried down here as soon as we heard something happening."

"Good for you, Sergeant, because we're almost spent. Now let's get out of here before any more of them turn up. At the very least, we've got cuts and bruises that need attending to."

There's certainly more than cuts and bruises here. It's all right for them. They're wearing visors. Ellen and I have hands clamped over our mouths as we try not to breathe in the dust. Fist probably does too, if we could only see her. It's not only the dust cloud that's making it difficult to see. It's the grit in our eyes as well.

Hands grab us and we're dragged to our feet. There's no ceremony here, just blind stumbling as we run through almost complete silence, accompanied only by the crunching of our boots. As the dust cloud clears, through tear-filled eyes I can see a growing, irregular circle of orange sky ahead of us. Beyond is a desert-like landscape, rolling folds of rust red populated with plant life. Purple fleshy creepers reach out around thick, bulbous cactus-like cores, interspersed with low bushes, and spiky grasses. Somewhere out there is Andranalapsis' ship, and that's an awful lot of open ground to cover with the Great Og almost certainly not finished with us yet.

Joined by three more troopers, we set out at a steady trot. Our eyes scan the horizon all around but particularly behind us where, in the middle distance, there sits the top half of the Great Og's pyramid. Rise follows rise in front of us, and it's from behind us they come. The Great Og really doesn't want his dinner escaping. There are things on the ground which are too big and too fast to be guards. There's something in the air as well, a black blob that might even be some kind of helicopter. The Empire of Og has air support, and we find this out now?

At the top of another rise, at last, the ship is sitting in the hollow below us. It's small and sleek, a horizontal, flattened-out cone, white and tinged with red from the light of the small sun above us. Its ramp awaits us, a stream of white light promising salvation, and it's not a moment too soon. The air support has opened fire, sending great plumes of rust red into the air and bowling two troopers down the slope in front of us. Troopers guarding the ramp rush forward to help while we follow them down the slope. At the same time, the Great Og's ground forces arrive. They're guards, all mounted upon two-legged beasts with great wedge heads and thick tails. They're the Great Og's cavalry but they're too late. Even as another firefight begins, we're climbing the ramp and it's closing behind us.

The ship bucks beneath us as it takes off. In the cockpit we can hear the flight crew talking. "Forget the ground forces. Target their bird. Take it down."

The ship accelerates. G-forces start to kick in. By now we're all strapped in.

"Incoming. Incoming. Taking evasive action."

As the ship turns and wheels, it's a good thing we are strapped in. If we weren't, there'd be broken bones everywhere.

"They have missiles. They're locked on."

"Deploy countermeasures. Now hit it. Let's get out of here."

The g-forces increase, and then fall away. On the cockpit screen, the red sky of Og has given way to the blackness of space.

"Okay, people. We're clear and coming in to dock. You're safe now."

The flight crew is happy. Captain Andranalapsis and his troopers are probably happy too. Ellen may also be happy but it's hard to tell. That leaves Fist and me, and I'm guessing from the expression on her face that I'm not the only one who's thinking frying pan and fire.

There's nothing for either of us to do but see where it goes, and where it goes first of all is a docking bay: a small hanger, all white walls and brightly lit.

Waiting for us at the bottom of our rescue ship's ramp are Major Drovenanthis and two subordinates. He smiles broadly as we come before him, offering Ellen a welcoming hand. "Captain Praganathulis. It's good to finally meet you in person. It's been quite a chase and not a little costly, but never mind. The First Security Directorate is more than pleased to have you back."

While Ellen accepts his welcome, perhaps a little reservedly, Fist is bluntly skeptical. "Yeah, about that. Who exactly are the First Security Directorate and how did you keep tracking us down?"

"Yes, you'll be the salvager. Welcome aboard." Major Drovenanthis offers her his hand. Fist isn't interested. "Well, never mind. All will be explained in due course. For now, we need to get you to the med bay and have all those cuts and other injuries looked at."

There's a quick handshake for me too, which is about as interesting as I appear to be. Then we cross the hangar floor to a portal, with Ellen and the major engaging in some off-and-on chitchat along the way. Fist and I follow while Captain Andranalapsis and his troopers disappear to somewhere else.

On the other side of the portal is the med bay. It's pretty standard, with beds and machines and cabinets, and white walls, brightly lit, with glinting chrome and glass. There's a medic too, dressed all in light gray and armed with an aerosol. Forget superglue. One spray from that and our cuts heal up right before our eyes. This could be my next Nobel Prize, along with several honorary degrees. This could become embarrassing, and all those big pharma companies that will be going out of business won't be pleased either.

After all the remaining grit has been flushed from our eyes, there's a quick examination. Once the medic has cleared us all, Major Drovenanthis directs Ellen back to the portal. "Now, if you will. The First Security Directorate is eager to debrief you."

"Debrief me of what? You've told me I'm Captain Travanis Praganathulis of the First Security Directorate. You've told me Veniramat is a distress call. Beyond that I don't know why I was out there, how I came to be aboard a Green ship, or what I was supposed to be looking for there."

"Yes, that's right. The Greens memory-blocked you. Unfortunately I can't give you any answers. That's First Security Directorate business, too highly classified even for a major to know. My job was to find and deliver you. Now that we're here, they're waiting for you planet-side."

That's nice of them, whoever they are. This First Security Directorate sounds a little too much like their version of a three-letter agency—y'know, FBI, CIA, MI6, KGB, FSD—and that is not filling me with confidence at all.

Drovenanthis tries again. "You know we've already jumped, yes? You are now in the sovereign space of the five worlds of the Quintessant, orbiting the capital planet Marshalin. Not even the Greens can reach you here. There's nothing to worry about. You're perfectly safe."

There's a loud snort which, of course, comes from Fist. "So you say. So what about our planet? We're gods down there, y'know."

"And I'm very happy for you. It was still there when we left, although not very communicative. Someone will decide in due course what's to be done about that."

"Someone? Did you miss the bit where I said it's our planet? We found it. That gives us the rights. There's our ship as well, still sitting there outside the Great Og's pyramid, unless you've rescued it too."

"No, it's still sitting there. Rest assured, we're keeping an eye on it too. Now let's get you planet-side. The sooner you're debriefed, the sooner your questions can be answered." Drovenanthis is smiling, but it's a crocodile smile. His two subordinates aren't. Fist could probably take them all without even messing up her braids. That would only leave the entire rest of the ghost ship to deal with. Well, there are three of us: the super spy, the salvager, and the hero of Og, except that we don't have weapons anymore. Captain Andranalapsis took them back before we arrived. Property of the FSD apparently. Everything has to be signed back in or questions will be asked and someone might end up assigned to some horrible ice world with a thousand miles of nothing in every direction and not even any vodka. Someone will figure that one out of course. There's always some guy who knows how to make liquor out of rocket fuel, or maybe that's rocket fuel out of liquor.

Anyway, Major Drovenanthis is still smiling. His subordinates still aren't. One of them approaches the portal, raises his left arm to the side of it, and says something. It opens, and there beyond it a white room is waiting for us. There are also four black uniforms, two of them armed and visored. The other two are standing with their hands behind their backs, very relaxed, very confident, very sure that non-compliance isn't even an issue. It isn't, and Ellen steps through easily enough. For her this is coming home, even if she can't remember it. Fist, tight-lipped and the most likely to balk, takes a moment longer.

Once we're all through, the portal closes behind us, and one of the officers steps forward to offer Ellen her hand. "Captain, welcome back. If you'll come with me? Your companions will be looked after while we debrief you."

The officer approaches the portal, raises her left arm, and speaks. It opens. This time there is a white corridor on the other side. The officer steps through, and again Ellen follows without even so much as a backward glance.

The portal closes and the second officer steps forward. He doesn't offer us his hand, but then he doesn't need to. Those two armed guards are still here. "Please, if you'll follow me."

He repeats the portal opening ritual, and there beyond is another white corridor. This one has doors spaced along it. I've seen this before. Last time it was all gray and it was Nosundomi. Wherever they've taken Ellen, it appears we're being taken to holding cells. No pressure though. The officer is still being impeccably polite, with those two armed guards to back him up. "Please."

Halfway along the corridor a door opens. There's no handle or pad, and the officer didn't do it. Somebody must be sitting in a control room somewhere watching us through invisible cameras. If there are cameras on the inside too, that could be a little awkward. At least it's not some pokey little cell. It's a moderately sized room done up like a lounge, with sofas and a coffee table. There's a large screen on one wall showing a nice soothing landscape: a meadow with tall grasses waving in a breeze and distant mountains beneath a deep blue sky. There's even the scent of wildflowers, the perfect environment to relax in before they start the nasty stuff.

"Please make yourselves comfortable. If you require anything, just say so and someone will be along shortly." As the officer finishes, the door slides shut and we're alone. Fist is at it instantly, feeling all over and around it for some hidden means of opening it, but there isn't any. We are locked in. It's the most pleasant holding cell anyone's ever been held in, but it's still a holding cell.

She moves to the center of the room. The officer said, "Just say and someone will be along shortly," and she means to test that out immediately. "Hey! How about you open the door?"

Of course nothing happens, even after she's called out two more times. So that's it then. We've been suckered. Fist mutters and fumes, but there's little point to that. Far better to make the best of it, or so it seems to me. There's another door in the opposite wall. It leads to a small bedroom with a washroom beyond. If they're both listening and watching, there's no way that's being used until absolutely necessary. The bed's another matter. The last time I slept in a bed was my not-very-long nap on Greeter Prime's god world. Before that it was in my own bed, and how long ago that was I honestly can't remember. Right now my husband might be making an appeal on local TV. Search parties might be out combing through woodland and culverts. My kids might be sitting there with one or other of their grandparents, asking when Mommy's coming home. At this rate, God alone knows if I'll ever see them again.

No. I refuse to think like that. I am going home, somehow. Whatever it takes, I will see them again.

~

Sometime later my eyes open. It takes me a moment to remember this isn't some hotel room, although there might be room service. I could certainly do with something to eat.

Back in the main room, the only thing that's changed is Fist. No longer fuming, she's sitting on the sofa, first of all staring at the big screen and then watching me as I sit opposite her. "You're awake then."

"Yeah. Sorry about that. You hungry? Because I am. Maybe we could order some food."

"You can try. They're not answering, or at least they're not answering me."

"Maybe that's because of your sunny disposition."

"Oh, ha, ha. Very funny. Anything else you wanna get off your chest while we're sitting here staring at somebody else's vision of paradise?"

"Nope. Can't think of a thing. Still, you could be a little less in everyone's face, y'know. What could it hurt?"

"It could hurt a lot, believe me, like it's probably hurting Ellen right now. Hasn't it occurred to you that we might not see her again? Hasn't it occurred to you that one of us is probably next? If they come for me I intend to be all over their faces and everywhere else too."

"Yes, it has occurred to me, but they're her people and they said debriefing, not interrogation. And since they probably know a lot more about this than she does, when she comes back we might actually find out what all this chasing about has been for."

"*If* she comes back. For all we know, she might be dead already. Debriefing, interrogation: It all sounds like torture to me."

"Yeah, well. There's torture, and there's torture. Where I come from, trying to renew your driver's license is a kind of torture, believe me."

I should have known better than to try flippancy.

"Renewing a driver's license, whatever that is. Is that one of those quaint little rituals you have on your world? Does it involve sacrificing someone to the god of driving licenses and then eating them? Well, this is just great. I'm stuck in a white room with a primitive."

"Do you think you could stop doing that? I've proven my worth here, y'know. It was me who figured out Greeter Prime's god world while you were busy sticking your fingers down your throat, and it was me who escaped the Great Og's kitchen all on my own, bringing a weapon with me while you were stumbling around in the basement. A little respect, y'know. That's all I'm asking for."

Fist snorts, and that's where the conversation ends. The landscape continues to play on the big screen. The minutes drag by, a silence made that much worse by the sulkiness of my only company.

Fortunately it doesn't last that long. The door opens and Ellen enters. Fist is instantly on her feet, fit to explode.

Ellen holds up calming hands. "Hold on. Everything's good. Just relax. No, shush."

Fist opens and closes her mouth. Somebody's face might be in serious danger at some point around here, but it's not happening right now.

Ellen has already turned to me. "So, Debbie, they want to give you an examination. It's nothing to worry about. Just sort of tying up the loose ends, that's all. They want you too, Fist."

"An examination! What kind of an examination? Didn't we just have one of those on their ship? And what loose ends? Do you know what this is all about or don't you?"

"I know some of it."

That only makes Fist more insistent. "Then tell us. What is going on here?"

"I can't, not yet. Like I said, there are loose ends to tie up. The sooner we get this done, the sooner everything can be explained. As to what kind of an examination, it's just a medical, like the Nosundomi gave Debbie when she had her chips implanted."

"So you say. How do we know what they did to you out there? You could be—"

"It's just a medical, okay. And they didn't do anything to me. Just relax, Fist. No one is going to harm you. So what do you say, Debbie? Are you up for it?"

Just a medical, like the Nosundomi gave me. "Are there going to be needles?"

"They'll want a blood sample, but that's all. No implants or anything like that. So what—"

"Why? What's so special about my blood?"

"That is what we'll find out, if there is anything to find out. Look, it's just a medical. The sooner it's done, the sooner it's over. So what do you say?"

Somehow I'm not entirely convinced. Nor is Fist, and we're both weaponless. So once again it comes down to a simple choice. Do what they want or remain in this cell, unless they decide to turn nasty.

"Okay, but it better be just a blood sample."

"Good. Let's get this done then." Ellen leads us out.

Waiting for us in the corridor are the officer who brought us here and four guards. Why we need them if it's just a medical is a good question, but Ellen has never lied to me before—not that I know of anyway. The portal at the end of the corridor opens, and beyond is another white room. This one is very different. There's a big chair in the center of the floor. It's laid almost flat with a large machine standing behind it, almost as if they've brought me here for an ultrasound scan. That doesn't seem very likely. There are more machines blinking and bleeping around three sides of the room, interspersed with tall cabinets, all chrome and glass. The fourth wall has a door at one end with a long window filling the rest of it. In there are more machines and cabinets, the whole thing brightly lit by a ceiling that's one big, seamless diffuser.

Waiting for us are two men and a woman, all in white gowns. The two men don't look at all like doctors. In fact they look rather like bouncers. Big, beefy, and glowering very unsympathetically, they are standing with their arms firmly folded. Somebody will be taking their medicine today, and that somebody is me. I could be wrong of course. They might be really cute and sweet. They just got out of bed on the wrong side this morning.

The woman is far more welcoming, rushing toward me with an outstretched hand. "Hi. I'm Doctor Molinapsis. You must be Debbie. I love your hair by the way. I might have to give that color a try myself."

She has a bright smile, hazel eyes and short, dark hair like Ellen's. She's also rather obviously trying to put me at ease. This is just an examination. Absolutely nothing to worry about. "Now let's get you up onto the chair so you can make yourself comfortable, and then this will all be over in just a few ticks."

So you say, but then I'm the one outer space is turning into a pin cushion.

"Oh, come now. You're not afraid of a little examination, are you? Up you go. There. First of all, I'm going to check your medical record."

As I lie back, still unsympathetically watched by those two bouncers, she produces one of those smartphone-sized ID readers very like the Nosundomi's. My left forearm is scanned. The result produces an expression verging on disappointment. "Hm. Nothing there. I'll run a scan. Lie back and hold still, please."

"Perhaps if you tell me what you're looking for I might be able to help."

"Now just lie back and hold still, please. This will only take a moment." She turns to the bank of machines behind me. The ceiling immediately above me turns pale blue. This is going to be one of those Nosundomi things with me pinned to the chair again while the doctor has her evil way with me. But not quite—there's a bar of red light that moves slowly from my head toward my feet but that's it.

We're done, with Doctor Molinapsis looking even more disappointed. "Very well. A blood sample it is then."

"Really. What is it you people are looking for?"

As the ceiling turns white again her only answer is a smile, and—surprise, surprise—here comes the needle. It's a very small needle, but all the same. I swear I'll never sit in one of these chairs again, not ever, and this time I really mean it.

"Now just a little prick and then it's all over. There, didn't hurt at all. Great. So you relax while we get this analyzed, and then we'll have a little chat." She has a very good bedside manner, a lot better than Splog's anyway. If she asked me for a kidney, it might be hard to say no. Fortunately she's satisfied with the blood sample and hurries away to the other side of the glass. Except for two of the troopers, everyone else follows, the door sliding shut behind them. They gather round to watch as she runs the analysis. It's probably fascinating for them, watching all that science in action. On the other side of the glass, it's pure boredom. What this place needs are some mood music, a few magazines to flick through, and a nurse to make small talk and take my mind off what's happening on the other side of that glass. Instead there are the two troopers, and they might as well be made of stone.

There isn't even one of those screens to show me a nice,

soothing landscape: maybe a forest with rays of early morning sunlight bursting through foliage, or a lake rippled by a breeze and the occasional fish jumping. There's only that glass and the group of people huddled behind it as they analyze my blood. Typical. They're all busily engrossed in their science stuff and the patient, me, can only stand on the sidelines wondering what's happening. Hello. Excuse me. Would somebody—

Then things suddenly become interesting. The analysis is done. Doctor Molinapsis is talking, pointing at the results. Then it's Ellen talking, looking bemused. The officer is next, with Ellen shaking her head. Fist is standing off a little, listening to it all. The two bouncers are listening too, and at the same time casting me glances that are a very long way from cute and sweet. Something isn't right, something about me. They've discovered something, or they've failed to discover something. Let's hope it's something they've failed to discover because it would be real disappointing to come this far across the universe only to be told they've found a tumor.

The discussion continues with Doctor Molinapsis once more pointing at her results. The officer listens and then wags a finger at Ellen. She shrugs. She might be in just as much trouble as me. The two bouncers are looking more and more unpleasant with every passing moment. Then Fist steps in. This could make things a whole lot worse. But no, everyone is listening. Ellen is being interrogated. Fist is gesticulating. Whatever she's saying, Doctor Molinapsis is nodding. The officer is nodding too. This is like watching a silent movie. Shame there aren't any of those text frames to explain what's going on.

One person who isn't nodding is Ellen. She's shaking her head. The discussion is now an argument. There are heated words and stabbing fingers, until Fist waves Ellen away. Now she turns to the officer. She's demanding something. Whatever it is, the officer hands it over. Belligerently stone-faced, Fist turns to leave. Maybe she's storming out, going home to Grinder. Ellen tries to stop her but the two orderlies hold her back. This is fascinating. I can't wait to see what happens next.

Disappearing from behind the glass, Fist enters the examination room. That thing she demanded from the officer is a sidearm. She very much intends to use it. Those two troopers don't stand a chance, except she's ignoring them. She's coming toward me. She's standing in front of me. She's pointing that sidearm at me.

"Y'know what? This is something I should've done the first day I met you."

"What? What are you doing, Fist?"

"What am I doing? I'm getting some payback, sweetie. You've been a pain in my ass all the way here, always whining on about your weird little planet with your weird little ways and your weird little words. Why did I ever listen to you? I could be sitting next to my old boss watching the sun set right now. Instead I'm here and it's your fault. Well, guess what, Earthling? This is where it ends."

Oh my God, she means it, and when Fist says she's going to do something she does it. She's coming closer, step by step, with a cold and merciless glint in her eye. She's piling on the pressure, enjoying the moment, and no one, not even those two troopers, is making any attempt to stop her.

"Hold on, okay, just hold on a moment. Look, Fist, if I've done something to insult you, I—"

"Insult me! You've done nothing but insult me. Every time you've opened your mouth you've insulted me!"

"Somebody help, please!"

No one does. They're all standing there watching.

"What is wrong with you people? Fist, stop, okay. Think about what you're doing. This is—"

"Oh, I am thinking about it. I've been thinking about it for some time, and now I'm going to blow your face off."

This chair has some mysterious hold on me. I can't get out of it. I can't crawl any deeper into it. My mouth is dry. It's suddenly become hard to swallow. My heart is racing.

"Fist, no!"

CHAPTER SIXTEEN

Doctor Molinapsis rushes in. At last somebody's going to stop Fist—except she isn't. There's a needle in her hand. I don't believe this. She's taking another blood sample.

"What the . . .?"

She leaves. So does Fist, shrugging as she lowers the sidearm. "Sorry about that. Had to be done."

"What?"

They're all back behind the glass, with Doctor Molinapsis busily analyzing her new sample. Everyone else is watching and waiting, except for me. This is beyond weird. This demands an explanation, and by God, I'm going to get one even if it kills me. Jumping off the chair, I head for the door but it's sealed tight. No amount of beating on it is going to shift it.

"Open this door, goddammit! Open this door, and tell me what's going on."

No one does, and that includes the two troopers who are still with me. They might as well not be here for all the interest they're showing. I could wreck the place for all they care. Well, okay then: The glass is next. Turns out it's unbreakable. All that my hammering on it does is have everyone on the other side staring at me.

"Will somebody please tell me what the hell is going on?"

The door slides open. The two orderlies march through it.

"Don't you dare! Don't you dare touch me."

They do, and very unsympathetically. They're dragging me away, and once again, no one is doing anything to stop them.

"Ellen! Fist! Why don't you do something?"

Ellen is watching blankly, as if this is some kind of waking dream to her. Fist has problems of her own. The officer has taken back the sidearm and the two troopers in there with her each have a hand on her shoulder. So that's how it's going down. Whatever Fist was doing a few moments ago, it's Ellen who's selling me out.

"Ellen, you bitch! Ellen, do something!"

But it's useless. The portal opens and moments later I'm tossed back into that most pleasant of all holding cells. Hammering at the door is as pointless as when Fist tried it. She's probably in another cell exactly like this one, and as for Ellen, well, this betrayal is total. I should never have listened to her. I should never have trusted her. I should've demanded to go home the moment those Greens were dead. Instead here I am, almost right back where I started, and this time no one is coming to rescue me. Fury grips me. There's no words for it other than pure rage. If screaming was enough Ellen would be squirming by now, but then she's all but emotionless and probably not capable of it. That bitch is so gonna wish she'd never been born.

Eventually the rage passes. There's no one here to pass the time with but myself. There's nothing to look at but that damned screen with its meadow of rippling grass. My God, can't they at least change the scenery? Time drags slowly by, increasingly filled with thoughts of home. I may never see it again. I'm trapped on a planet that might be a million light-years from Earth. I have no friends, no allies, and I've probably been declared an actual intergalactic bioterrorist.

Home. Volunteers must be out by now. It won't be just woodland and culverts they'll search. It'll be vacant lots, rivers and streams. It could take days, with a little bit more hope lost for each day that nothing is found. At the end of it all there'll be regretful condolences, maybe a memorial service, and an open missing person's file. And then everything will go on as before, with nothing left of me but some old photographs and videos. God, I hope my husband doesn't spend the rest of his life obsessively watching them because that would be too awful. Even thinking about it brings me to tears, with more tears of desperation heaped on top because God alone knows what these people mean to do to me.

Sometime later the door slides open. It's Ellen, with Fist behind her, and both of them are wearing officers' uniforms. Don't know why, don't care why; all I'm seeing right now is red. But before I can make a move toward Ellen, Fist leaps forward to place a hand over my mouth and whispers into my ear, "Don't make a fuss. You know they're listening. They're watching too so we need to get out of here now."

Not before a small matter of treachery has been dealt with, we don't. I struggle, but Fist isn't about to be argued with. "It's not what you think, okay? We'll explain later. For now, we need to get out of here before alarms start going off everywhere."

Ellen is saying nothing, which is probably a good thing. Well, okay, maybe this is a rescue. They better have a damned good explanation though because one of us is not forgetting about any of this any time soon.

Meeting Fist's cool but determined gaze, I nod my agreement. We walk out into the corridor, with Ellen leading the way and Fist keeping a firm hold on my arm.

"Until we're out of here, you're our prisoner and we're taking you somewhere else. If anyone challenges us, you let Ellen do the talking. So just be patient and keep your mouth shut. Can you do that?"

I'll think about it, and Fist takes my silence as assent.

"Good. All we need is enough time to get out of here."

By now, we've reached the end of the corridor. Ellen raises her left arm to the portal and says something. Nothing happens. She tries again. Still nothing happens.

This is all very familiar to me, but not to Fist. "Open the damn portal, will you?"

"I can't. They must've canceled my ID."

"Canceled your ID. What d'you mean, they've canceled your ID?"

"I mean all portals in the Quintessant are ID-activated. If you're not cleared on the system, you're blocked. We need to find some stairs and fast. We're running out of time."

At the other end of the corridor is a door. It's also ID-blocked but Ellen quickly solves that problem with a few well-placed shots from her sidearm. There's a stairwell on the other side. Portals must be like elevators. If the building catches on fire, use the stairs. The same goes for daring escapes from security compounds. We clatter halfway down to the next landing. The door there opens. An officer and two troopers burst through, weapons raised in readiness. Ellen is quicker, putting all three of them down. That's one way of doing the talking, I suppose. Picking up the officer's sidearm, she thrusts it at me. "Time's up. Take this. We're fighting our way out."

She and Fist head for the next flight of stairs. I don't know how big this compound is but fighting our way out doesn't seem like such a good idea, especially when we've just been presented with a much easier alternative.

"Wait. We need an active ID to operate the portal, right? Well, we've just got ourselves one, haven't we?"

The officer is lying there at my feet. Come on, guys, it's simplicity itself. It takes them a moment to think it through. Maybe her ID died with her. Maybe not, because Ellen is springing into action again. "You two carry her. I'll lead."

She's already back up the stairs before we've figured out how best to carry the officer. Fortunately she's not too heavy. By the time we reach the door, Ellen's halfway along the corridor. There are sounds from above and below us. More troopers are on their way. We're not hopelessly cornered yet though, until the portal opens in front of us. Ellen opens fire. Troopers on the other side fall. The portal shuts. Thank God for energy busing or whatever it was that the Nosundomi guard on Demaroven called it. We reach the portal. Ellen slaps the left forearm of the officer to one side of it and barks a destination. The portal opens and we step through.

We've entered an office. It's shabby, in the way only underfunded public sector offices can be. There are hard-wearing carpets, with several untidy desks scattered around and walls plastered with posters: information, instructions and photographs of several unsavory-looking characters. It could be a police precinct in any big city. Over the other side from us are three officers, two men and a woman, all sat together at a desk chewing the fat. Crime must be way down in this precinct.

Before they see us, Ellen whispers, "Third Security

Directorate. They don't know yet so we're going to walk out nice and easy."

That piques my curiosity. "How many security directorates are there?"

"Shush. Start walking."

We make it perhaps a third of the way across the floor before one of them notices us. "Can I help you?"

"No, we're good thanks. You can get back to your busy day." All three of them are watching us now, and Ellen's comment isn't making us any friends.

"Because FSD's got it covered, right? Us boneheads would just mess things up."

"Pretty much, but we'll be sure to let you know if we need any grunt work doing."

We're almost across the office. A few more steps and we're in the clear. The TSD officers have already lost interest. "FSD, huh? A bunch of . . ."

While they're busy bitching, we step through a door into a reception area. There's a long counter, posters on cream-colored walls and hard seating. It's about as welcoming as its bleak lighting. At least it's deserted.

With Ellen and Fist still wearing their own clothes beneath their discarded uniforms, we step outside, and it's like, wow. This city makes New York look vertically challenged. It's ten times taller and ten times brighter. Somewhere up there is the sky unless these buildings reach all the way up into space. Down here at street level, neon is everywhere: storefronts, restaurants and bars. Immediately above are big flat-screen billboards enticing the lazy crowds wandering by beneath to buy everything from soap to spare part surgery, pens to politicians, and everything in between. There are even holograms projected down onto the sidewalk. None of the beautiful people walking through even notice them. And they are beautiful people, all perfectly formed, perfectly manicured and perfectly dressed, like walking mannequins and with about as much expression on their prettily painted faces.

Out in the wide, wide street there are vehicles sliding by almost soundlessly: great, fat, sleek ones, bulbous-nosed, encrusted with chrome and with smoked windows almost too narrow to see out of. They could be out of an old movie and filled with wise-cracking gangsters on the prowl for someone to slap around.

"Those things are beasts. They must guzzle gas like there's no tomorrow."

As she peers along the street, Ellen replies, "Gas? If by that you mean hydrocarbons, we stopped using them a long time ago. Everything is electric, generated by fusion reactors and delivered through cables buried beneath the pavement, like your Wi-Fi."

She's looking for something—an FSD SWAT team, maybe.

"Is that why you don't have flying cars?"

"No. We tried that once, but a pile-up is a pile-up and having idiots joy riding in flying cars turned out to be not such a good idea. Too much hot metal and too many body parts falling out of the sky."

The very next second something does fall out of the sky, splatting loudly and unpleasantly onto the sidewalk away to our left. It's a body, or what's left of one after it's pancaked. It's horrible, truly awful, and my hands go straight to my mouth. Everyone else continues to stroll by, not the least bit concerned, even the ones spattered with blood. This is too weird, an entire planet as emotionally dysfunctional as Ellen. It doesn't even seem to bother them that whoever this person was who just committed suicide, they might have landed on someone and taken that poor unfortunate with them.

"Oh my God. What the hell?"

"Don't worry about it. This happens all the time. We'll talk about it when we've got you safe. Right now we need a cab."

"A cab! Seriously? Somebody just jumped and you're looking for a cab?"

Without answering, Ellen sticks her hand out. Almost immediately a red monster with indecipherable writing on its side glides to the curb. We get in, and it's not a moment too soon either. Even as we disappear into traffic half a dozen FSD guards pile out of the precinct office to scan the street for us. They don't appear to notice the mess on the sidewalk either.

"Isn't anyone going to—"

Urgently, Ellen whispers, "Be quiet. These cabs are monitored so don't say anything."

That's me told then, and Fist as well. There's nothing for us to do but settle back into the deeply squishy upholstery and wait for Ellen to tell us what to do next. A couple of blocks away she does, and we take another cab. By the time we step out of a third the bright lights and sky-high buildings have been left behind. The buildings here are still tall but they're shabbier. The street is shabbier too, with graffiti and litter and people hanging out in doorways. Others hurry by with their heads down and their hands thrust deep into their pockets. Every city has its downtrodden poor hidden away in some ghetto, I suppose, and Ellen has brought us slap bang into the middle of this one.

While Fist is looking around with as much concern as me, Ellen is almost looking pleased with herself. "Okay. So far, so good. Our next step is new IDs. When they scanned me they took all my credits, but I'm guessing they didn't take yours so paying for what we need won't be a problem. After that we'll do a little light shopping so we look like tourists. Then we'll portal up to the docking station and buy tickets for the shuttle to Volumundus. It's a resort world so there'll be lots of people passing through. Once we're—"

"A resort world? You have a resort world?"

My astonishment is barely noticed.

"Well, it's more of a moon, but yes, we have a resort world. Don't get too excited though. We're not actually going there. The tickets will get us through security and boarding. Once we're on the other side we steal the shuttle and jump out of this system. Simple and elegant, right?"

Not if your name's Fist it isn't, which she makes perfectly clear by commenting, "Yeah, real simple. So what's plan B?"

"We'll worry about that later. For now, this is TSD territory. They maintain civil order, street crime and stuff like that. It'll take a while for the FSD to liaise with the TSD, argue over who's in charge and who gets credit for the arrest, etc., etc. We should have enough time to get in and out. From here we walk. It's a couple of blocks this way but keep your eyes open and your weapons ready. This is also clan territory."

That's reassuring. Walking down a darkened street with lurkers watching from doorways isn't exactly a fun place to be but, fortunately, no one bothers us. We must be walking with way too much attitude for that. It's for sure that they are taking note though. Runners will be running and bosses will be thinking, *Three women, on my turf, as brazen or as dumb as can be. Maybe there are credits to be made here.* My sidearm remains firmly in my hand. Resorts have visitors but they also have attractions and I certainly don't intend to end up as one of those.

We come to a building that looks no different to any of the others. Ellen knows it and takes us down a side alley even darker than the street. Hidden away at its end is a single eye-level red light which Ellen reaches up to press. "Hey, you there?"

After a few moments a voice replies, "Yeah. Who're your friends?"

"Doesn't matter. We got business to put your way, if you're interested."

"Always interested in business. Come on up."

There's the click of an opening door. We step through and then climb dark and dingy stairs to a modestly lit second floor. Waiting for us there is a man as slovenly shabby as his surroundings. A haircut, shave, shower, and clean clothes wouldn't go amiss. His eyes are bright enough though.

"Wasn't expecting to see you again. Vancy K's still lookin' for you, y'know."

"Vancy K's a schmuck. Now we doin' business or what?"

"Yeah, sure. Whaddya need?"

"New IDs and passes for the docking station."

"Okay. I reckon I can do that for five each."

"Five each, huh? I tell you what I'll do. You keep your mouth shut, like you never seen us, and I'll make it an even twenty."

"Deal. It'll take a few minutes so make yourselves at home. There're cans in the fridge, if you want."

Well, this is a side of Ellen I haven't seen before: the hard-boiled doll who ain't no moll. That's a story waiting to be told, but not until my story has finished, the one I'm sitting bang in the middle of without even a clue as to what's happening or why. Once we've cleared enough junk from a couple of tattered sofas to be able to sit down, it's time someone started telling it.

"So, Ellen, you said you were going to explain all of this. I don't know about Fist but right now, I'm sitting on the edge of my seat, literally."

There's a pause, with Ellen staring into the distance, probably collecting her thoughts. Or it's so bad she's trying to figure out how to let me down easy. Come on, Ellen. It's my story. Give it to me.

At last she bites the bullet.

"About thirty years ago a new drug hit the streets. It quickly earned the name D, short for Devil Wings because it quite literally makes people think they can fly, until they hit the sidewalk. I mean, seriously, there are people falling out of the sky, like the one you saw earlier. And they develop other abilities as well: strength, speed, and absolute fearlessness. They also became highly disturbed, fearful, and paranoid. The First Security Directorate was tasked with finding out what this drug is and where it's coming from.

"We identified it eventually, and we established that the clans were supplying it. The next step took us a while but we finally figured out that the clans were being supplied by the Greens. And that, for some time, was where the trail ended, until the decision was made to infiltrate the Greens. I was the one tasked with doing that. I still can't remember exactly how I did it but the rest of it I know now because I've read the files."

"Okay. So that's why you were on that Green ship. But what does any of this have to do with Earth? What does any of this have to do with me?"

"Unfortunately it has everything to do with you. The last piece didn't fall into place until we gave you that examination. The first blood sample contained nothing. After Fist walked in there and threatened to kill you, the second sample was full of it."

"So Fist sticks a gun in my face and I start . . . Wait. You're talking about adrenaline. D is adrenaline."

CHAPTER SEVENTEEN

Shocked hardly begins to describe how I'm feeling right now. For Ellen it's just another line in her report. "If that's what you call it. The fact remains. The source of D is Earth. The source of D is you."

"But how can that be? You're human, the same as me. You must be able to make adrenaline."

"Clearly we aren't. Your body can make D, ours can't, and that includes Fist's. I can't explain it. No one in the FSD can. The whole matter's been referred to the Council of Experts."

"The Council of Experts?"

"Yes. They've been running the Quintessant since the end of the last war. That was centuries ago. It's possible our lack of adrenaline has something to do with that, but that's just conjecture. The Council of Experts will investigate. We can only wait for them to pronounce upon it."

"Because they're experts and experts are always right until they're not and even then they're not wrong. So where does that leave me? Where does that leave Earth? There are civilizations all over the universe. We can't be the only ones who make adrenaline."

"No, but you are the only ones who are virtually defenseless. There could well be others, but you're the ones the Greens somehow stumbled across. They're greedy sons of bitches, always on the lookout for a profit and they don't care how they get it. Somehow they figured it all out. They abduct you, scare you into producing it, and then milk you for it. Then they bring it clear across the universe and sell it on our black market. There were more than enough clan bosses here willing to help them and they all got rich out of it. Now they protect themselves by buying up officials, security directorate officers, maybe even council members. It's a huge problem."

"Are you kidding? The Greens are the biggest drugs cartel in the known universe and we're their opium poppy, nothing more than a herd of cattle to be milked? I don't know what you're laughing at."

I mean it. What's so funny, Fist? Please do tell me, and she does. "Oh, come on. You gotta admit it's pretty amusing. Some weird little planet no one's ever heard of turns out to be undermining one of the most advanced civilizations in the known universe. And you with your red hair have just become the most important person in this part of the known universe. I think that's hilarious."

At least Ellen is still taking it seriously. "Hilarious or not, Fist is right. It's not just the Greens anymore, or Grinder, or the Xvr. The council wants the source shut down. That was the point of my mission, to find it. They don't know where Earth is yet but they'll find out."

"And then what? Are you saying they'll attack Earth?"

"The supply of D must be stopped. That means wiping

out the Greens or wiping out the means of production. The Greens are everywhere. Earth is one planet. As far as the council will be concerned, wiping out Earth will be the more achievable option."

"The more achievable option! Are you for real? They can't do that. Earth is my home. I've got a family there. I've got relatives and friends. Hell, I've even got people I don't like very much there, but none of them deserves that. We have to stop them, or stop the Greens."

"Oh, so you don't want Earth to be wiped out but you'll happily wipe out the Greens."

And thank you again, Fist. What I really need right now is a snarky comment like that.

Then it gets worse because Ellen hasn't finished digging a hole for me yet. "We need to deal with the problem that's in front of us right now: namely, you. News of you will leak out. Maybe it already has. You're a walking, living, breathing source of D right here among them, and every single clan boss on this planet will want to get their hands on you. The one that does won't need the Greens anymore. The one that does eventually won't have any competition either. He or she will lock you down, milk you and maybe even try to create an entire farm off you. That's why we have to get you out of here and as far away as possible."

"Well, great! I guess it's true what they say. You're not paranoid if everyone actually is out to get you, and your entire planet as well. So what about you? You're prepared to risk everything you lost and found for me?"

"I already have. I can't remember much about my previous life; you already know that. All I know about this is the files they showed me. You and me, we're friends, aren't we? Shipmates? We've survived the Greens, the Xvr and the

Great Og together. So has Fist. There's an entire universe of trouble waiting for us out there, with more to come, but we'll figure it out. We'll find a way. So what do you say? Us versus the universe, and the universe better watch out." Ellen holds out her hand, palm down.

With barely any hesitation, Fist places her hand on top. "Sounds like fun. Us versus the universe it is then, and the universe better watch out."

Sounds like fun, she says, like we're just popping out for a bottle of merlot. Well, us versus the universe is pretty full-bodied and likely to be very red and green and who knows what other colors as well. But then, you gotta do what you gotta do, right?

They're already committed, and Fist isn't appreciating my hesitation. "Hey Earth girl, it's your planet we're pledging to save."

"Us versus the universe it is then, and the universe better watch out. I guess that means we've just become the three musketeers."

As my hand lands on top of theirs, Ellen and Fist gaze blankly at me. If we ever do make it back to Earth they're going to have some serious reading to do.

Ellen's contact calls us into the room next door. It's filled with screens, blinking boxes and cables. If the state has everything tagged, including the cabs, this must be their version of low-tech. Our IDs are changed with a single sweep of something that looks like a barcode reader, and we have passes for the docking station. We're good to go: back down the stairs, along the alley and out into the street. That's as far as we get. Waiting for us are six meatheads and one slick-head.

The latter gives us a big toothy smile, the kind that says

he's da guy. "Good evening, ladies. Now, which one of you is the milker? It's okay, I already know." He stabs a finger at me. "You'll be coming with us."

"I don't think so." It's seven against three, but Fist probably thinks those are good odds.

Slick guy's smile turns icy. "I don't need you two but the milker is coming with us, so why don't you show some smarts and walk away?"

Weapons are being drawn. There's going to be a fight, but not the one everyone's expecting. Spotlights light up at both ends of the street. As they glide toward us, a whirring sound comes from overhead and spotlights appear there too. We're lit up like a circus ring, and the ringmaster's voice is booming, "This is the Second Security Directorate. You will all lay down your arms and lie down with your hands behind your heads."

Slick guy and all his goons look behind them. Suddenly they're not so sure of themselves. Fist is in her element though. "Us versus the universe, right?"

No sooner have we agreed than she draws, aims, and shoots out one of the spotlights above us. Before anyone else can react, she shoots out the other one. The SSD immediately fires back from both sides and up above. Slick guy and three of his goons go down in the first burst. The rest of us duck for cover behind the two cars they came in. Two of them are away to our right. The third is with us. Fortunately their cars are bulletproof, which makes sense if they're the local mob.

The two goons over there are returning fire, which isn't particularly getting us anywhere. With blue tracer bouncing around all over the place, our goon appears to be waiting for us to tell him what to do. Well, that's meatheads for you. If they're not completely clueless they're in a competition to see who can run out of ammunition first, and it's probably not going to be the SSD.

Us girls can do better, or at least Fist can. "You two stay here and help keep them busy. I'm going hunting."

Before anyone can object she's off, running at a crouch along the sidewalk. Somehow the SSD troops fail to notice. Perhaps meatheads have their uses after all. Speaking of which, Ellen and I add our fire to theirs. All the other spotlights are quickly taken out, and in the pale street lighting we can see the black-visored SSD troops firing from behind their vehicles. Leaving them to the goons, Ellen opens up on the flying machine, its underside hovering above us like a gray ghost. I help her, filling the air with tracer like lasers at a rock concert. Come to think of it, some heavy metal would just about complete this scene. Maybe when they turn my bestselling memoir into a movie, I can make sure to mention it.

Meanwhile back in the real world, another goon has gone down to our right, but away to our left the SSD fire is lessening. They must've realized they've got something else to worry about, that something else being a particularly aggressive salvager called Fist. The flying machine is having second thoughts too, suddenly whirring away into the night sky. That leaves only the SSD troops away to our right, and all of us turn on them. The firefight is quickly over, with what's left of the SSD turning tail. The other goon to our right has shuffled off to the great clan in the sky as well, leaving only our goon who rises with a huge grin on his face. "I guess we showed them, right?"

Ellen smiles back at him. "We sure did."

Then she shoots him in the head, which seems rather ungrateful to me.

"What did you do that for? He was on our side."

"No, he wasn't. They came to take you, remember?

Besides, we need their vehicle to get out of here and I rather doubt he was just going to hand it over."

Well, there is that, I guess. All the same, though.

"They're gonna be really pissed when they find out, aren't they? The SSD and the godfather, by which I mean their boss."

"Wouldn't be at all surprised."

Fist strolls over to join us. "Not bad for a few minutes' work, wouldn't you say? Now, since they were kind enough to leave us their vehicles, how about we get out of here before any more of them turn up?"

Not bad at all if leaving the street littered with bodies is your thing. A quick getaway is another matter. Both of these vehicles are locked, with somebody's thumbprint needed to open them. Since dragging seven bodies over to find out which one works isn't really practical, rather gruesomely seven thumbs are cut off. When the one that works is found, Ellen slips it into her jacket pocket. And this is supposed to be the most advanced civilization in the known universe, according to Fist.

The inside of the vehicle is really plush: more deeply squishy seats with plenty of legroom, and view screens if anyone feels like watching some local TV. No one does, and once Ellen has programmed the autopilot, we're on our way as smoothly as gliding on air.

"So how far is it to the docking station?"

Ellen glances at me. Apparently I haven't been listening. "The docking station is in orbit. We'll have to find one of their outlets and portal up to it. The shuttle leaves in just over two hours. So, first of all, since we need to look the part, we're going shopping."

"Yay! Oh, come on. You gotta like shopping."

Some deeply unamused looks say otherwise, and a short

but silent drive later we pull up curbside in the middle of more bright lights and crowds of evening strollers. The vehicle is dumped. Its owners might have a tracker on it. So might the SSD if that's how they found us out in the sticks. As we mingle and blend, once again I'm taken by how beautiful they are. Both men and women are all made up and wearing weird-shaped hats, dresses and suits, svelte or full-bodied, nipped and tucked, all of them in shimmering chameleon fabrics. This isn't a sidewalk so much as a catwalk, and as we walk among them, I barely notice the holograms we're walking through.

After a couple of blocks we come to a mall. Inside are more casually gorgeous people browsing their way past brightly lit stores filled with all sorts of shiny things while buy-me music fills the air. We're hitting the clothing stores, each of us with an allowance shared out from what credits Fist and I have left and with instructions from Ellen to buy one piece of luggage each as well.

About an hour later, I'm strutting my stuff in a mid-thigh dress with a plunging neckline front and back. It's basically metallic silver but every movement I make causes it to shift and flow through rainbow colors like some kind of living tie-dye. It's a little like wearing a kaleidoscope. The shoes are silver too, and so is the chunky jewelry. Hey, this is outer space. Everybody gets to be whatever they want, including a mom with two kids.

Ellen and Fist don't quite see it that way though. They turn up looking like they just left job interviews, in chic but staid pantsuits and sensible shoes, and Fist isn't at all impressed with the choices I've made. "Really? You couldn't find anything more conspicuous? Maybe we should strap a big flashing red light to the top of your head."

"I'm blending in, okay, looking like all the beautiful people. Besides, we're supposed to be heading to a resort world, aren't we? We should be looking like we mean to have fun, not going to a business meeting. You look like a pair of asset strippers, instead of . . ."

Maybe not. Giving Fist more ammunition out of my own mouth isn't going to work any better than it did last time. There's something else far more important to deal with anyway. On the far side of the concourse two men have appeared. Stone-faced with slicked-down hair and wearing the kind of long leather coats it's easy to hide weapons under, they're clearly on the lookout for something.

"Girls, I think maybe we ought to get outta here."

Ellen hasn't seen them yet. "Why? We've got new IDs, unless my man sold us out, which is unlikely since he thinks I'm a clan assassin."

And now they've seen us. Okay. Time to get real. "Fire! Fire!"

Every face on the concourse turns to look at me. On Earth they'd all be running for the exits. This must be what it looks like when an entire civilization decides adrenaline is surplus to requirements.

Frowning, Fist asks, "Why are you shouting fire? There isn't one."

"Because no one comes running if you shout rape."

Ellen chips in with, "But you're not being raped either. The only thing you're doing is making everyone look at us."

"My God, Ellen, will you just look!"

At last she does, and Fist too, and not a moment too soon either. Those two men are making their move. They're coming straight at us with hands thrust into their coats. Everyone else is standing watching like this is some kind of street theater.

"Oh my God! Quick! Run!"

Ellen and Fist aren't listening. They're drawing their weapons, because that apparently is what people do when their only response to danger is cold calculation. Those two men are nearly halfway toward us. Their own weapons are now barely concealed. There's going to be a firefight in a crowded mall. There are going to be bodies everywhere, with an audience of onlookers not even thinking about self-preservation.

"No, you can't do that. Look at where you are. Look at all these people. You can't start shooting here."

Somewhat surprisingly, Fist is the first to get it. "Yeah, you're right. Come on. We best get out of here before a whole lot more of them turn up."

They already have, with two more appearing in the distance. That settles Ellen's mind too and we set off with our suitcases trundling behind. The crowd closes in around us, blissfully unaware of the tragedy they were so nearly involved in. They hamper us, getting in the way and forcing us to weave among them, but they hamper our pursuers too. The mall stretches ahead of us, seemingly endless. Then every screen in the concourse is suddenly showing a big head, and she's not helping either.

"Fellow citizens. We have just been informed by the highest authority of the presence of an intergalactic bioterrorist among us."

So now it's official, and just to confirm it, there's a great big photo of me on the screen.

"This woman is considered to be extremely dangerous. If you see her please retreat to a safe distance. Second Security Directorate personnel will be with you to deal with the situation directly."

Well, this is good. Now we've got three security directorates after us, not to mention the now six leather-coated guys who are on our tail. At least the crowd clears in front of us. They might be as vapid as sheep but they're obedient sheep.

With the way ahead clear, we run. The other end of the mall comes into sight, but that's the end of the good news. There are more of them waiting for us. We've run out of road. As we trundle to a halt, one of them swaggers forward to meet us. He's wearing a great big grin on his fat, round face like he's just won the lottery. As far as he's concerned, he probably has.

"Well, look at this, guys. We just caught ourselves an intergalactic bioterrorist." He comes to me, leaning in until he's barely inches from my face. "I know someone who's very interested in your body."

"Why? Does he want to lick it?"

He chortles. "I wouldn't know about that. All I know is he wants you. Now hand over your weapons. We need to be somewhere else before the SSD turns up. And you can dump those suitcases too. You won't need them where you're going."

With little choice in the matter, Ellen and Fist grimly comply.

I'll be damned if I'm giving my suitcase up though. "Oh, come on, man. I just spent an entire month's salary on party clothes. Don't you want to see me all dressed up nice and ready to party? Come on, baby, drink it all in. Wouldn't you want to party with me if your boss wasn't taking it all for himself?"

Apparently not. He's not even bothering to smile anymore. Oh well. It was worth a try. "I said, dump the suitcase."

"And I said no. I'm the one he wants, remember? You want me, you take my suitcase as well."

He thinks about it. He can't lay a finger on me and we both know it, or at least that's what I'm hoping. Everyone else is looking at me like I'm crazy. It's just a suitcase. Leave it. But the SSD are on their way. They could be here at any moment.

As much as he doesn't like it, at last he accepts it.

"Okay, you can keep the luggage. Now get moving."

"Why, thank you, sweetie. I knew you'd understand. Now give me your arm. That's right. We'll walk out of here like we're gonna party all night and everyone will be jealous of you."

Two people who definitely aren't jealous are the two dark clouds trailing behind us. Their scowls could blister paint. It wouldn't be any surprise at all if Ellen and Fist thought my performance was the first step in me selling them out. That's okay. Like the Xvr, my dour date hasn't done his job properly. He hasn't checked my suitcase. He doesn't know about the weapon I have stashed inside.

Parked up curbside are two chrome-encrusted monsters. I slide into one, with my date and three of his goons filling the rest of it. Once Ellen and Fist have been pushed into the other one, with more goons surrounding them, we slide away into the neon brightness. What lies ahead of us is an unknown. What lies behind isn't.

"Baby, aren't you afraid the SSD are going to track us?" Right now I'm rather hoping they do.

He's smiling again though, blithely confident. "Why? You don't like my company? Forget about them. Our vehicles aren't exactly to spec. So long as we're on the inside they can't track us. And even if they could, who's to say we don't own them? One call and it all becomes a big misunderstanding. 'This is not the woman you're looking for.' So sit back, enjoy the ride. We'll be there soon enough."

Turns out the ride is over sooner than he expects as another chrome-encrusted monster flies out of an intersection and sideswipes the vehicle Ellen and Fist are in.

CHAPTER EIGHTEEN

Our driver brakes hard, bringing us to an abrupt halt in the middle of the street. He also has an impressive command of some pretty colorful language. Parts of it don't translate very well but the gist of it is, "Learn to drive, you idiot!"

My date sees it differently. "That doesn't happen unless they disengaged the safety protocols. Everybody out." Stabbing a finger at me, he adds, "Not you. You stay here."

The other vehicles have stopped maybe twenty feet ahead of us, one on each side of the street. There's a whole crowd of people wandering by barely interested. We just about avoided a shootout in a mall. With goons piling out of vehicles on both sides of the street, all of them pulling firearms, somebody needs to do something before it ends in a bloodbath here instead.

Fortunately there's a breathing space as one of somebody else's goons calls out from the other side of the street, "Hey, melon head"—or so my ULD says—"You didn't really think you were just going to walk away with the prize, did you?"

Melon head, also known as my date, calls back, "In case

you haven't noticed, clown boy"—again, so my ULD says— "we outnumber you."

"Not for long. We got more guys coming so why don't you be a good"—my ULD doesn't even try to interpret his insult this time—"and hand her over."

While this fascinating discourse continues, I open my suitcase and rummage through clothes that will now never be worn outside of the store. They looked so good in the changing room. Sidearm in hand, I slide across the seat and step out onto the sidewalk. The crowds have stopped wandering. There's that lack of adrenaline again, and the poor fools don't even know it.

Before me is twenty feet of no man's land. Not a problem. My dress is a lightshow, my walk is a sashay, and that ought to be enough to have any man's jaw dropping.

Three steps in and my date notices. "Hey, didn't I tell you to stay in the car?"

"Yeah, but you know how it is. Us girls never do what we're told."

"I mean it! Get back in the car!"

Sorry. No can do. I'm beyond the nose of our monster now. The goons taking cover behind the one in front of me have noticed too. They're watching, jaws slowly dropping. An increasing number of the crowd has what I'm guessing must be their phones out. They're videoing it.

Across the street, clown boy is also watching. "Is that her? No one shoot! Any of you hit that woman and you'll be collecting debts in a mining colony for the rest of your life."

That's right, boys. I'm the prize, and there ain't a damn thing you can do to stop me.

That doesn't stop clown boy from trying though. "Hey, beautiful. Why don't you come on over here? We can offer you a way better deal than those mongrels."

Sorry. Got my own deal in mind.

"Oh, come on, baby. We can work something out."

My date's reply turns the air blue. Not sure how that'll play on all the streaming services those videos will be uploaded to. It's a pity because me and my shimmering dress walking through this neon wonderland with a small army of goons pointing their weapons at each other and unable to fire a round could be irresistible viewing. A star is born, the angel who walked through the valley of death and prevented carnage. I could be an overnight sensation with advertising deals and my own cheesy sci-fi show, *The Girl from Planet X* or something like that. All those security directorates might think twice before messing with a property like that.

I arrive at the rear of Ellen and Fist's chrome-encrusted monster. They're still inside, but the goons with them are all staring up at me as if they can barely believe the heavenly intervention they've just witnessed. Time to break the spell before somebody else does. "Hey, boys. Y'all better close those mouths before you catch something."

That's enough to wake one of them up. "Boss said you're to get in the car. Get in this one now."

"No, I don't think so."

He turns his weapon on me. "Don't make me shoot you."

"And deliver damaged goods? Figure it out, numb nuts. You can't shoot me." My sidearm is leveled at him.

"I can shoot you though. Hell, I can do whatever I want."

"Yeah? Well, how about we shoot your friends instead?"

"Then I start shooting and you still can't shoot me. Guys, come on, it's not that hard. Now be good, put your weapons down, and move away from the vehicle. We'll be taking that too."

Some sheepish glances are exchanged. Yeah, I know, arm candy does what it's told, not the other way around. There are two faces looking up at me from inside the vehicle as well: Ellen and Fist. They can barely believe it either. The mom from Earth just turned gangsta. Who knew?

At least the goons are convinced. Laying down their weapons, they raise their hands and back away.

"There you go. So easy a five-year-old could do it."

That produces some sour looks. My date shouts something from way behind us, but no one is paying him any attention. Ellen is already out of the vehicle, gathering up weapons and throwing them to Fist in the back. Once she's done I follow, and she jumps in front to take over the driving, gliding us toward the next intersection even as the SSD comes howling by. Those guys we left behind, they really aren't having a good day at all.

Fist, on the other hand, is. Wearing a huge grin, she might even have forgotten about my dress. "Way to go, girl. Not only are you an intergalactic bioterrorist but you might also have started a clan war. Y'know, I'm beginning to think you Earthlings are way too crazy to be let loose on the rest of the universe."

"Weren't you the one who said if it's crazy enough for normal people to run away from then it's crazy enough for you? Besides, this is a normal day in Chicago. Now can we go shopping again? I've got nothing to wear."

Both Fist and Ellen burst out laughing at that, with Fist adding, "You are completely insane. If Earth ever develops portal tech I may have to find a different universe to live in."

"You can rest easy on that score. We're a long way from escaping our asylum yet."

A block further on and the crowds stroll by as if nothing

has happened. Well, if bodies falling from the sky mean nothing to them, what's a little clan war? Traffic is sparse but there's still enough for us to blend in. Not that it would matter if anyone was inclined to take notice. The SSD are busy giving someone else a hard time.

All the same, going nowhere isn't much of a plan, as Fist points out. "So what are we doing now? I'm guessing we aren't walking into an outlet and portal-teching our way out of here anymore, not with every clan and the regular authorities on the lookout for us."

"We're safe enough for now. That guy told me their vehicles aren't exactly to spec. So long as we're inside, they can't track us."

My attempt at reassurance doesn't convince Ellen. "Maybe, but that only makes this vehicle the problem. For all we know, these clans have their own means of keeping tabs. They could be closing in on us right now. We need a way off this planet and fast, and if we can't use any portal tech our only option is a spaceport. There are plenty of them around, private and military, mostly for transporting cargo. The problem is getting to one. If we can do that, we should be able to steal a ship like we planned to before."

"Or we could persuade someone to give us one."

"Really? We're gonna persuade someone to give us a ship? Oh, I can't wait to hear how the crazy Earth lady is gonna make this work."

Fist is laughing again, but Ellen is less dismissive. "You have a plan?"

"Sort of. Look, if this vehicle is tracked, it's only a matter of time before they find us. We're going to have to deal with them sooner or later, so I say let's make it sooner. Park up and let them find us. When they do, let me do the talking."

"Because you're gonna make them an offer they can't ignore."

"Well done, Fist. You almost got that down perfectly. But yeah, I'm gonna make them an offer they can't ignore. Don't worry about it. I got this."

She shakes her head. Ellen says nothing. We drive on, leaving the bright lights behind. In another run-down suburb with poor street lighting and darkened doorways, we slide to the curb and wait. Huddled figures slow as they walk by. They check out our vehicle and then hurry on. No one from around here is about to mess with the clans.

Inside our vehicle the silence grows slowly more awkward, until Fist can no longer contain herself. "Y'know, this has to be the most ridiculous escape plan anyone has ever thought of. I mean, who just sits here waiting to be caught? Can't you at least tell us why we're doing this? What this big plan of yours is?"

"No."

If I did that they might both flip out on me. What Fist needs is something to keep her mind off it, something that might lighten the mood for all of us.

"Does this thing have a radio or something like that? Listening to some music might help pass the time."

Ellen reaches down to press a button.

The interior fills with music, the kind of late-night thing that's supposed to send you to sleep, but Fist still isn't satisfied. "So you're not going to tell us your plan then?"

"No, I'm not. Just trust me, okay? You want off this planet? What I'm offering will get us off this planet."

"Well, fine. Don't tell us then. It can't be any stupider than this."

Oh, it can be and it probably is, but it's the only plan

we've got and it's too late to back out now. Two vehicles slide into view behind us. As they pull up to the curb, one in front and one behind, Ellen and Fist are given a quick reminder.

"Let me do the talking, okay. If they don't buy what I'm selling, we're no worse off than before."

"Except for the bit where we're now their guests."

"Oh, just get out of the vehicle, will you? My God, we were already their guests until I got us out of it. That was me, wasn't it, Fist? I'm the one who got us out of it?"

She glowers but silently gets out. Everyone else does too, all of us toting hardware and eyeing each other up like it's the last-chance saloon. There are four goons behind us and four more in front. Fist watches our rear. Ellen backs me up as I take a step forward.

"Hey, boys. We were beginning to think you might've lost interest."

Some of them are watching us. Others are watching the street, the darkened doorways and the even darker alleys.

"Oh, come now. You're not expecting an ambush, are you? If we wanted to turn you in to the SSD we would've stayed where we were."

One of them steps forward. He's almost indistinguishable from the rest, apart from his air of command and the faint smile he manages to crack. "It's not the SSD we're concerned about. It's the other clans, but then you're way too resourceful for that, aren't you? You take on two clans and make both of us look like fools. You take our vehicle, and then you just sit here like you've got all the time in the world. Perhaps you should explain what the deal is with that."

"The deal is we want to talk to you on our terms."

"On your terms."

He casts an eye over the four goons behind us. The three

behind him, he takes for granted. "There are eight of us and three of you. Those don't seem like very convincing terms to me."

"Really? You want me to explain it to you again? You can't—"

"Yeah, yeah, we know but, you see, here's the thing. The boss has decided you can manage without a leg, maybe even an arm. So long as the rest of you is intact, we're good to go."

"And you'll risk that, will you? One misplaced shot and you'll risk me bleeding out. Then you and your boss get nothing. Or you could listen and understand that what I can get for you is so much more. Plus if you start shooting, so do we. You wanna risk losing a leg and maybe a whole lot more? Why don't you give your boss a call and ask him if your insurance covers that, assuming you have medical cover of course. I can't imagine someone in your line of work would, what with the high risks involved."

He tries to stare me out. "You do realize it will be a very short firefight?"

But it's not going to work. "You do realize you'll be shooting at your own men and they'll be shooting at you?"

That gives him pause for thought as he glances again at the four men his tactical genius has placed behind us. Dumb. Or maybe it's not his decision. Maybe his boss has been listening the whole time and now he's receiving orders. "Okay, but we'll be taking those weapons first. Boss gets awful nervous around guns, especially when they're being held by a woman. This wouldn't be the first time one of them offered him a sweet deal only for him to find out she was an assassin sent by some guy who ain't here anymore, if you take my meaning."

I do, but that's okay. His boss will be perfectly safe with us, unless it all goes pear-shaped of course.

Disarmed, Ellen goes in the first vehicle and Fist in the last. I'm back in ours with two of their goons to watch over me. No one's talking so there's nothing to do but watch the world slide by. First of all the slum gives way to more bright lights, the third such area we've been through. This city must be huge, a sprawl that goes on forever. Beyond that the buildings diminish, becoming apartment blocks then individual plots with all manner of houses. There are glass boxes like fish tanks, giant pods under-lit like ships that might take off at any moment. There are rectangles on stilts and squat towers and anything else that the fevered brain of a mad architect might dream of. There are also clean streets and trees and parks and bright lighting, and even the occasional jogger. It's not so different from any upmarket suburb on Earth, where even now the whisperers might be saying my husband did it. *That's right. He buried her somewhere out in the woods. Look at him sitting there, being so strong for the kids. The gall of the man, but we know. Yeah, we know what you did.*

Slowly the plots grow larger, the trees crowd together, the lighting becomes more discreet, and the streets turn into lanes. Then the walls appear, too high to climb but floodlit from underneath and razor-wired above. These people don't want unexpected visitors and, just to be sure, every gateway has armed guards. At one of them we turn in. The gates swing gently open and our vehicles follow a winding gravel drive. On both sides is parkland, close stands of trees and shrubs with tasteful statuary scattered carelessly about. There are more guards too, loitering on the edge of pools of light cast by ornamental lamps.

All of this is nothing compared to the mansion that appears ahead of us. The architect who designed this wasn't just mad. He must've been stoned as well. It's like someone blew a small mountain of bubbles out onto the ground and then turned them all to glass. Mirrored and lit up from without, it might also be some kind of Christmas tree that somebody hung way too many baubles on.

Our vehicles slide around a fountain, coming to a halt before seeping stairs. They lap layer upon layer as if some liquid had been spilled and left to set level by level until they reached the flattened ovoid funnel of an entrance. Within is a hall like the inside of an egg. It rises several stories, each one with a balcony from which more security watches. Spiraling staircases connect them all but we're led downward into a more functional world of corridors and doors with keypads, coming finally to a room that looks like an executive's office. There's a rich carpet, and big screens on the walls. On one side are sofas and a coffee table. On the other is a long table lined with chairs. At the far end is a huge desk cluttered with knickknacks and one of those huge throne-like chairs. That immediately has me thinking short man syndrome, and I imagine a little gnome perched on his throne, barely able to see over the desk.

That's not what enters the room through a side door though. There are three of them, all looking like accountants. While two of them hang back, the third comes to stand before us. He's getting on for six feet, lean, perfectly manicured and wearing a plain navy suit. His gray eyes take us in one by one before finally coming to rest on me, his lips parting in a thin smile. "You must be the woman of the hour, if not the century."

"And you must be the godfather, the don."

"I don't know what either of those terms means, but I am the head of this clan. You can call me Max, by the way. And you, I believe, are called Debbie."

He holds out a hand. Even as I shake it, Fist takes the opportunity to stir things up. "You must be a pretty insecure clan boss, judging by all the security. You expecting a war?"

His gaze wanders indulgently toward her and then, meaningfully, back to me. "Somebody already started a war. That's something we usually try to avoid. It's bad for business. It's quite an achievement though, considering you've only been on this planet for, what, a couple of hours? As for the security, it's a sensible precaution, nothing more. Now I understand you have a deal to offer me. Please, be seated."

Ellen, Fist and me sit on the edge of one sofa. He sits opposite with the coffee table between us. The other two accountants stand behind him, looking down their noses at us, their super-computer brains probably already calculating risk factors and profit-to-loss ratios. That already amounts to one hour of the boss's valuable time, plus the use of three vehicles and several goons who have other things to do, other people to intimidate. Add to that the whole war thing, and right now the balance sheet is seriously in the red. My offer needs to be good, very good, but then it is.

"You want D, right? You currently get it from the Greens but you want me because that way you can cut them out."

He nods, his smile fixed halfway between a hyena and an alligator.

"What if I could offer you an alternative? Direct access to the source, cutting the Greens out entirely. What if I could double, even triple, the supply?"

Ellen throws me a sharp what-the-hell-are-you-doing? glance. Just bear with me, okay? I knew you would react this way but don't fly the plane into the side of a mountain yet, not until our host has been coaxed on board anyway, and he doesn't seem at all inclined to buy a ticket yet.

"Cut the Greens out entirely. Double or even triple the supply. Those are some pretty big claims you're making. Perhaps you'd be good enough to tell me exactly how you intend to live up to them."

"You know how the Greens obtain D, right? Of course you do. That's why you want me. I'm the only one on this planet who can make it. So how much do you think you're going to make out of milking me? How much do you think you would make out of breeding a herd of me, if that's even possible? Your clan wasn't the only one out there looking for me. Do you think you could make enough out of me to supply them as well as yourself? What if you had the sole supply, and enough of it to put them all out of business too?"

"That would indeed be a most interesting proposition, but you still haven't told me exactly how you intend to achieve it."

"What you call D, we call adrenaline. Where I come from, we've been manufacturing it for years under the name epinephrine. We have entire factories churning the stuff out. To be honest, I'm surprised you people have never thought of that."

"We have, but it's not that easy. Officialdom is expensive. So are politicians. The security directorates can't always be relied upon to mind their own business, and there are the other clans with their own interests to protect. Let's just say some of them aren't that forward-thinking. So these factories: I'm assuming somebody owns them. They'd be willing to sell off-world, would they?"

"They won't care. Believe me, there's nothing big pharma likes more than another billion a year, no questions asked, and no liability. I don't know how much you're paying the Greens per unit but I'm willing to bet we could supply cheaper. Think about it. You could undercut the Greens and the other clans.

Two birds with one stone. You could corner the market and own this world."

He does think about it, but that ticket still isn't being bought. "Here's an alternative: You tell us where your home world is and we'll set up our own supply. Or you could refuse and then we'll show you how very persuasive we can be."

CHAPTER NINETEEN

Several big, ugly men enter the room. It's obvious they have no good intent in mind.

Before things can turn nasty, Fist chortles. "You don't actually think we'd bring that kind of information with us, do you?"

Our host holds up a hand. The big, ugly men stop.

"Where she comes from is called Earth. I can vouch for that because I've been there."

She hasn't, but he doesn't know that. Ellen has, but right now she's not saying anything.

"Only two parties in the entire known universe know the coordinates of Earth: us and the Greens. I don't think the Greens are in any hurry to hand those coordinates over, do you? As for ours, they're safely stowed away on the database of our ship. So whatever means of persuasion you're considering, it won't do you any good. Only our ship knows the location of Earth, and you'll need at least one of us to access the database. It's biometrically protected. You'll need a retinal scan and it will have to be at body temperature."

Wow. Another whopper, or at least it is as far as I know. It makes our host stop and think though, holding Fist's gaze as he realizes we're not quite the pushovers he thought. "And is there anything else I ought to know?"

"Yes. When the FSD finally caught up to us we were . . . Well, let's just say we outstayed our welcome. We left an awful lot of very angry locals behind us, along with our ship. We may have to use a little persuasion of our own to get to it. Now, imagine how disappointing it would be if you only took one of us along and that one of us ended up dead before you could reach our ship."

Well done, Fist. You've silenced him. His eyes wander. One hand tugs at a cuff, but there are no aces up there. The two accountants are looking a little uneasy too. Something big, red, and nasty must be flashing inside their heads. One of them leans down to whisper into his ear. Whatever that one says, after listening for a few moments Max waves him away. There's an entire planet at stake here and greed is a very good motivator. He'll even accept partners, however begrudgingly, and once more he meets Fist's unflinching gaze.

"You at least have the coordinates of where you left your ship?"

"No, but the FSD does. You have contacts within the FSD, don't you?"

"We do."

Another moment of thought and the decision is made. "Very well. We'll obtain the coordinates. Then we'll take you there—with an escort, of course, because we don't want you disappearing on us. You take my people to this Earth. You show them these factories and you obtain a sample. You bring it back to us. If everything checks out to our satisfaction, we'll have a deal. Since it will take a little while to obtain those coordinates, may I offer you the hospitality of my home? Please, order anything you want . . . except a vehicle, of course."

With everything settled, we're taken to a room on a lower level. There must be as much of this mansion below ground as there is above, with security everywhere. Our host wasn't joking. He really doesn't want us to leave, even if we could find our way out. There might be a control center buried deep beneath us, a darkened room with people peering at CCTV screens as they wait for a mouse to make the wrong move.

This room is another perfectly appointed cell: deep carpets and heavy furniture of some exotic wood, all grained and whorled so that a person could waste their entire life just trying to trace a finger around it. There are also the usual screens, each showing a different pretty scene—a stream burbling through woodland and snowy mountains beyond flowery meadows—and some sort of art installation that makes absolutely no sense at all to me. It's very plush, very stretch-out-and-forget-all-your-troubles, but it's still another holding cell, and one of us isn't at all happy about how we got here.

"Are you serious about this?"

As Ellen fixes me with a steady gaze, Fist tries to redirect the conversation. "I don't know about you two but I could do with something to eat. The last time we ate was with Greeter Prime and we all remember what happened with that, right? Could we get some food in here, please?"

Almost immediately the door opens. There it is: They're listening. While Fist deals with the guy, I try to deal with Ellen, coming close enough to whisper, "Don't say any more. You could ruin everything."

"I don't care! I want an answer. What d'you think you're doing?"

"I'm getting us off this planet, like I said I would. Now, for God's sake, keep quiet."

Our order is in. The door closes. Fist stands in front of it, watching and waiting. We all know what's on Ellen's mind. It's the very reason I didn't tell them my plan while they could still say no. There's an argument here that can't be avoided but we can't have it in this room with them listening.

"Is there a washroom? Why don't we all go freshen up while we wait for our food?"

"Sounds good to me."

Fist heads for the only other door. Ellen doesn't. This is about as angry as I've ever seen her and as stubborn too, although that pretty much comes with the territory. With my hand on her arm, she has to be almost dragged after Fist.

As soon as the door is closed behind us I turn on every faucet I can find, which has Fist confused. "Why are you doing that?"

"Because this is how we do it on Earth. Keep your voices down and they won't be able to hear us. So, Ellen, what am I doing? I'm getting us off this planet. That's what you want, isn't it?"

"Getting us off this planet! You're selling us out, both your planet and mine." Ellen doesn't quite get the keeping-your-voice-down bit.

Fist does, but she's not getting the bigger picture. "Yeah, I gotta say it looks an awful lot like that to me too."

"I'm not selling anyone out, okay? And, by the way, you helped seal the deal."

My words are greeted with barely a change in Fist's expression. For now she's staying very much on the sidelines. "Hey, this is your argument, not mine. I was born ship-side, remember?"

"Really? So what happened to us against the universe? Look, we get off this planet, we use Max's minders to get our ship back, and then we dump them. It's that simple."

It's that simple to me anyway. Not so much to Ellen. "Until the FSD finds us again. And what if we can't dump them? What if we end up stuck with Max's minders and we actually have to go through with this?"

"My God, will you stop being so anal about it? We get off this planet and figure the rest out later. Come on. We take the first step or we're stuck here with whatever it is they mean to do to us, and I already know what that means for me."

"Yes, but it's not all about you, is it? The whole point of my mission was to find the source so we can stop the flow. If this plan of yours doesn't work out, if we can't dump the minders, we become the flow. You do understand how that's a problem for me, don't you? It's my people running amok out there and jumping off tall buildings, and you've seen what that looks like for yourself."

Okay. Maybe it does need some more thinking about, some reassurance for Ellen that this isn't all about me. "Look, Fist has already said it. When we left Og we left some very angry aliens behind us. They're not going to just give us our ship back. So long as we keep our heads down, it'll be Max's minders who take all the fire. If we're lucky they'll all end up dead. If not, there'll be a lot less of them to deal with. Once we've got the database we find another ship so the FSD can't track us. Then we go back to Greeter Prime and persuade him to take on the Greens. Is that not enough for you?"

"Not really, no. What was that you said, Fist, about if, if, if? Well, here we are with more of them. *If* we can dump Max's minders. *If* we can get our database. *If* we can find another ship. *If* we can even find Greeter Prime again. So why don't you answer the question you're being asked? If any of those ifs goes wrong, we end up controlling the flow with a partner who's going to expect delivery and a competitor who's not going to take any of this lying down. How does that help my people? How do you mean to deal with that?"

"Your people? I thought you said they weren't your people anymore."

Trust Fist to be unhelpful at exactly the right moment.

Ellen fixes her with a stare. "I said I couldn't remember my life here. That doesn't mean they're not still my people, and even if they weren't D is a scourge, a curse. I wouldn't wish that on anyone, not even a bunch of pirates like you."

Oops. That's definitely not the way to get Fist on your side.

"Salvagers, not pirates, and space is a very big and wild place. Anything could happen out there and no one would ever know about it. We could run into the Greens or Grinder or the Xvr. Or someone might accidentally get blown out of an airlock so, on the whole, I think I'm moving toward the suck it and see approach. We get off this planet first. Then we figure the rest out."

This is not good, even if one of them is finally agreeing with me. Ellen is squaring off to Fist and Fist isn't backing down. Apart from anything else this washroom is way too small, as nice as it is with its duck egg-green decor and its gold fittings. If they're listening, let's hope they're not watching too. Apart from being way too pervy, us clearly not all being on the same side isn't going to help our case with Max at all.

"Okay, everyone just back off and calm down. I say we get off this planet. Fist says we get off this planet. Come on, Ellen. Us against the universe, remember? And the universe better watch out. Apart from anything else it's the only choice we've got, and not taking it won't help anyone."

The staring contest continues for a few more moments. Then Ellen nods and we're all one big happy family again—well, almost. Her reluctance is obvious, or at least as obvious as it can be, but that's something to be dealt with later.

Back out in our comfy cell, a cold buffet has arrived. It's not the feast Greeter Prime served up but it's just as varied: cold cuts of strange meats, white and salty or red and peppery, vegetables in different-colored sauces, breads, and a purple-colored drink that could almost be wine. It's all delicious and our meal passes in near silence, although whether that's down to the food or because no one dares say anything is an open question. All that does pass between us are brief requests for this or that. It's probably for the best, otherwise somebody might end up storming out. Then out of sheer embarrassment no one would look at each other, and food would be toyed with in an awkward silence until everyone could escape to their rooms for the rest of the night. But then no one is going to storm out. There's nowhere to storm out to, which makes the silence even more awkward.

It doesn't get any better once we're done eating. Ellen flicks one of the screens over to an entertainment channel, then settles back to stare at it. What we're all watching with varying degrees of disinterest is some sort of game show. There's a studio filled with lights and colors, three contestants standing behind podiums, and a host who moves things along with that usual mix of affableness and time management. How the scoring system works is a mystery—probably only Ellen understands it—but every so often the audience applauds and everyone quietly moves on. The whole thing is somehow lacking. There's no whooping and hollering, there's no real excitement or emotion. It's people doing things in a world without adrenaline where no one really ever fully engages with anything. We do it because it's there, and then we move on to the next thing. A stream burbling through a mountain valley would be more interesting. Hell, even the adverts are dull: Buy this because it does this, next.

Thankfully the torture doesn't last too long. With my eyelids drooping toward terminal closedness, the door opens. Our host has news. We're taken back up to his suite to find him still sitting on that sofa with the two accountants standing behind him. It's almost as if they haven't moved, although the accountants are looking a little less like the share price just fell off a cliff. There's another man too, staring grimly as he stands to one side with his arms folded.

"Ladies." Our host smiles, motioning for us to sit before him again. "We have the coordinates. A ship is being prepped at our own private spaceport with all the clearances already taken care of. Why don't we have a drink to seal the deal and then you can be on your way?"

"Sounds good."

It does to me anyway. Ellen and Fist are keeping their opinions very much to themselves.

"You said you were going to send some guys with us."

"Indeed." He waves a hand toward the fourth man. "This is Mr. Katzakulis. He also answers to Katz. He and his men will be your escort, which means he's in charge. He'll want to see this Earth and these manufacturing facilities you spoke of. Do I need to suggest that he is a man you don't want to disappoint?"

"Oh, I'm sure we'll get along fine. It'll only take us a few hours once we've found our ship."

"Good. Well, drink up and we'll have you on your way."

One of the accountants doubles up as a bartender, delivering four tiny-stemmed glasses filled with a colorless liquid. We all down them in one, and it's impossible not to grimace as the bite hits the back of our throats. This planet must have its own version of Siberia where the alcohol content is the same as the degrees below zero. Our host doesn't suggest a second shot, which is a good thing, or we might all end up going into space Russian-drunk. On the other hand, that might be preferable, all things considered.

At the bottom of the frozen steps beyond the mansion's funnel mouth, three vehicles are waiting for us. There are also eight men, all of them as uncompromising as Katz. Our host meant what he said: We're no longer in charge. It's the same arrangement as before with Fist in the first, me in the second, Ellen in the third, and all those men piling in wherever there's room. Before I climb in, one of them offers me a coat. It's a simple thing, plain brown and ankle-length with a high collar. Our host, the perfect gentleman, must think it's a little chilly for me out here. Or maybe not. The goon who hands it to me couldn't care less, although it's pretty clear I will wear it whether I want to or not. Max must be thinking something else then, possibly that my dress stands out like a pole dancer at a nuns' convention and we don't need the attention it might draw. He's such a dear to be looking out for me like that.

Our vehicles glide back down the drive, taking a different route beyond the gates to another part of this endless city. This area looks industrial, a square grid sprawl of long, low, windowless warehouses and factories. There are towers and silos too, all pointing like the boughless trunks of dead trees into the pre-dawn sky, all around them a mess of pipework crawling like ivy. Everything is gray in the yellow lighting of the streets and lots. It's a barren scene with not a single soul in sight and yet all the plants and factories are working, with driverless forklifts moving pallets in and out.

Most of these lots are enclosed by high-security fences. The one we come to has a wall. Our host doesn't want the world to see what goes on inside, not from the ground anyway. High gates slide open as we approach, allowing our vehicles to speed inside like a presidential motorcade, before rolling shut behind us. We come to a halt off to one side of a square surrounded by warehouses. In its center is a ship, powered up, lit up and looking an awful lot like a stealth bomber. Our host said we have all our clearances, but maybe there are times when he doesn't want the authorities to see this ship's comings and goings.

Cleared or not, somebody doesn't want this ship leaving. Even as we get out of our vehicles, spotlights shine down and a great booming voice drowns out the faint whirring of their flying machines.

"This is the SSD. You will all lay down your weapons and surrender."

Those guys sure do get around.

Looking over at Katz, Fist is decidedly unimpressed. "Well, this is good. I thought your boss had cleared all this."

"He did, with our contacts, but we're not the only interested party. There are all the other clans, all with their own contacts, and the regular authorities. The whole thing is like one big dysfunctional family. We're all the same blood. We all want the same things but don't anybody dare step out of line. Family get-togethers are the stuff of nightmares."

By now troops are abseiling to the ground, and the voice is booming again. "Lay down your weapons. Now!"

Katz isn't about to do that though, but what he is going to do he's not so sure about. SSD troops are on two sides of us, at least a dozen of them, plus who knows how many others still in their flying machines. All their weapons are trained and ready. Most of Katz's guys are trained and ready too, crouching behind our vehicles. It's a standoff, or at least it is for them. For me, it's perfectly simple: the same deal as before. If this is some other clan wanting to get their hands on me, they don't dare open fire. And if this is the Council of Experts wanting to know the location of Earth, they still don't dare open fire. Or I'm completely wrong and we're all about to die.

While everyone else stares down their gun barrels waiting for someone to make the first move, I begin the long walk toward that ship. Every SSD weapon switches to me, and the big, booming voice isn't quite so certain anymore either.

"Hold your fire. Hold your fire. You, stop. Do not take another step."

I keep walking. Fist appears beside me, wearing that huge grin of hers. "I was wrong about you. You're not insane. You're not even in the same universe as the rest of us."

"Aww, thanks. Now run."

We're halfway toward the ship and eating the ground up fast, even with me in heels.

"Stop! Stop! Arrest those women. Do not let them board that ship."

Some of the SSD troops in front of us make a move. Behind us, Katz's guys open fire. We're not waiting around to enjoy the light show. The ramp is here and we're in the hold. Close behind is Ellen. Then comes Katz and one, two, three of his guys.

The rest of them are still out there in the meat grinder, but Katz isn't in the least bit concerned about that. "Get us out of here. Everybody hold on to something."

Whoever he's talking to, the ship shudders, rises and

powers upward from the ground. The ramp is closing, but not fast enough for the third of Katz's guys. Desperately scrambling but failing to find a firm hold, he falls toward the ramp, disappearing through it while it's still half open. The rest of us grab on to anything or anyone. For me, that's the floor. It's an array of bolted-down metal plates stamped with a regular pattern of holes. As I slide toward that now three-quarters-closed ramp, I manage to jab my fingers into some of them. It's just about enough to keep me safe until the ramp is fully closed and the acceleration has fallen away.

Katz is first to his feet. Now he is showing some concern. There were supposed to be eight men coming on board with us. There are two and both of them have been hit, one of them only slightly, the other seriously. With blood dripping through the holes in the floor plates, it's obvious he's not going to make it. Just a few days ago I might have been physically sick at the sight of that. Too much murder and mayhem have flowed under the bridge since then. Besides, the SSD have unexpectedly evened the odds, which was always the plan anyway. Then the ship shudders again. We've jumped. Someone is up there flying it. That's okay. Katz's guy has given up the ghost. It's still evens then, or it would be if we had any weapons.

Now we discover Ellen's taken a flesh wound too. While Fist and I take a look at her and Katz talks to the one semi-fit guy he has left, our mysterious pilot steps down into the hold. He's lean-faced and beady-eyed, wearing plain overalls and a cap. He could be the guy who came over to fix the plumbing only to end up coming along for the ride. He could be, except for the weapon he's carrying.

"This it? This all you got aboard?"

Katz nods. "Yeah. Don't worry about it. Three of us will

be enough. We've jumped, right? We're free and clear."

"Yeah, we've jumped. We're in dead space. You'll find first aid kits in the locker over there."

"Good."

Katz works his way through the rest of us, issuing each order with a stabbing finger. "You watch them. You and you, deal with their wounds. I'll be up on the bridge."

That's us told then, and very manfully it was done too. Surprisingly as I follow Fist over to the locker, she's being remarkably quiet about it, which has me asking, "What do you want to do? We could jump him easily and then take them out as well."

"We could." Keeping her voice down, she opens the locker, taking one first aid kit out for herself and handing me another. "Or we could let it play. We still have a very angry Og to deal with. The plan was to let them soak up the fire and then make our move. I say we let them continue to think they're in charge until suddenly they're not. Now, I'll deal with him. You see to Ellen."

And that's me told as well. Well, okay then.

As I walk over to Ellen, she looks up at me like something really bad is about to happen. "What was Fist saying?"

"That we should let it play."

"So she's not going to try and take that one out then."

"No. We stick to the plan."

She relaxes a little, but not too much. "Good. Now the question is, do you know how to use an aerosol?"

I give her a teasing grin. "Nah. I'll just bang you over the head with it."

"That's what I'm afraid of."

"Afraid. What happened to all that super-spy training they must have given you?"

"It's not my training I'm worried about. Now, let's get this over with."

And indeed the first aid kit turns out to be not much more than one of their magic aerosols. Ellen's wound begins to heal over in a matter of moments. It would appear deeper healing takes longer though, and she's still nursing the wound as she climbs to her feet. Katz's guy will be limping for a while longer too.

CHAPTER TWENTY

By the time we've finished patching up Ellen and Katz's guy, we've jumped again. Katz calls us up to the bridge. His guy comes limping along behind, his weapon in hand and the dead guy's weapon slung over his shoulder. That's not so good, and it's still nagging at the back of my mind that we should've taken him when we could. But then, as Fist said, we have a plan. We're the salvager, the super spy and the nut job, the puller of irons out of fires, and we're not in the fire yet.

The bridge we arrive in is small and compact compared to the Green and Lepoorunt bridges. It could almost be the interior of a stealth bomber cockpit, although I've never been inside one. There's a small window on both sides and two big ones in front. Beneath the big ones is a more moderately sized main screen and smaller ones on either side. Beneath them is a D-shaped console with the one chair already occupied by our pilot.

Katz, standing next to him, is looking rather pleased with himself. Never mind the dead guy in the hold. "So we've arrived at the FSD's coordinates and we're about to head down to the planet. Anything you want to tell me before we land?"

Not really. We'd rather like it to be a surprise.

But, of course, it was never going to be. The Great Og's system, with its small, red sun and two little planets, is replaced on our main screen by the head, neck and shoulders of an Ogian. It might be the same one we spoke to before, with the same attitude.

"You have entered the magnificent and all-conquering system of the Great Og, Glorious Creator and Emperor of—"

Its big beady eye becomes even bigger and beadier. "You! You"—my ULD is struggling, or maybe it's too embarrassed to translate—"You shall feel the wrath of the Great Og for a thousand orbits. All the known universe shall witness the infinite terribleness of your—"

"Yeah, yeah, yeah." Fist might almost be yawning. "How's your battle fleet doing? Have they found the Xvr yet? Or is that just as imaginary as everything else? Now, we want our ship back. Prepare yourselves because we're coming down there to get it and if we don't get it, our wrath is going to be pretty impressive too."

"Your ship! Your ship! The Great Og claims right of ownership over everything in his empire. It is not your—"

"Such a whiner. So are we doing this or not?" As she abruptly breaks off communications, leaving our pilot looking a little peeved, Fist is ready to go.

Katz isn't, and no one is going anywhere until he's satisfied. "Didn't I just ask you if there was anything you wanted to tell me before we landed? Like, for instance, the fact that these creatures aren't exactly pleased to see you. And what's this about a battle fleet?"

Fist is blithely dismissive. "It's nothing. Imaginary.

Everyone on this planet is delusional. Would you believe they think their Great Og is emperor of the entire known universe? As far as they're concerned, we're all his subjects. Oh and by the way, if he invites you to dinner, just say no."

Katz digests that for a moment, and then tells our pilot, "Initiate automatic targeting. Destroy all hostiles on detection."

After he makes several taps on his console, the main screen zooms in, expanding one of those two planets into a gibbous purple ball. A few more taps and our pilot says, "Destiny, set course for selected destination. Initiate automatic targeting. Destroy all hostiles on detection."

The view on our main screen expands outward again. There's the faintest of tremors beneath our feet. Our ship is moving and that tiny dot in the center of our screen is growing. Everyone is silent, watching and waiting for whatever the Great Og is about to do.

Everyone except me. "Who's Destiny?"

Our pilot replies rather distractedly, like a person who has far more important things to do than explain the obvious to an idiot. "It's the onboard computer."

Now this is more like it: a computer you can talk to. There appears to be something missing though.

"Doesn't it talk back?"

"No. Give it a voice and it never shuts up. Who needs that when we've got women?"

Well, okay then. It's always good to know where you stand, which is something our pilot will find out in the not-too-distant future. In the meantime, sorry for the inconvenience but I have another silly question.

"Is there anything else out there besides those planets?"

"No."

"Nothing at all?"

"No. Nothing at all."

Ellen and Fist throw me glances. They know. Greeter Prime's god world is gone. It could be this ship can't detect it. It could be they've orbited to the far side of the sun. It could be they've jumped and we'll never find them again. That would be disappointing, and not only because I rather liked Greeter Prime. He might only have been an android but he was the nicest android I've ever met.

Meanwhile the purple disk of Og has grown large on our main screen, and now little silver dots are rising from its surface, which improves Katz's mood no end. "Imaginary, huh? They're all delusional and there's nothing to worry about?"

With Fist not offering a reply, Katz addresses our pilot again. "You might want to think about taking some evasive action right about now."

"You got it. Everybody grab a hold of something because we're going for a ride."

We can see them through our cockpit windows now, little dots that are quickly resolving into small attack craft. Our pilot takes manual control, making a joystick appear, and now it's almost a video game. At first our player heads straight for them. Once we're in among them he begins to duck and weave, threatening to throw those of us who haven't taken his advice around the bridge like ping pong balls. At the same time our weapons open up, streaming tracer in every direction. The return fire comes in. We can hear it popping off the hull as if we've flown into a hailstorm. This doesn't sound good at all but Katz is calmly dismissive.

"Don't worry. This ship is purpose-built. They're not going to penetrate the hull with that fire."

That's a relief. Living inside a popcorn bag is all we have to worry about. Poppity pop, and then pop some more. One by one, as our pilot plays chicken with the Great Og's battle fleet; they detonate into little exploding suns, leaving nothing behind. Then the few that remain try to fly straight at us. The Great Og's last resort is kamikazes. One of them successfully hits the hull and the entire ship shudders under the impact.

Katz is not so laid-back about that. "What in the . . .? I said evasive action. That means avoid them."

Our pilot isn't laid-back about it either. "Will you shut up and let me concentrate? I'm trying to fly a ship here. Destiny, damage report."

This is where you need a talking computer. Our pilot very quickly skims the information that's appeared in a window on his console. Then he's back to piloting the ship, not even thinking to tell us the bad news.

Ever so thoughtfully, Katz translates. "The hull's buckled but it's not yet compromised. One or two more impacts like that though, and it's likely to be a different story. Avoid them, for pity's sake. Avoid them."

Our pilot doesn't reply. He's too busy. Another one is coming in. There's a loud boom but the ship doesn't shudder. Our fire must have taken that one out before it could impact the hull. Any sense of relief is short-lived though. That one is quickly followed by another. This one makes it through, shaking everything hard. The damage report window is scrolling fast. Katz doesn't bother to translate. He doesn't have to. This time an alarm is going off. Something is seriously wrong.

Our pilot hits the gas and we run before the two that are left. They're trying hard to catch us but they can't. One by one, our fire catches them and they puff brilliantly into nothingness. Looks like we've made it to the next level, which puts a grin on our player's face, but it's only gallows humor.

"Onward and downward, people. Let's hope we don't burn up on re-entry."

Og now fills our screen, purple interlaced with rust red. More dots rise to meet us. This time they're missiles. The ones that get through explode close by but they're harmless, little more than scatter gun pellets pinging off the hull. As the launches peter out, our nose pitches upward. Og becomes an arc filling the bottom half of our cockpit windows and main screen, and then the atmosphere hits. This is not my first time riding this rollercoaster. It is my first time with a damaged hull and that curtain of fire filling our cockpit windows, and there's a very definite air of trepidation filling the bridge. Every one of us is hanging on grim-faced, waiting for that instant when we all burn.

It never comes, and down we go through wisps of cloud and occasional tracer fire until the Great Og's city of pyramids grows beneath us. At around fifty feet we halt and hover. There's an entire ground army waiting for us. All of them open fire. From outside it must look like we're not hovering at all. Instead we're being held aloft by a myriad pulsating strings of light. Destiny fires back, mowing them down by the hundreds, until the rest turn and run. Even the emperor of the entire known universe can't make the saner of his followers choose to stand in the face of certain death.

We're now hovering over a square littered with corpses. This has become an alien invasion movie, and we're the aliens doing the invading. As terrible as the carnage is, we have other business to deal with. A little way in front of us is our bunny ship, or at least what's left of it. These guys have been busy, and what's left of it looks like the shell of a car in some deprived neighborhood. All that's missing are the bricks stacked under the wheel arches.

"Well, great. Does that mean they've looted our database as well? So what do we do now? Start shooting up the city until they beg us to stop?" That would be Fist's first thought, except we've already done that and there's been quite enough death and destruction here for me.

Maybe there has been for Katz too. "No. We land, go in there, and talk to them. We've already shown them what we can do. The threat alone should be enough to get us what we came for."

"And if it isn't? You expect us to walk in there empty-handed?"

Nice try, Fist, but Katz doesn't look like he's buying it. He's supposed to be the sheepdog herding us toward Earth, but that only works if the sheep aren't armed. What a universe that would be, with gangs of woolies toting military hardware and hunting down sheepdogs everywhere. There'd have to be safe houses and underground railroads and sheepskin disguises for the dogs to go out in while steely eyed rams at checkpoints bleat to see their papers. But, officer, I identify as a sheep.

Not that Katz will ever identify as a sheep. He's way too alpha for that. But now that he only has one man to rely on, he does see the sense of arming the flock.

"There are plenty of weapons lying around out there. Just don't get any ideas."

As if we would.

Our ship touches down. Four of us disembark, with Ellen staying aboard to keep an eye on our pilot. As they rise again to hover behind us, Fist and I grab an Ogian weapon each and we begin our advance toward the Great Og's pyramid. Katz, Fist and me are in a line. His guy is limping along behind. The square is deserted, silent as an open grave. There might be nothing at all left alive on this planet, except, of course, there is. They're hiding, probably peering through door cracks and over windowsills at the wrath from above that's descended upon them. The chill air is still, with the smoke from all those fires hanging like the threat of mist, and the hairs on the back of my neck are bristling. It wouldn't surprise me at all if all those corpses were to start rising, their arms outstretched as they shuffle toward us moaning for their revenge. All that's missing is the music, something suitably eerie to make the audience barely able to watch.

The entrance to the Great Og's pyramid looms before us, an almost black hole with who knows what beyond its event horizon. It turns out to be not very much. All the dull, orange-lit passageways that were full of guards before are just as empty as the square. Up ahead is the Great Og's chamber, still and silent beneath the great weight of darkness above all those glowing globes. Sitting at the bottom of the steps leading up to the purple nest is one of them. With a crest and cloak large enough to prove his importance, he watches closely as we approach but makes no attempt to rise. Perhaps he's the one chosen to negotiate with us, the picker of the short straw, while the Great Og himself watches from the shadows.

He certainly wastes no time coming to the point. "Have you come to humiliate us again? To make us witness the death of our empire even as our sun dies, leaving us in the gathering darkness until we who were once so great likewise flicker and fail?"

Wow. That was almost Shakespearean. It is to me at least. Not so much to Fist, who's taking it upon herself to do the talking. "You're not the Great Og. Where is he?"

"Ah, such is the fall of Ogs. When we are young we take our place upon the great nest and cast our loving cloak about all our cherished worlds. But time wearies us. It grinds the kernel of our good intentions into grist, leaving only the husk of cruel experience. Wisdom is a curse when ignorance is such bliss. Woe it is—"

"So the Great Og is dead?"

"Dead? Do I not sit here before you? Am I not a creature of flesh and blood and brains and feelings? I am the Great Og, perhaps the last in that long and noble line. My predecessors strode the universe like raptors. Civilizations were hatched to rise and fall under our protecting wing, entire systems transformed from barrenness to plenty beneath our guiding hand. And now we are fallen. Now we—"

"So the Great Og, the one who was here before you, *is* dead then?"

"Sadly, yes. Our new Chef is preparing him for his final service even as we speak. So shall—"

"What? You're going to eat him?" Katz's surprise passes like water off an Og's back.

"Of course. His brain might have been curdled but there was greatness in him once. What better way to honor him than to pass that greatness on to his successors, as it has always been? In truth we should have done it a long time ago, but such is the way of things. Quiet perseverance is always so much easier than the casting of our lots into the winds in the uncertain hope of betterment. He wasn't doing any real harm of course, until you turned up. You came, you saw, you exposed the hollowness of our pretensions. Now we are laid low, unable even to resist uninvited guests. Which reminds me: Why have you come back?"

"We want our database. You can keep the rest since you've pretty much junked it all anyway. You can call it payment if you want."

The new Great Og takes a moment to mull over Fist's offer. "An interesting concept. We should accept payment for something we already own with something we already own. Excuse me if I'm missing something, but this seems to fall a little short with regard to the commonly accepted principles of commerce. Do you have any other suggestions with which to both fascinate and bore me?"

"Yes. How about we open fire again? How about we lay waste to your city until you give us what we want?"

"Ah." The new Great Og nods knowingly. "We are all the creatures of our pretensions and you, it would appear, are nothing more than a pirate."

"No! I'm a salvager, not that it matters. Look, we're not trying to extort anything out of you. Well, maybe we are, but it's our database so it doesn't count."

"Such is the privilege of power: that all things are as the mighty ordain them to be. Regardless, your new proposal is much more persuasive. I accept your terms. Your database will be returned to you as soon as we've found it. That may take a little while since everybody and their chicklets took a piece of your ship. Souvenir hunters—what's a body to do? In the meantime you shall enjoy the best of our hospitality, although I shall presume that you will not take it amiss if I do not invite you to my predecessor's funerary feast."

"You can safely presume that. As for the database, sooner rather than later would be good. I'm presuming you don't want us hanging around any longer than is absolutely necessary."

"Oh indeed. I quite see your point. Very well, then. The last great act of the Empire of Og shall be the return of your database, and none shall oppose it. Now leave me. I feel the weight of all our lost futures bearing down on me."

Poor old Og. What he needs right now is a big hug. He's not getting one though.

Fist has another demand, something that hadn't even

occurred to me. "There is one more thing. While we're here, we'd like our rock back too."

"But of course. And is there anything else you'd like? A leg or a wing perhaps? Maybe even a whole breast?"

"No, I think we're good. We'll be back later. Need I say you don't want to disappoint us?"

"Oh indeed. Disappointment is so . . . disappointing."

Leaving the Great Og to his disappointment we head for the exit, silently and watchfully.

That lasts until halfway along the passageway when Katz can't contain himself any longer. "How long ago were you here?"

Since Fist is busy keeping an eye out for guards, I reply, "About three hours ago, maybe four."

"And how long were you here for?"

"About an hour."

"So am I getting this right? You were here for about an hour three to four hours ago and in that time you caused a coup?"

I nod, with maybe a hint of smugness. "Yeah, that sounds about right."

Taking that as her cue, Fist steps forward rapidly, turns and levels her weapon on Katz. "And now we're making it two for two."

Well, this is interesting, and thanks for the heads up by the way. Of course I knew we were going to take him at some point but a little bit of a warning would've been nice, a nod or a wink, something like that.

Katz takes it in his stride, even managing to crack a smile. "And here I was thinking we were all after the same thing."

"Oh, we are, but our plan is slightly different from yours. Now ditch the weapons or I'll ditch you."

His guy is just plain confused. "Boss?"

Not that he's about to do anything. My weapon is now leveled on him.

"Boss?"

Katz draws a breath. He'd like to. He'd really like to, but he's not that stupid. Letting that breath out, he tosses his weapon to the floor. As his guy does the same, Katz is still fixed on Fist. "So what was your plan, if you don't mind me asking?"

"Our plan was that you would soak up their fire, and then we would take our database and disappear. But I guess you'll be coming with us now, so start walking, nice 'n' easy. That's right, go on. Debbie, you pick up their weapons."

Yes, ma'am.

However reluctantly, Katz and his guy lead us back out into the square. As soon as we're seen, our ship lands and we pick up the pace. One double-cross a day is enough. If the new Great Og knows of ours, he might try one of his own. The double-cross that comes is straight out of the blue though, and it's Katz who stabs a finger at our pilot as he delivers it: "Full systems shut down."

So that's why he was smiling. He thought he had an ace up his sleeve.

Perhaps he should have shown it to our pilot before he tried to play it. Now that he has, our pilot is not so hot on the idea. "Really? You want a full systems shut down on a hostile planet with a damaged hull? I don't think so."

"Fine. I'll do it myself. Destiny, full systems shut down."

Our pilot grins. He even manages a little chuckle. "Yeah, unfortunately voice recognition is on. Destiny will only take orders from me."

Katz takes a threatening step forward. "Well then, perhaps

you should remember who you work for."

"Oh, I know very well who I work for and it isn't you. So while we've all got nothing better to do than threaten each other, I suggest we inspect the hull. You all heard that alarm. We might very well be leaking atmosphere."

No one could possibly argue with that, as much as Katz would like to.

Oh wait, I forgot about Fist. "Are you serious? You want to tell the Great Og how close he came to taking us out?"

"We're not going to get very far if we're venting into space. I'm not talking about a full repair, only enough of one to get us somewhere else. There's none of them out there. For all they know we'll be making a routine inspection, nothing more. So what about this database of yours? Are they going to deliver it or do we shoot the place up some more?"

"They're searching for it, or at least that's what they said."

"Exactly. It's entirely possible they aren't finished yet, so we need to get this done fast and be out of here as soon as they deliver, if they deliver. So who's coming with me?"

I must say, this pilot seems awfully commanding, a man who expects to be obeyed at least as much as Katz, if not more. But then he is the one flying the ship, which sort of makes him god. In return, all Katz can do is quietly fume. His guy still doesn't have a clue what's going on. Ellen appears to be out of it again. Maybe her shoulder is still bothering her. That leaves Fist and me, and Fist is a doer not a waiter. "I'll come with you. Just make sure you don't get any ideas."

"Oh, please. We're inspecting the hull and you're the one with a gun. What am I going to do? As for the rest of you, I suggest you keep your eyes open just in case."

That leaves four of us, all standing around waiting for someone to say something. Katz and his guy are over by the opposite wall with me keeping an eye on them since Ellen is still distracted. There's definitely something on her mind and it might not be her shoulder. There must be something we can talk about, something not too controversial. I've got kids. Perhaps I should talk about them. On second thoughts, that might give Katz a weapon to use against me. Being abducted by aliens, even human ones, is the last thing I want happening to them.

As we begin to hear faint scrabbling sounds from the topside of our hull, it's Katz who decides he has something to talk about. "So this Earth, the planet no one's ever heard of but everyone suddenly wants to find—you given any thought as to what's going to happen when someone does find it?"

"Someone already has. That's how this all started. The Greens have been milking us for years."

"Yeah, because you're the source of D. The Council of Experts wants to wipe you out. The other clans would do anything to get their hands on you, and the Greens are out there with their own interests to protect. And those are just the enemies I know about. How many others did you make as you blundered your way across the universe?"

"Is there some point to this beyond you thinking we're too dumb to have figured all this out for ourselves?"

"You made a deal. You honor that deal and we can see to it that the Council of Experts never find Earth. The other clans'll have to go through us to get to you, and the Greens won't be able to stop us. You should think about that before you go blundering around some more and make a whole lot more enemies. After all, it would be ironic, don't you think, if the Greens turned out to be the ones protecting Earth?"

If nothing else, it's persuasive. I certainly haven't thought about it like that before. But then, of course, undermining me is what he's trying to do, and that at last wakes Ellen up. Casting him a quick glance, she turns a cool gaze onto me. "If he opens his mouth again, shoot him, somewhere it'll really hurt. Just try not to kill him, not yet anyway."

That shuts Katz up.

CHAPTER TWENTY-ONE

The bridge is deathly quiet again. The square outside is quiet too. For maybe half an hour, all we can hear is the faint clunkings and scrapings of Fist and our pilot doing whatever they're doing on the topside of our hull. When they return, they're both smiling. That must mean job well done, unless it means something else. There was an awful lot of clunking and scraping. No, they couldn't have, not right there on top of our ship with the whole of Og watching. Of course they didn't. They patched up the hull, that's all.

That's what our pilot says anyway. "We'll need to put her into a shop as soon as possible but we're good to go, enough to get off this rock anyway. So what about this database? How long do we mean to wait for them to deliver it?"

"We don't." Turns out staring at the main screen isn't the only thing Ellen's been doing. "They've had more than enough time to find it. For all we know, the Great Og knew where it was all along. They saw how hard we came in to get it back. If I was them I'd be thinking if it's that valuable to us, how valuable might it be to someone else? The empire of the entire known universe could do with some friends right now, and knowing the location of Earth could make them an awful lot."

That's all the encouragement Fist needs. "So we're going back in then. Same routine as before, except those two don't get weapons."

Not according to Katz we're not. "If you want our cooperation, we go in armed. You don't know what's waiting for you in there. They might have your database, or they might have changed their minds. Think about it. They've seen five of us. They're going to figure there can't be that many more and all they have to do to avoid our ship's weapons is stay underground. So if you want us going back in there, you give us weapons."

Well, he does have a point, even if Fist and Ellen are exchanging doubtful glances.

"Oh, don't worry. We're not going to double-cross you the way you double-crossed us. This is about getting to Earth so missy silver dress can hook us up with an endless supply of D. Or maybe you've forgotten that in all this excitement."

Missy silver dress! Really? "My name is Debbie, thug life, and how could I forget when it's my home world we're talking about? I say we give them some weapons, for now, but one wrong move, understand, just one wrong move."

"Sweetheart, one wrong move and we're all dead. Now, are we doing this or not?"

We are, with the same routine as before. Ellen and our pilot remain aboard and the rest of us walk the walk. Katz's guy isn't limping so much. That magic aerosol must have worked its way deep into his wound—that or it's all that nanotech we're carrying to keep us safe from everything. Everything except each other, that is. The square remains silent and deserted. That doesn't mean we're not being watched. That doesn't mean there aren't big yellow beady eyes staring at us through crosshairs every step of the way. Each of us has one eye on the lookout for them. Fist and I have the other eye on Katz and his guy, and they're almost certainly doing the same to us. There's no honor among thieves, which we're not, whatever the Great Og might think. More importantly there's no trust either, but that's a problem to be dealt with later.

The great, dark throat of the Great Og's pyramid takes us in. Now there are guards—not many, just enough to make a show. The Great Og's confidence is growing, which means Katz could be right. Our host might be planning something after all.

We walk warily on, entering the great chamber. There he is, still sitting at the bottom of the steps leading up to that great purple tangle of a nest. There are more guards standing partially hidden in the shadows. They all seem fairly relaxed, just hanging bro, unless they're waiting to be given the word, with more of them lurking out of sight. If this is to be some kind of ambush, if this is to be our Alamo, the Great Og will need them. But then, wrapped in his feathered cloak, he seems fairly relaxed too, so much so that he might almost be sitting on a clutch of eggs, although he would probably consider that to be hens' work.

He waits for us to come before him, head jerking slightly as he fixes each of us in turn with an intense gaze. "How delightful, and your timing is so perfect too. I think maybe you must have the gift of foresight because, see? We have found your database and your rock."

A wave of his hand brings one of the little ones scurrying

forward, in its hand a tiny black sliver not much larger than a thumb. Two more follow, carrying our container between them.

"There. Our business is now complete. As interesting as this experience has been, I find most things in life are best taken in moderation. I wish you farewell then, certain in the knowledge that an entire universe awaits the pleasure of your company. I would not wish to deprive them of it for a moment more than is necessary."

"Yeah." Taking possession of the sliver, Fist turns it over once before pocketing it. "I think we'll be taking the copies as well, if it's all the same to you."

"Copies?" The Great Og is surprised, shocked even, but not very convincingly. "You think too much of us. Our world has just been turned upside down. You have invaded and conquered us with one ship. You have caused the downfall of my predecessor and all his grand delusions. All that we have left, I set to searching out the cause of this catastrophe, delivered only moments ago into your hand. How could we have had time to think of making copies, let alone execute the doing of it?"

"Oh, my heart bleeds for you. Now, if you want us to leave, hand over the copies."

Katz and his guy are watching all those lurking guards. None of them are making a move but, and this might be my imagination, there does seem to be a few more of them. That might be a threat, or simply a move the Great Og is making while he continues to play with Fist.

"I am wounded. I am cut to the gizzard. That you should think me so underhanded, so sly, so lacking in good faith that I would try to trick you, and in so obvious a manner. Let the ground swallow me whole. Let the stars fall and all our tomorrows be as dust. Let—"

"Yeah, yeah, yeah. Now, I'm only going to ask you one more time. If I don't get an answer I like, maybe we'll overthrow you. This planet looks like it could do with some competent leadership."

The Great Og's head bobs up, a single great, yellow eye fixing Fist with what might be a first hint of steel. Negotiating is one thing. Calling an emperor incompetent is quite another. That sort of thing is usually best left to a kid.

Nor is it my imagination anymore: There are more guards, and Katz is getting nervous. "Can we get this over with and get out of here while we still can?"

Taking a step forward, Fist holds the Great Og's gaze and there's no doubt about the steel in her eyes. "The copies. Now. Then we'll leave and you'll never see us again."

The air thickens. The tension is like butter. For the second time on Og, we might not get out of here alive. All it'll take is one nervous trigger finger. The Great Og must be thinking something like that too. If somebody does let fly he'll be sitting right there in the middle of it. Then Chef might have to prepare another funeral feast, and without this Great Og having tasted a morsel of his predecessor. The horror of it.

"Indeed." He waves another of the little ones forward. "I see that you do have the gift of foresight. My apologies, but you cannot blame a body for trying. What kind of a universe would it be if trying were a crime? Not a very inventive one, I should think. So please then, again with my apologies, accept these in good grace and go forth in peace."

Two more slivers are delivered into Fist's hand. She weighs them, slowly and deliberately, and Katz isn't the only one who thinks it's time to leave.

"Are we done? Because our situation isn't getting

any better."

As she pockets the slivers, Fist nods. "We're done, and may I say what a delight it's been doing business with you."

The Great Og nods too. "The delight has been all mine. And may the universe reward you as your endeavors deserve."

You too, sweetie.

As tempting as it might be to say that, we leave in silence, nice and quiet because we don't want to spook anyone. It's a slow walk back through the passageway with the glowing globes above us and every guard eyeing us as we pass by. If looks could kill, that square beyond the entrance would be as unreachable as Jupiter is to everyone on Earth. I can drop by there any time I want, of course, along with Saturn, Uranus, and all the rest. Maybe I should. I'm sure NASA would be grateful for the free samples: a little piece of Saturn's rings here, a vial of Uranus' atmosphere there. And think how many billions of tax dollars I'd be saving them. No need to send any missions, guys. If you need more just let me know.

Well, it's the thought that counts. For now we still have that square to cross, littered with the reasons why no one is shooting at us. While we're crossing it, with Katz and his guy carrying the container ahead of us, another thought occurs to me. "D'you think they might have more copies?"

Fist shrugs. "Dunno. Sometimes it's best to just cut and run."

"But if they do—"

"If they do, we'll deal with it later. For now let's quit while we're ahead."

Our pace quickens. Ahead of us our ship has already landed. The ramp is open. We're almost sprinting by the time we reach it. An emergency evac would be good right now, like the one we did on Ellen's home world. It doesn't happen.

Up on the bridge, Ellen and our pilot are waiting for us. She's looking vaguely pensive.

He's in no hurry to go anywhere as he says, "I take it you were successful. You have the database?"

Fist produces one of the slivers. "Yeah, we got them."

Our pilot nods. "Good. We don't need him anymore then." Suddenly there's a weapon in his hand and Katz's guy is dead.

Katz could be next, followed by the rest of us, except Ellen now steps in. "Everybody relax. Our pilot has been keeping a secret. Turns out he's XSD, Special Security Directorate. Lower your weapons. Lower them now."

That's sufficient for Fist and me, just barely, but Katz is not remotely inclined to obey. "I don't care who he is. He just shot my guy dead. And who exactly is this XSD? I've never heard of them."

"Good." Our pilot lowers his weapon. "If you had, we wouldn't be having this conversation. Now that you have though, the XSD is the security directorate that watches all the other security directorates. My name is Major Popolanopsis. You can call me Pops for short, if you wish. And since I am now the ranking officer here, I'll be taking charge."

Fist throws Ellen a look but, like the man said, she's only a captain.

"Listen to him, okay? And, Katz, lower that weapon. He might still shoot you."

Katz does as he's told, sullenly, but he does it. In a way, I feel for him. That curious grin Pops was wearing when we arrived has become way too superior.

"So then, here's the deal as the XSD sees it. Maintaining an orderly society is hard enough without throwing something like D into the mix. The Council of Experts may have thought that suppressing the production of adrenaline would help create the perfect society but, like all experts, they failed to see the bigger picture. They failed to understand the cold-bloodedness of greed, corruption and the thirst for power. A certain amount of corruption is inevitable. A limited supply of D on the streets is tolerable. Some might even say it's desirable. A person high on D isn't getting up to anything else, after all. Then the FSD decides to go looking for the source and, surprise, surprise, they find it. So now we have to step in. We've already got a clan war. There's no way we're going to allow you to fan the flames by giving them an unlimited supply to fight over. A solution has to be found. It may or may not include the destruction of Earth. That's for me to decide once I've seen—"

A weapon goes off. Pops yelps, following it with a string of curses, and now it's Fist who's wearing a curious little grin. "Oops. Sorry. Finger must've slipped. Is that your foot? You should go aerosol that before it turns bad. Maybe Katz would like to help you. Make sure you leave those weapons behind as you go though. And while you're about it, take the dead guy with you."

I'm grinning too. Sometimes you simply can't stop yourself. Ellen can't stop herself either. Fist is such a bad girl. Katz certainly thinks so. He's not grinning at all. Before Fist shoots him too, and she's clearly thinking about it, he dumps his weapon on the floor. Pops has calmed down enough to do the same, and he's glowering as well. Suck it up, boys. Neither of you is in charge anymore.

Once they've sorted themselves out, with Katz and Pops carrying the dead guy between them, we have the bridge to ourselves, and Fist is our captain again.

"So then, what d'you say, girls? Shall we get off this rock?"

Without further delay, we're powering our way back into space. No missiles are chasing us so the Great Og must be staying true to his word. The purple planet beneath us settles to fill the bottom third of our cockpit windows and main screen. All we need now is somewhere to carry out permanent repairs and then it's on to Earth. That thought fills me with a pang of longing. It's only been a few days and yet I can hardly wait to see her again—the blue splendor of her daylight side with clouds and continents, and her dark side draped with jewels and necklaces of light like some dusky eastern beauty.

Then an alarm goes off, loud and furious, and Fist is stabbing at the console. "Proximity alert. Looks like the Great Og was stalling after all."

Katz rushes back onto the bridge. "Jump. Jump now."

Pops comes limping behind him but it's too late. A dull clang reverberates through the ship as something impacts the hull. All our systems go haywire, with every screen becoming a distorted mess of static. The lights flicker. Destiny is having a nervous breakdown, and we're dead in the water.

We're all stunned into silence for a few moments. Then the main screen comes back online, and gazing out at us from it with an incredibly smug grin is a lean-faced man with cropped hair and cold, calculating eyes. "Hello, Katz. Greetings from the Rose Street clan."

"Yawla, how did you get out here?"

"Our mutual friends. They're not at all happy with your boss trying to cut them out of the loop. I don't think your clan will be supplying D to anyone anymore. In fact all the other clan bosses are already discussing how they're going to carve up your territory."

"Really? You don't think the regular authorities might have something to say about that?"

"No. They don't like people who rock the boat either. Not that it's any concern of yours because you're never going home. None of you are ever going home. You know the rules, Katz. Stick your head above the parapet and it gets shot off. There's also the small matter of these three. They stole a Green ship, wiping out its whole crew in the process. Some more of them are here with me and they very badly want to have a word with them."

It's been a busy hour for double-crosses and reversals of fortune. For Ellen, and for me, this is one reversal too far. "The Greens? You're selling us out to the Greens?"

"Absolutely. The Great Og was most accommodating. You wiped out half his troops and he bought us enough time to arrange everything. And now that he too has the coordinates to Earth, the Greens have offered him a deal: a once-a-year shopping spree, an open buffet with all you can eat, that sort of thing. He's looking forward to it very much. Now, I strongly recommend you prepare yourselves. The Greens have gone to no end of trouble to arrange a welcoming party for you. I wouldn't be at all surprised if they've even gone so far as to buy a cake. Besides, you don't have any choice. You have a mine attached to your hull. Not only has it shut you down but it's also rather explosive." Yawla's grin is growing more smug, his gaze even more coldly triumphant. "Nothing to say? Good. We'll be with you shortly then, and you might want to consider laying those weapons down."

He disappears and our main screen once more looks over the horizon of Og into the blackness of space. Katz is scowling at it like a man who very much wants to kill something, preferably Yawla.

Pops, on the other hand, is looking inscrutable, apart from the occasional wince. His highly trained mind must even now be running through scenarios, plotting strategies, figuring angles, and all the rest of it. If so he's not coming up with very much. "So, ladies, what do you propose we do?"

Katz is the first to answer. "We fight. Any of them sets foot on this bridge, we blow them away."

"No!" Ellen is adamant. "We do what we always do. We let it play out and wait for an opportunity."

That only causes Katz to explode. "Wait for an opportunity! Are you out of your tiny mind? You heard what he said. It's that or the Greens, and I'm not about to enjoy their hospitality for a planet I've never even seen."

"Yes. I heard what he said. Did you? We're not going anywhere until we've dealt with that mine, which we're not going to do from here. So we be patient. We bide our time. We'll figure it out. We always have so far. Think you can do that?"

She probably doesn't need my support but she's getting it anyway. "Quite apart from which, that planet you've never even seen is my home. I have family there. The Greens are already milking us. Now they want to help the Great Og cull us, with one of your clans signing off on the deal. If you think I'm going to die here in a pointless firefight with all of that hanging over my kids, I suggest you think again."

Fist weighs in too. "Sounds about right to me. Us against the universe, that's what we agreed. We're going to save Earth even if I've never seen it either. And since, like us, you've got nowhere else to go, perhaps you ought to sign up too. Like it or not, we're the only home you've got left so deal with it."

But Katz isn't. In fact he's having a real hard time of it, fisting and unfisting his hands as he tries to come to terms with being powerless. "I knew it. I knew this would happen. Trust a woman and she'll always screw you over. I told Max not to do it. I told him to forget the whole thing and dump the three of you in a ditch. Would he listen? No, and now look where—"

"If you're quite done." Looks like Pops is about to deliver his vote. "So far as I'm aware, only two people aboard this ship have ever escaped the Greens. Perhaps you ought to try listening to them."

"Listen to them! 'Us against the universe?' Can you hear yourself? It's us against the Greens and every clan back home, and probably every security directorate as well. You think they won't be coming after us too? Isn't that enough of a universe for you, or are there more? How many enemies have you made out there?" For some reason, Katz is looking at me.

"Well, let's see. Not too many I think—apart from all the ones you just named, there's the Xvr, because we didn't give them their rock back, and Grinder, because he didn't get his ransom money. There's the Lepoorunt as well, an entire family of bunnies who've probably found out by now that we killed their relatives, stole their ship and sold off their cargo. We've seriously annoyed the Demaroven too, but that's about it, I think, for now anyway."

Katz shakes his head. "Unbelievable. Absolutely unbelievable."

Really? Try being me. I went to bed a few nights ago with the certainty that no one had ever received a signal from aliens and probably no one ever would. Now here I am, perhaps a billion light years from Earth, there are aliens everywhere, and a growing number of them want to throw us welcoming parties, which may or may not include cake. Of course annoying them doesn't help, and we're very good at being annoying. Some of them want us dead. Some of them want to give us a psychological examination. Some of them are out for what they can get, and what they all want to get is me.

On the plus side, at least I know I'm not paranoid. Well, you've got to take what consolation you can, especially when there's a big black rim closing in around the edges of our view. It's barely perceptible against the blackness of space, but clearly defined as it slowly devours the Great Og's purple planet. The Green junkyard ship is swallowing us whole, the aperture closing like the ending of some old movie. All that's missing is the final caption, the one that says *fini*. It's all over. The whale has won and we have all become Jonahs. A final clunk says our ship has been secured, and that's that. We've been caught by the Greens.

A NOTE FROM THE AUTHOR

If you enjoyed this book, I would be very grateful if you could write a review and publish it at your point of purchase. Your review, even a brief one, will help other readers to decide if they'll enjoy my work.

If you want to be notified of new releases from myself and other Alkira Publishing authors, please sign up to the Alkira Publishing email list. In return you'll get a free ebook of short stories and book excerpts by Alkira Publishing authors. You'll find the sign-up button on the right-hand side under the photo at www.alkirapublishing.com. Of course, your information will never be shared, and the publisher won't inundate you with emails, just let you know of new releases.

OTHER BOOKS BY REMI DEWITT

The Alien Who Woke Earth

If God gave you a gift, would you change the world or would absolute power change you?

Have you ever wondered if aliens are out there?
If so, why aren't they contacting us?
Maybe they think our world is too messed up.

In this metaphysical first-contact adventure, a young girl called Devon certainly thinks so. When an alien robot with awesome powers falls out of the sky, she sets out with it to put the world to rights.

This isn't so easy when she doesn't know who is responsible for messing things up.

Everyone she meets along the way has their own idea of who is good and who is evil. But how can she and her AI

friend tell the difference? Who should she believe or trust?
And who deserves to be punished for their sins?
Playing God isn't easy.

www.ingramcontent.com/pod-product-compliance
Lightning Source LLC
Chambersburg PA
CBHW051251210726
48287CB00002B/442